2

Passion's Race

DREAM BIG! AND FOLLOW THAT
PASSION.

Christine Mazurk (signature)

CHRISTINE MAZURK

D1314620

DEDICATION

To John, my Ironman.
My true love, best friend, and training partner.
Thank you for sharing this journey with me.
You believed in me from the start and were my rock in
times of uncertainty.
This story was possible because of your unconditional
support and love.
Then, now, and always—I love you!

ACKNOWLEDGMENTS

First and foremost, I thank my husband, John, for encouraging me never to give up. For always sharing his observations about the story line, characters, and cover design. Our love of racing and a lifetime of love inspired this story, and the additional edits in this second edition make it an even richer story. Our son, Michael, and our daughter-in-law, Veronica, for their continuous support. Thanks for sharing this with all of your friends.

Thank you to all my friends—Annette Blair, Jeanine Spikes, Julie Schroeder, and Rachel Singpurwalla—for cheering me on and critiquing my work. With a special shout out to my sister in spirit and best writing buddy, Lynn Jenssen. Whether we're sitting across from each other in one of our homes, talking on the phone, or communicating on-line, we seem to know what the other needs. Thank you for that.

Thank you to Carole J Greene, editor extraordinaire, for her keen eye and her long-term partnership. To Catherine Jenssen, my angel Mama, thanks for teaching me that family is all about the heart not necessarily about bloodlines.

Thanks also go out to Drew Murphy and Shannon J Murphy, my go-to Guam pals. Blanche Marriott for her technical proficiency. Doug Koch for his movie-star name. Dr. George Cierny for his medical expertise. Nancy Brooks and John Ruppel for stirring my passion for writing.

Available Now
by
Christine Mazurk

Sisters Of Spirit Anthology: Identity

Mystical Connections

Passion's Race

Coming Soon

Passion's Spirit
(read excerpt at the end)

Chapter 1

The twenty-mile mark.

The rich smell of the earth hung in the air, and she breathed it in as she filled her lungs with oxygen. Her long, powerful legs propelled her forward—closer to the end. CJ Fallon caught sight of Kate Brooks, her best friend and volunteer photographer, who had a knack for capturing CJ's quest in digital form. Seeing Kate, camera aimed and ready, gave CJ a burst of energy, and she pushed her pace.

She thought about earlier moments from the day—the announcer shouting that she was among the top ten females out of the water, and beating her bike goal by over seventeen minutes—both kept her determined to finish strong. While the goal for most age-group participants was to finish before midnight, her goal in Ironman New Zealand was an age-group win and the chance to compete in Kona, the Ironman Championship of the year, held in Hawaii every October.

The crowds lining the streets screamed words of encouragement, punctuated by the loud clang of cowbells. They shouted, "Good on you," which at first sounded like curse words, but she soon realized it was the Kiwi's version of "good luck." She absorbed their cheers, using them like fuel in her blood. The muscles in her legs worked like the pistons of a well-tuned machine, and she focused her strength on crossing that finish line.

"Nice pace," a young guy with a mop of chestnut hair said as he fell in step with her. "You're looking good." The camaraderie of a shared passion bonded the racers, and compliments and support were handed out without hesitation. That he was a pro made no difference. They compared strategies and ran side by side for the next few miles. It helped ease the fatigue of the day.

"Need to keep Coach happy with a top-ten finish." His form remained relaxed as he chatted.

"I finished fourth in Florida last November. One minute down, one spot away from an age-group slot."

"Ouch." He screwed up his face, which made her laugh.

"Exactly, so I'm determined to earn my place today."

"You go, girl." He picked up speed, waving over his shoulder as he pulled away with ease.

She tried to catch him but he pulled farther ahead. Not long after, she turned the corner and closed in on the finish line, another woman several hundred yards ahead of her. The sun darted behind the clouds before popping out again to spotlight her opponent. She couldn't read the ink on her calf, had no idea if they were in the same age group, but she focused on the woman's feet, matching her turnover. She lengthened her stride, her pulse racing, and closed the distance between them. As she got closer and closer, she noticed the *P* inked on the woman's leg. Her pulse skipped. She was chasing a pro.

She dug deep, her heart and lungs hammering, her feet pounding the pavement, and she continued to reel her in. As if in slow motion, the two of them inched closer to the finish line, the gap between them shrinking. Her lungs were ready to burst, but when they entered the finishing chute, CJ surged, using every ounce of energy to run the woman down. The crowd roared.

With five yards to go, the noise level tripled. Everyone jumped to their feet, cheering as the race unfolded before them. Breathing hard, her arms up and pumping by her sides, she propelled herself and crossed the line first. The clock read 10:17:21—her best time ever.

A volunteer placed the medal around her neck, and she stepped aside, bending over to gulp the air her lungs craved.

"You give me run for money. *Goot* job." The woman she beat, her breath settling, offered her hand. Only then did she recognize the pro as Bella Zeebroek, the Belgian-born triathlete. "You should turn pro." She chuckled. "No, don't. Then you truly give me run for money."

Amazement shot through her as she shook the woman's hand. "I can't believe I beat you. You're awesome."

"Like you, yes?" Bella squeezed her shoulder and smiled. "Will watch behind me in Kona. You like flame burning, hot and goot. I bet you strong in the tree events." She held up three fingers.

As Bella stepped away, CJ felt a light tap on her right arm. She turned and a brilliant pair of green eyes, fringed with long, dark lashes and thick brows, captured her. They were deep green like the trees in a forest just before sunup. Her breath caught.

Stunned, she took a moment to study the rest of the face—ruggedly handsome, jaw set, intense, covered by a day's growth of beard; fine lines that spoke of his time outdoors etched around a sensual mouth and those eyes; all topped with thick, dark hair, wind-mussed, and gorgeous.

His right hand reached out for hers, and she took it,

feeling the calluses, and the strength in his grip. His lips pursed, just before his grin flashed, and he nodded what seemed his approval.

"Great race," he said as he shook her hand. "You have spirit."

Her heart toppled, a response lodged in her throat, and heat lingered long after he released her fingers and walked away.

"You're star struck." Kate raced over. "But who wouldn't be—with Nick Madison? I had the biggest crush on Jens Voigt, watched the Tour de France every year, and then Madison came along." Her friend made a fanning motion with her hand.

"Am I supposed to know who Nick Madison is?"

"Pro cyclist, almost won the Tour de France. Quit after a major crash, disappeared, only to reappear some years later to coach an all-male team of professional triathletes."

CJ smiled. "A coach congratulated me on my finish. That's a first."

Another first for her: the electricity that spiraled when their hands touched, and the look in his eyes, the tone of his praise—all sent shivers up her spine.

* * *

Back two weeks already, and CJ had yet to call her parents to share her news. Her age-group trophy stood radiant and proud at the edge of her desk, a solid reminder. In October, she would compete in the Ironman Championship of the year.

With only a few minutes before her first department walk-through, she picked up the phone and dialed. She held her breath as it rang.

"I'm going to Kona," she said when her mother answered.

Her mother replied with her usual aplomb, "That's well and good, dear, but does it pay your bills?"

Gritting her teeth, she responded in her *perfect daughter* voice. "I see your point, Mom. I got excited and wanted to share my first-place finish. I guess I should get back to work now." Disappointment settled in the pit of her stomach as she hung up. Once again, the dull ache in her heart confirmed their non-existent relationship. She should be used to it by now, but it still hurt. She tried over and over to earn her parent's respect—straight A's, athletics, earning her Masters, climbing the corporate ladder—but to no avail. No matter what she accomplished over the years, they, no, *she* considered her a failure. That knowledge sat like a burr beneath her skin. Yet for some ungodly reason, she never gave up hope.

Back to work, she reminded herself, shaking off the hurt.

As general manager of Haley's department store, she took total responsibility for the results within her building, and with Spring Sale only a few days away, she had plans to execute. With one last look at her trophy, she left her office to walk through the sales set-ups with her department managers.

She walked the men's floor, set to perfection—sale merchandise up-front and center with the flare of a good merchant's touch, well signed, crisp, sized, and ready to sell. "Well done, Steve. Your staff did an outstanding job."

She smiled and nodded at the sales people flanking their boss, and a flurry of high-fives spread through the group. It made her happy to know she led an enthusiastic group who valued results as much as she did. She thanked them again then headed across to the women's ready-to-wear department.

The results the store netted through her leadership

three years ago had won them a total remodel. The store gleamed with new fixtures, tiles and carpeting. They'd torn down walls to open up the selling floors, making it more inviting for customers to shop, an incentive to increase store sales for her employees.

But one manager seemed unwilling to accept her responsibilities.

Betsy, the ready-to-wear manager, stood waiting at the edge of the tile. CJ sensed apprehension in her stance and, right away, spotted a few concerns in the set-up, but she held her tongue and let Betsy take the lead.

Betsy knew the expectations of a strong presentation—key items front and center, aisles clear, sign package ready to go—but Betsy's attention-to-detail had taken a hike in an area or two. And when Toni, the Divisional Manager, joined them, CJ caught her troubled look. Yet Toni did nothing to address the issues.

She shelved her annoyance that the Divisional Manager stood on the sidelines waiting for her to point out the problems; that would be dealt with later...in her office with the door closed.

Her smile remained professional, her voice calm, as she pointed at one section of the floor, the most obvious blunder. The clearance merchandise looked like a garage sale—one where the owners heaped the merchandise on tables, uncaring of the jumbled mess.

"Is that how we set up clearance merchandise?" CJ walked over and fingered the now wrinkled clothing. "These need to be hung, steamed, and sorted by percentage off, then by category and size."

She walked toward the other side of the department to discuss the next issue, but neither manager followed. They stood embedded as if part of the carpet, eyes wide and mouths gaping.

Following their gazes, she turned to see Nick Madison approaching. Nick, the coach who congratulated her on her New Zealand finish. He *was* handsome, she had to admit. His dark, almost brooding, presence caught the attention of many, including several customers standing at the cash wrap, waiting to pay. Activity stopped. The sales associate looked confused. Either she'd forgotten how to ring the register or her brain had gone to lunch.

CJ simply wondered why this powerful and sexy man, dressed in Armani Exchange jeans and an Ironman polo, decided to shop in the women's sportswear department of her store in Daytona Beach, Florida.

His powerful stride carried him across the floor, where he stopped directly in front of her, hand extended. "Hi again."

The same brilliant pair of green eyes captured her. As it happened in New Zealand, her breath caught, but this time, her heart hammered with his nearness.

"Hello." Her fingers hovered just out of reach. When she took his hand, she shook with caution, afraid he'd notice her unease. "What can I do for you?"

"Can we talk?" He flashed that smile, the one that unhinged her the first time they met. "In private?"

What could he want with her? Why had this famous athlete suddenly popped up in her life? Just by standing there, he created havoc in her carefully planned day.

"I'm busy." Nerves made her tone sound clipped, so she softened that with a smile. "Perhaps we could meet later?"

"Look, what I have to say won't take long." A frown settled between his brows. "I traveled from California to talk to you. The least you could do is spare me a few minutes."

True. And she did want to know the reason for his visit.

Turning her attention to the two managers, who ogled him without embarrassment, though he seemed not to notice, she said, "Let's meet back here at two. We'll continue then. In the meantime, why don't you handle the clearance goods?"

She touched his arm and indicated he should follow her.

* * *

Nick did just that. He followed her, enjoying the natural sway of her lean, athletic body as she made her way up the escalator, across the second floor, and through the kids' department. In that short skirt, her legs looked endless. Her stride seemed a mile long, like that of a competitive runner.

They stepped into her office and she closed the door, but she did not take a seat. Instead, she rested her hip on the edge of her desk, her arms crossed, as if to shield her from what he might say. Her expressive, tawny eyes remained level as she took his measure and waited.

"You impressed me with your race in New Zealand."

"That's kind of you to say." A puzzled yet humble expression played on her face. "But you needn't have traveled so far to tell me that."

"You're right." He took a breath and continued. "I watched you run that pro down. Saw the determination in your stride. You placed ninth among the pro women, and I think you possess the potential to win, not just as an amateur, an age-grouper, but as a professional."

She moved. For a moment, she stood over him, unsure, then she shifted to her chair and sat down, the desk now a barrier. A look of fear took hold in her eyes, darkening them to topaz. What he'd said must have spun her head.

"What exactly are you saying?"

He reached across and lifted the trophy from its place, balancing the weight in his hand. "I'd like to coach you to be number one." He took advantage of her shock to go on. "We have a stable of strong sponsors. All you have to do is sign."

He didn't mention that if the team didn't produce a winner this year, the sponsors were threatening to withdraw.

She said nothing.

"I'm offering you a professional contract," he stated to clarify. "With my team."

"But you coach an all-male team."

"You could change that."

"I don't know what to say." Elbows resting on the surface of her desk, she laced her fingers in front of her mouth, but he caught the slight trembling in her hands.

He stood, placing the trophy dead center of the desk in her line of vision, then paced. Back and forth, back and forth, the hushed brush of his shoes against the carpet the only sound in the now tension-filled room.

"It won't be easy," he continued. "It takes time and effort, commitment and dedication, discipline and the ability to listen to me. You'll race more often than you're used to, and push yourself harder than you ever have, but the sponsorships mean money for the team. A win would mean money for you, minus my twenty percent, of course."

She stared at him as if he spoke a foreign language she didn't understand.

He stopped pacing and placed his hands, palms down, on either side of her trophy. "One last thing; you'd need to quit this job." His final statement hung in the air between them.

"Excuse me?" She sprang out of her seat.

"You can't manage a department store and be a full-time Ironman triathlete at the same time." He shrugged. "This opportunity is golden."

"For you, maybe." She leaned in, her eyes sparking. "Are you nuts? Look, I've worked hard to get here, to prove my worth. I can't just walk away, especially in this economic crisis."

He pushed off the desk. "A win would pay more than you've ever dreamed of. Certainly more than you make here." He hiked his brow, angled his head. Did she see cockiness? He smiled, thinking she might. "I'm offering you a new, exciting career."

"One I might fail at." She sank back into her chair as if her legs no longer supported her, the statement tainted with what sounded like her lack of self-confidence. "You're asking me to walk away from a solid and steady career. After six years, I can't do that on the dream that I might win."

"My job is to make it more than a dream." He pierced her with his stare. "You're already good. You proved that in New Zealand. Just think how great you could be if you focused one hundred percent of your time on training. With no distractions and a team of tough guys to push you, you could be a winner in no time."

She shook her head, looking down at one of the reports on her desk. "It's unrealistic."

"It's not." He reached out, gently lifting her face with his fingertips, forcing her to look him in the eye. "Confidence and determination—what I saw when you beat that pro. That's what will get you there."

Her teeth worried her lower lip. He wanted to smooth away her angst with his thumb. Instead, he dropped his hand.

"Look, it's a lot to digest. A stranger walks in and asks you to change your life as you know it, because he believes you have something special." Reaching into his pocket, he pulled out a business card. "Think about it. Let it sink in. I'm going to hang around for a few days, take in Daytona, maybe drive up to St. Augustine to see the Fountain of Youth. Why don't you put a list of questions together. Call me when you're ready to talk."

He walked to the door. With his hand on the knob, he turned and winked. "It's only fair to warn you, Ms. Fallon, I won't take no for an answer."

* * *

CJ stood, staring at the card in her hand, his name branded in her mind. Nick Madison—Coach. His offer echoed in her head. The thoughts it evoked bounced through her blood and a tingle of something prickled her neck. Fear, excitement, disbelief, she didn't know which.

By winning her age group, she attracted the attention of a world-renowned coach who wanted her to alter her life, walk away from her comfort-zone, her secure world. Apprehension danced in her belly and her palms broke out in a cold sweat. Could he be serious? About her abilities, her chances?

A sizzle of a dream flared near her temple then dissolved. No way. She already had a career—and a stable one at that.

She set the card on her desk, afraid it might disintegrate in her fingers. Letting out a sigh, she dropped in her chair, the chaos in her brain making it difficult to breathe. Of course, she couldn't accept his offer. Dreams did not pay the mortgage. Hadn't her mother reminded her of that this morning?

Again, the card drew her eye. *Team Fear US*. It taunted her. Was it the play on words, or did the name mock her? She was afraid. Of his offer, of what it meant. What if she wasn't good enough? What if the abilities he'd seen had been Luck carrying her across the finish line?

Yet…this tempted her.

She reached in her drawer for a legal pad and made two columns. At the top of one, she penned *Pros*, on the other, *Cons*. Under the second header, the list grew quickly. *Leave a steady and safe career. Enter volatile world of professional athletes. Train with a group of testosterone-filled strangers. Piss off parents. Disappoint boss. Risk everything. Fail. Become poor. Lose house.* She could think of a hundred reasons why *not* to, but she had yet to write one that supported a *yes*.

She had work to do, the biggest sale of the year to set. March sales out-produced all other months except the holidays. Her career meant everything, so why did she feel so torn? Why did the thought of swimming, cycling, and running as her *job* send a thrill up her spine?

What if she could *win*?

Confusion propelled her to reach for her phone. She dialed Kate. Her best friend would be a good sounding board. "You'll never guess who just left my store," she prompted as soon as she heard Kate's voice.

"Let's see, with the track nearby—a racecar driver? Jimmie Johnson? Danica Patrick?"

"No. Nick Madison."

"Whoa, what was he doing there?"

"He wants me to quit my job and sign with his team," she blurted. "He thinks I have the ability to win."

A low-pitched, gravelly "Whoop" popped out of the phone.

"Kate, I can't do it." Pushing out of her chair, she paced, agitation poking at her shoulder blades. "It's crazy."

"It's an offer of a lifetime," Kate said. "Think of it as a new thing to prove, that motivates you. Look, CJ, opportunities like this don't come along every day. Why can't you do it?" she asked, heat sparking her words.

"I just can't take the chance."

"You're afraid you'll fail, naturally. But what if you

don't? What if you do win? What if this is your true calling?"

"I can't imagine."

"Well, kiddo, you'll never know if you don't try, but then what do I know about taking chances?"

CJ laughed because they both knew Kate had taken risks her entire life.

Kate had walked away from her family at fifteen. Sure, she'd been pregnant, but she thrust herself into the unknown to break the cycle of monotony, the tedium of becoming a farmer like the generations before her. She took a huge chance and survived, made a better life for herself and her child.

Kate remained silent and it made CJ wonder: *What if?*

Grabbing the legal pad, she flipped the page and scribbled questions. They flowed from her pen, all thoughts centered on those two words. When done, she read them aloud to Kate.

"Did I miss anything? What else do I need to know?"

"Salary, potential, timing. Expectations and the pressure you'll feel from those. The dynamics of the team and where you'll fit. I think you've covered it all."

"Well," nerves made her voice hitch. "I guess I better call him and hear him out."

"Call me when you've decided and we'll celebrate." Kate's throaty laugh filled her ear. "Just think, one day I may be able to say, 'I knew you when.'"

"Oh, please."

She hung up and dialed his cell, but impulse made her set an appointment on Anastasia Island for tomorrow morning at 7:00. Her day off, the beach—her usual place to run a ten-miler—she told him to wear his running shoes. Did she think she could run him into the ground? And why did that thought make her giddy? Or was it her competitiveness coming to the surface?

A devilish smile swept her lips as she left her office to finish her walk-throughs. Toni and Betsy were waiting for her at the bottom of the escalator.

As she stepped off, Toni pounced. "So...who was he? What did he want?" She fanned herself with her notes. "Man was he sexy."

"I didn't notice." She laughed and entered the department. "He came to follow up on my age-group finish, to ensure I accepted my slot for Kona."

"Oh, so that's why he traveled from California." Betsy stared at CJ, an incredulous look on her cute, plump face, her cheeks rosy. "That's awesome."

"Very exciting," Toni added.

"Yes, I didn't expect such personal attention." Though she didn't come clean with the real reason for his visit, she floated across the floor, because *his* attention made her toes curl inside her Via Spiga pumps.

She steeled herself against the onslaught of foreign emotions, and turned back to her job. "Shall we get back to work?" she said, as she waved her hand toward dresses.

The two women nodded, but they also exchanged glances as if they knew something more had occurred.

A secret smile crested. If they only knew.

Chapter 2

The sun climbed, its rays dancing across the rippled water like a million scattered jewels. Pelicans and seagulls gathered on the large expanse of white sand as if an important meeting had been called. Nick smiled at that picture as he sat waiting behind the wheel of his rental car, windows open. The breeze ruffled his hair, and when he breathed in, the salty tang filled his lungs.

Last night he followed CJ home, keeping a discreet distance. Not only for the need to see her again, but also to gauge if she took his offer seriously. From the way she tore into the garage, barreled through the front door, and reemerged soon after, wearing running shorts and a bra top, he guessed his offer made an impact. She collected her mail, tossed it inside, before hitting the beach for an aggressive but abbreviated run.

He liked her style. In each stride, she attacked the possibilities, pondered a huge and difficult decision. *Leave a career and trust a stranger?* With each burst of speed, sand flying beneath her shoes, he wondered what she'd decide. Her phone call to arrange this meeting had disclosed nothing.

Afterward, when she sat on her front porch, sipping from a sports bottle, he simply wanted to touch her. The way she held her shoulders made her seem so vulnerable. She appeared tiny beneath the buttery-yellow walls of her two-story, cottage-style house, and for some reason that tugged at his heart. Whatever the explanation, his hope intensified that she would sign the contract.

To retain the sponsors and their money, he needed a winner on his team. He approached her because of her talent, but as the lone female, could she rocket his fame? Especially, if he took her from nothing to superstar in less than one year. Would that grant him enough credibility to recruit big names?

A copper-colored Jeep pulled into the lot and parked next to his rental—CJ's. He thought yesterday, as he did again this morning, it suited her—top down, windows open, Lyle Lovett crooning from the speakers.

She jumped down, waved to him. Her smile seemed relaxed, her stance neutral. Spikes of cinnamon-colored hair emerged from the edges of the Ironman cap she pulled on her head. She looked young and fresh...and rather cute.

He smiled back, got out of the car, and tucked the key in the small pocket in the waistband of his shorts. "What a beautiful morning. Do you run here often?"

"Every chance I get," she said as she started for the beach. They walked in silence until they reached the edge of the water. "I usually start here, run north to the tip where beach meets park. I turn at the wall of rocks. Round trip is about ten. Is that good for you?"

"Yup. Do you want to talk while we run?"

She nodded and started them at a steady, unhurried pace. "Once I get answers, I'll need some time to think this through."

"I understand." He looked at her, trying to read her expression. "But you should know, the team starts training in mid-April. I'd want you with them."

"But," her footsteps slowed, "that's three weeks

from now."

"Ah huh. No added pressure, right?" Picking up speed, he fired over his shoulder, "Come on. Let's hear those questions."

It took her a moment to catch up, her breathing heavy. Should he slow the pace? Or did the time-crunch to make a decision overwhelm her?

She left nothing to chance, her specific questions well thought out. As he answered each one, he tried to solidify the offer, get her to recognize this as a chance to make a name for herself. Maybe that's what scared her.

When he watched her race, her strength and confidence drew his attention. Yet in their two brief encounters, he caught a glimpse of self-doubt. She competed now as a hobby. Did she possess the fortitude to race against the pros? Would she step out of her safe world?

For the sake of the team, he needed to convince her.

"I checked your times online. Pretty impressive. You finished every race you started and showed improvement with each. I think you just need a push to peak, and I'm damn good at pushing." They turned and headed back, and he wondered at her silence.

He listened to her breathe, watched her belly expand as her lungs filled with air. Her shoulders relaxed as she picked up the pace, and he allowed her time to think.

He scanned the almost deserted beach, admiring its beauty. A magical place—serene and peaceful—it made him think of the moon. Only with the ocean lapping at the sand, smoothing it, firming it, creating the hard-packed surface CJ admitted she loved.

A line of pelicans floated overhead on a current of air, their graceful flight calming. He watched them sail by as he soaked the warmth of the sun into his skin. Next to him, CJ's stride changed. He caught her watching him from the corner of her eye and anticipated her move.

She kicked forward; he did not react. She pulled ahead. He pretended to struggle, slowed. Exaggerating his breathing while behind her, he gasped.

Her shoulders squared and he imagined her smiling, because she punched the accelerator. She gapped him but only for a moment. He counted three heartbeats then pounced. He flashed by her, laughing, and once again her stride changed.

She threw all her energy into the chase and caught him with less than half a mile to go. Her move, though tenacious, fed his determination. He dug deep, opening his stride as he increased his turnover. And when he reached her side, he wrapped his arm around her shoulder and yanked her toward the surf.

She tripped, pulling him with her, and he rolled to take the impact, her body covering his. His heart gave a quick punch as their laughter filled the air then got drowned out by the waves crashing over them.

Soaking wet and covered with sand, he sat up.

"I'm pretty good at pulling, too." That earned him a splash in the face, but her grin remained easy. "So, Ms. Fallon, what are you thinking?"

"That you're a goof."

"Besides that." He stood and offered his hand. Pulling her up beside him, he brushed sand from her cheek, then bent to retrieve her cap. He deposited it on her head before turning to walk toward the cars.

She fell in step with him, rearranging her cap and tucking wet strands beneath it. "Why do you want a girl on your team?"

"I need a winner." He shrugged. "With you, I'd have two shots, one in each division."

She chuckled. "Why have you coached all men, then?"

Her nose crinkled, and a spurt of adrenaline shot

through him. Man, she *was* cute. Just one of the reasons he resisted signing females—emotions rarely got involved with men.

"I never thought about it. Coming from all-male cycling, it seemed natural to concentrate on the men. But when I watched you chase that pro, saw the passion in your eyes, I altered my thinking. Want to start a new trend?"

"Will you sign another girl?" She strode toward the parking lot, tension etching the lines around her mouth.

"Depends," he answered, "on how well you do your first year."

"How will the guys feel about having me on their team?"

"Can't answer that, but you'll certainly benefit."

"How so?" She stopped, turning to lean against the spare tire at the back of her Jeep. She took a deep swig from her water bottle, shifting weight from one foot to the other.

"Are you kidding? Training with twelve strong guys, you'll either improve or get run over." He thought about how that sounded. He needed to persuade her, not scare her. "But something tells me you'll have them eating out of your palm before race season ends."

Twin spots of color rose to her cheeks and she looked away.

"Hey, do you eat sushi?"

That brought her gaze back to him. "Yes. Why do you ask?"

"Thought we could do dinner later. There's a little place on San Marco in St. Augustine."

"Fusion Point." She nodded. "I know it well."

"Would give you time to evaluate this morning's information, and I could answer any other questions that come up, tonight." He unlocked the car, reached in for the white hotel towel he left on the seat. He offered it to her. "What do you say?"

"I don't think so." She shook her head gesturing at the towel. "I need time to think."

"Look, I don't want to rush you, but the quicker we resolve your issues, the sooner you can decide." He wiped his face, threw the towel back in the car. "Besides, it's just dinner."

* * *

CJ arrived early, intrigued that Nick picked Fusion Point, her favorite restaurant, as the place to have dinner. She smiled at the men behind the bar. Artists in her mind, because with delicate slices and colorful curves, they created platters of sushi almost too pretty to eat.

"Evening, CJ," a waitress greeted. "Will you be dining alone tonight?"

"No, I'm meeting a friend."

The young girl nodded, grabbed two menus, and walked her to a corner table.

Apprehension knotted her belly as she sat down. The wait amplified her uncertainty. Would he think she meant to accept his offer because she agreed to have dinner with him? And why exactly had she agreed?

When Nick entered the room, CJ studied him. He walked over, his posture confident and strong, yet somehow agile. He reminded her of a panther stalking his prey. He pecked her cheek before sitting down, and warmth rushed her body as if hot tea coursed through her veins. She swallowed hard.

His good looks made her heartbeat quicken, which so wouldn't do. He'd be her coach, for goodness sake— if she signed with him, that is. Focusing on the drink menu, she pushed the attraction aside.

She ordered a cold Chardonnay, he ordered Kirin beer. When he raised his bottle to make a toast, his knuckles skimmed hers, and the heat moved to her face. It wasn't the wine, because she had yet to take a sip. She reminded herself that this man expressed interest in her sports abilities, nothing else. His focus remained for her to make a drastic change in her life, to have her throw caution to the wind, but for what?

A chance at fame? A dream of glory? What if she couldn't handle either?

"To you, next year's champ," he said, winking.

"I haven't said yes yet." That smoldering stare of his set her on edge, added to the nerves already humming through her.

"You will." He took a swallow, watched her. After a minute, he sat back and added, "Put your concerns on the table."

She recited her list from memory then in a rush whispered, "But I'm so torn. It is an unbelievable offer."

He brought his face closer to hers, his breath warm against her skin. "CJ, I never make emotional decisions. They're always sound and well planned. I approached you because I believe in your abilities." He touched her hand, a light brush of skin against skin. "But this decision rests on your shoulders, yours alone. I don't want you to regret it…either way."

"I thought you said you wouldn't take no for an answer."

"You'll say yes." His lip twitched. "You're standing on the edge, waiting for that tug. I think I mentioned I'm good at both pulling and pushing." He reached out his hand, as if daring her to cross over.

His advice was accurate, she thought. This decision must not end in regret.

"Would I race Kona as a pro?" She pulled her chopsticks apart to avoid looking at him. A weak attempt to calm the squirrels rampaging her system.

"When you sign…" He paused, regaining her

attention. Then he dipped his head as if to say *I-understand-your-turmoil.* "You'll give up your age-group slot. We could get you into Kona as a pro, but as your coach, I wouldn't recommend it."

"Why not?"

"You won't be ready to win by October. A smart plan is necessary to build strength and speed. I'd say prepare for Wisconsin, which is six months away. Race it in early September. Then instead of racing in the championship, you rest through October, rebuild, and race to win Florida in November."

"Did you say win?"

His answer: a simple nod.

Platters arrived and Nick surprised her when he shared his sushi eating ritual.

"I'm a stickler about eating sushi," he said, grinning. With his chopsticks, he pointed. "We take turns picking which roll we'll eat, alternating until two pieces of each are left. Then we rank those—favorite to least favorite—and eat those in whatever order we choose."

It didn't fit her image of him, but then again, rolling in the surf with him hadn't either.

She almost giggled as he explained the process but stabled it behind her most professional smile. His playfulness popped out at the oddest moments, making him awfully cute, boyish at times. Though looking into his eyes right now, she noted all man.

He allowed her first pick, while he stirred wasabi into his soy sauce, and the ritual began.

After tasting the first piece, he continued, "Wisconsin's rigorous, hilly bike-course challenges. Racing it would strengthen you for Florida. You train in the Florida wind, your advantage over the others. As a flat and fast course, you'll dominate." He pointed to the tempura battered one. "I think you shoot to win Florida, and next year you start with an early race, maybe New

Zealand again. Then do Kona. You'd go in ready to compete against Miranda Carfrae, Leanda Cave, and Caroline Steffen, some of the top pro women."

She added a little wasabi to her own soy and stirred it, while his plan took root.

"With Wisconsin as your first pro race, and a win at the championship the following year, the media would view your journey as amateur-to-winning-pro in thirteen months a major coup for our team."

Her turn. She picked the one with the avocado on the outside, ate it, then sipped her wine. "Makes sense, but I've tried for six years to get to Kona. I'm ready to check it off my goal list."

"So your goal shifts a year, and you go as a pro, a much bigger deal." He finished his beer and held up his bottle to indicate to the waitress to bring another. "More wine?"

"Please." She nodded.

"Again, you concentrate on a win first," his tone leveled. "Then do Kona." They polished off the last few pieces. Pushing aside his plate, he centered his bottle of beer, wrapped his powerful hands around the base. "I like the fact that you set goals, and I'll help you meet them, but you have to trust me."

She, too, slid her plate to the side, her fingers resting against the stem of her wineglass.

"Other concerns?"

She hissed out a breath, her nostrils flaring, then took a small sip before blurting, "Fame-and-fortune or failure, what if I'm not good at either?"

Not meant as a question. She let the statement churn.

He sat watching her, his expression considerate. After what seemed an eternity, he sighed, his shoulders dropping. "Fear of failure, I understand, but what about fame scares you?"

His words skimmed her flesh, lifting the fine hairs on her arm. By emphasizing her own fears, had she cracked open a window into his soul? Had his failure as a cyclist edged him toward fame through a different venue—coaching? Because he'd quit, did he demand more from his team?

"Why'd you quit your Come-back Tour?" The question popped out of her mouth. "Ouch, sorry." She made a face to convey her insensitivity.

"You know my history." Something changed in his eyes and that cocky gleam disappeared. "I lost the edge, that cut-throat need to win, hence why I chose to coach triathlon."

"But there's still competition, right?"

"Yes, of course, but triathlon is more like a tribe. There's always a chief, but the others respect him. They may vie for his position the following year, but it's more like a family." He shook his head. "It's difficult to explain."

"I understand the camaraderie of the sport; I've felt it in my races. But as a pro, doesn't that change?"

"No. You saw how Bella reacted when you beat her. After a long exhausting day, those were her true feelings."

A fresh wave of heat flushed her face. "How incredible was that?"

He lifted his beer. "Care to kick that up a notch?"

* * *

After leaving the restaurant, CJ sat at her desk in her home office, hoping the rhythm of the ocean would calm her frantic mind. Nick's answers to her questions flipped about in her brain, confusing her even more. An unbelievable opportunity, but one issue nagged.

If she followed this dream, she risked disappointing

her parents—no, her mother—yet again.

She always compared her to her brother, Gordon, two years older and a college drop-out who lied about his accomplishments, but could do no wrong in their mother's opinion. He sold cars for a living—not a bad way to make money—while still living under their parents' roof. She, on the other hand, graduated with honors, got a job and climbed the corporate ladder.

Just after her twenty-third birthday, Haley's recruited her to be a store manager, but because her new position took her to another state, exactly seven hours away, her mother disapproved of her decision to accept it.

She never understood why Gordon was the golden-child and she was the misfit. As a child, she spent every waking moment trying to please, but for some reason it never worked. Was it disappointment? Jealousy? Or pure and simple hate?

Her entire life, CJ yearned for a close-knit family, a tribe, as Nick described triathletes. In her real family, emotions stayed buried, problems got swept under the rug, and passionate displays were forbidden.

Would Mom think her stupid or flaky for wanting to leave her career? And how could she justify walking away from a career in which she worked so hard to succeed? Store Manager of the Year three times in a row, along with the other prestigious awards she earned. What did she risk by quitting? Was there any guarantee that she could come back?

In these economic times, no.

Feeling nauseous and a little unsteady, CJ decided to call a peer for a professional and objective view. Kate, also her best friend, would lend an honest slant.

She hit speed dial and doodled on her pad as she waited for Kate to answer.

When she put down her pen, she glanced at the

strange images that filled her legal pad: an island with one tree, broken at its base, flames licking at the wound. *Well, how odd?*

"Hey, kiddo, how'd the chat with the hunk go?"

"He's convinced I'm going to sign," she said as she flipped to a fresh page on her pad.

"And you're still not sure."

"That's why I called you. Help!"

"Talk to me, CJ. I'm sure you've over analyzed every detail, made lists, re-evaluated, so what is still not clear?"

"How am I going to relate to twelve male teammates, and a coach who sometimes knots me up inside, when I don't get along with my brother or understand my father?"

"You sit in boardrooms with the CEO and VPs. That doesn't intimidate you. Why should playing with boys?"

"They're competitive ego-maniacs."

"Yeah, and you'll kick their asses. So?"

"Workwise, is it stupid to leave what I've established? What if I suck as a pro?"

"What do you have to lose? You're an excellent manager, CJ. Managing a store, you can do in your fifties and sixties. Can you be a professional Ironman triathlete at fifty?"

Others described Kate as a crude, cutthroat businesswoman with a biting sense of humor. CJ thought of it as a shield, but she'd never before felt the sting of it. Cutting, but honest. *Ouch.*

"Cee, when are you going to start making *you* happy?" In contrast, Kate's nurturing attitude filled a gap CJ's own mother had left. "Look, get out of your comfort zone. Take a chance and see what you're capable of. Again, I ask, what do you have to lose?"

CJ rubbed at the kernel of tension coiled in her

neck.

"I understand it's a huge step, a scary one at that. But either way, follow your heart. Go after your dreams. If you want to continue climbing the corporate ladder, fine. But if you take a year off to chase a passion, see where it leads you, what's the issue? I'd say jump in with both feet. Like swimming, don't stick your toe in to test the water; jump in—heart, body, and soul. Do this because *you* want to."

* * *

After a restless night, with Kate's words spinning in her head and weird dreams waking her every hour, CJ now sat in her office at work, sipping some strong coffee, contemplating. Did she know what she wanted? Did she understand what would make her happy?

She thought she did, that is until Nick Madison entered her life. Now, she wasn't sure.

She was twenty-seven. Did it make sense, at this stage of her life, to continue striving for the possibility of marriage and a family she may never have? Did she have the courage to step out of her comfort zone, to chase a dream and risk possible failure? Could she jump in and see what she was capable of?

What was the downside if she did?

Her success as a store manager would remain part of her accomplishments, but what if she could make a name for herself as a pro? Did she fear that the world as she knew it would forever be altered?

Was that a bad thing?

She took another sip of her sweetened brew, digesting her situation.

Sunlight streamed through her office window, a brilliant spear that grazed her shoulder and illuminated her trophy. The small plate that held her name, place, and age group glowed. And she knew. One option just won the tug-of-war.

Chapter 3

Peering through the clear glass door after ringing the bell, Nick watched CJ hop down the stairs. She finished wiping her hands on a dishtowel before opening it.

She wore faded blue jeans that sat low on her hips, no shoes, and a small white tee shirt that stopped an inch above her navel. The only pieces of jewelry were a fabulous chunk of silver that hung above the vee of her top, and a titanium bar in her belly button. With no makeup and her short hair tucked behind her right ear, her natural beauty called. His heart stumbled.

She eyed him from beneath her lashes as he handed her the single yellow sunflower, a touch his aunt, the woman who raised him, would applaud.

"Come in." She swung open the door, stepped aside.

Above his head in the open foyer hung a large modern chandelier, a glass orb like a crystal ball hanging suspended between the dark metal swells that held the bulbs.

"Do I get a tour?" He wanted to understand her choice of furniture. Just as her vehicle and the music she preferred conveyed her individuality, so would her decorating sense.

She seemed shy as she led him down the hall. Laundry room. Office, nicely done in dark wood furniture set upon a throw rug of muted jewel tones. In the corner stood an oversized chair and ottoman of dark chocolate leather, rich and tempting one to sit. Did she curl up with a book, a sports magazine, or perhaps her store's reports? Did she doze there after a tough workout?

The guestroom sat at the other end of the short hall, done in simple shades of green and Tuscany yellow, warm and inviting. The bathroom nestled between the two rooms pleased in sage and vanilla tones with candles glowing on the counter next to a basket filled with rolled hand towels.

"Go through." Her smile hadn't yet reached her eyes, but as he opened the door, her enthusiasm grew. "You should appreciate what I've done with the space."

This room ran the length of the back of the house— he guessed thirty feet by fifteen. Workout machines stood like little soldiers lining the walls—a wind-trainer, leg press, weight bench, inverter, elliptical and treadmill.

"Nice." He let out a whistle of appreciation, his gaze settling on her body. No doubt she used each one. "Your own personal gym."

"Yup, got everything I need right here. Backyard included for long runs and swims when the ocean water is warm enough. When it's cold, I use the heated pool down the road." Her eyes lit up, her passions clear, and something in his belly shifted.

An awkward silence settled, but she broke the tension by giggling when her stomach growled. "Come, I have wild salmon waiting to hit the grill."

He followed her up the stairs, stopping at the top.

"Wow, this is incredible." Family room, dining room, and kitchen opened to a deck overlooking the beach and ocean, her backyard as she called it. The half-moon streaked light across the top of the water, which rolled in gentle swells.

Through the large open windows, the surf curled around the sound of Lyle Lovett singing an off-center song about someone being ugly from the front.

During the day, he imagined those windows let in an abundance of light, but now, she had the kitchen lights dimmed to a warm, soft glow. Three thick candles sat on a plate in the center of the island where she stood preparing the last of the salad.

"Could you open the wine, please, while I get this started?" She grabbed the platter of fish with one hand, reached into a drawer with the other and handed him the corkscrew. "Glasses are left of the sink, first upper cabinet." She stepped out on the deck, leaving the door open. "I hope you like salmon."

"Love it." He opened the Chardonnay, carried a glass of it out to her. Leaning his elbows against the rail, he relaxed. "Since you told me to bring the contract, is it safe to toast to you joining the team?"

Her shoulder lifted in a quick jerk, almost like a nervous twitch. She put aside the platter and turned to look at him. "My stomach's in knots, but yeah, I'm doing this."

"Yes." He punched his fist in the air.

Another one of the sponsors had called this morning threatening to pull out if he didn't produce a winner this year. He needed her now more than ever. She might just save the team. "You won't regret this. Want to sign now?" He pushed from the rail.

She laid a hand on his arm, holding him where he stood. "After we eat is fine."

"Sure." He sipped, resting back against the rail. "By the way, nice of you to do this. Not necessary, but nice."

She lifted her glass, mimicking his phrase from the

day before. "It's just dinner."

The deck light from above pooled in her eyes, making them appear a few shades darker than the wine they shared. Drawn into the depth of them, he stared. Everything disappeared but those eyes. Dark lashes skirted the edges, the worry in them, cool and calm, but with jade specks sparkling like trust clinging to the edge of fear, as if afraid to let go, afraid to fall. He felt he gazed into the window of her soul—trespassed—and an electrical current shot through him. When she blinked, he came back to reality, a little off-kilter, but no longer trapped inside her skin. He shook his head to readjust, to close down the emotions pushing to the surface.

"Nick?" She stared at him like he'd grown an extra head.

"Sorry." Lyle now sang about riding a pony on his boat, and her expression softened. He sipped, too quickly, as he tried to hide his embarrassment, turned his concentration to the fact that she might redefine the team.

"I'm going to dress the salad." She stepped inside. She either hadn't noticed his unease or chose to ignore it.

Again, his thoughts drifted.

She'd made her decision, yet after everything they talked about—mainly her concerns—how would she feel about the other deal he made today? The deal he made with his best friend, Mike Dawson?

He thought for a second of letting her sign then telling her, but that would be wrong. He might be demanding, difficult, even a bully about getting his way, but he was not deceitful. He'd work it into the dinner conversation and pray it didn't change her mind.

She reemerged carrying a large bowl and the bottle of wine. She set them on the small glass table, artfully arranged with colorful dinnerware and rustic silver. In a slim vase in the middle of the table rose the single flower he brought. Napkins the color of buttercups bloomed from thick, heavy-looking water glasses of deep amber, a pitcher of ice water nearby. Reaching for matches, she lit the one stocky candle that complemented the rest, then turned to fetch the salmon.

"Shoot. I forgot the bread." She spoke over her shoulder, her hair—the color made him think of aged cognac—tumbled to frame her face. "Nick, would you mind? It's in the oven."

He nodded and stepped back into the kitchen. On the counter near the oven sat a wooden cutting board, a large knife, and a basket with a cloth draped inside. He sliced the warm bread, filled the basket, and carried it outside, all the while trying to decide how to share his news.

Five bites into dinner, Nick sat back and picked up the bottle of wine. He topped off both glasses then cleared his throat. "I made another deal today that I think you should know about before you sign."

"You signed another female?" She tossed an impish grin his way.

"No." He shook his head, chuckling. "My best friend owns a resort on a tropical island. Tourism is down for him at the moment, so he offered to let the team stay there at an incredible discount while we train. It's my second home. I helped him build the resort, and I stayed there between my cycling disaster and my coaching. The terrain is perfect; mountainous with several challenging climbs, and flat spots with gusty winds. In my opinion, the best possible conditions for us to train in, to get us ready to win."

"Sounds wonderful. What's the problem?" She stabbed some spinach and a slice of red pepper from her salad.

"It's halfway around the world. Mike lives on Guam."

Her fork stopped short of her mouth, and she stared at him.

"What is it? Once in a while, I see doubt flicker in your eyes. Does location matter?"

"Giving up my job and moving to the other side of the world with fourteen men—all strangers—doesn't quite fit into the compartments of my organized brain."

"Oh." What could he say to comfort her? "Concentrate on your fitness level, think of how strong you're going to be." His mind shifted to those endless legs. *No, don't go there.* Shit, her with him and thirteen other men?

She stood, grabbed her wine glass and edged to the rail, looking out at the water. Her shoulders tensed as she stared at that black ink, and an urge struck him; he wanted to hold her.

She spun around. "Let's sign this thing before I do chicken out."

"Okay." He stacked the dirty dishes to keep his hands occupied. He carried them in and set them on the counter but remained silent, watching her.

Skirting around him, she entered the living room and sat down on the love seat. As she grabbed a pen from the side table, a determined look flashed across her face.

He wished he could read her thoughts, understand what made her tick. It would help him push the right buttons in her training.

"Well?" She stared at him, those liquid eyes huge pools.

He set the contract on the coffee table and succinctly covered the details on each page, showing her where to sign.

When she put the pen down and stood, he moved. *Reflex,* he told himself, *not expected.* Instead of shaking her hand, he kissed her, sealed the deal with his mouth. It just happened—a flash of lips like lightning ripping the sky, hot and hard, smoking against cold stone. Steam rose in his blood.

Maybe he reacted to the tense slant of her shoulders. Maybe he wanted to bolster her courage, wipe away her doubts. Whatever the reason, it rocked him to the core.

CJ stepped back, a nervous laugh escaping her gorgeous mouth, but she quelled it and shoved her hand between them. "Umm, Nick? Is that how you celebrate all of your contracts?"

"Ah, no. Of course not." He blinked. His mind clouded.

"I didn't think so." She moved forward and jabbed a finger in his chest. "Let's get one thing straight, Coach. Just because I'm a woman doesn't mean you can take advantage of me. You got that? I expect to be treated like one of the boys."

Smiling, he held up his hands and backed away. "Fine. Okay, fine." He put the papers back in the envelope, tried to regain some balance. Embarrassed by his blunder, he shifted to business, his tone gruff. "The guys will be ready to go in three weeks. Will you?"

"Do I have a choice?" Her hand remained up, a barrier between them.

"No. You're now part of my team." He patted the envelope. "You take orders from me. Oh, did I mention you need to get a physical before we go?"

"Anything else I need to know?" She crossed her arms over her chest.

"Basic gear, including bikes, will fly with us. The rest will follow in a container. I'll set everything up and email the specifics." He headed for the stairs, paused, and turned back to look at her. "In the meantime, should you need anything, you know how to reach me."

She nodded, their gazes locked, and an odd sizzle filled the space between them.

Attraction, strong and hot, flared, but it was awkward. They'd just met. He knew very little about her, and now he was going to be her coach.

He cleared his throat. "Thanks for dinner. I'll show myself out." He shifted his stance, gave a quick nod, and turned to leave.

Nick closed the door with a firm click and drove back to the hotel, his emotions raging. Man, she turned his brain to mush. He needed to get a grip and figure out how to handle five months on a tiny footprint of an island with his new star pupil. Especially after what happened tonight.

* * *

The front door snapped shut, a punctuation to the decision CJ made tonight. She'd signed the contract— her first bold step to a new career—but Nick's kiss jumbled things. Could she ignore it, pretend it never happened? His lips unearthed sensations she couldn't afford to feel.

Would he heed her warning and treat her like one of the guys? Could she tamp down the feelings he stirred and remain strong in his presence? She'd better, because she was a fool to think he might want more than a professional relationship. He was her coach, nothing more, but the thought of living on an island with him and twelve male athletes spun her head. Panic snaked through her belly. She moved to the sink and filled the dishwasher in an attempt to calm her nerves.

The song on her Nano stopped and within seconds the sound of Moby started, filling the air. A far cry from Lyle, whose lighthearted music entertained. Moby's music evoked deeper emotions. It was as if the change in beat mirrored her upcoming move. A new world awaited. Her heart skipped in her chest. She was closing one chapter and turning the page to find out what would happen next.

She loved the feel of the wind in her face and the sun on her skin as she ran for hours. She loved the freedom she felt when riding her bike. She loved slicing through the water under her own power. And now those disciplines would be the basis of her new job.

Excitement took hold. CJ finished cleaning up in the kitchen then went downstairs to plan. Sitting at her desk, she made a list of what she would need to do over the next three weeks. Combing her fingers through her hair, she thought hard about her preparation and the list grew: resign; write a resignation speech; call the family doctor for an appointment; coordinate that with a trip to Atlanta to bring parents into the loop; make a separate list of what she'd need for a five-month stay in Guam, including equipment, tools, and nutritional supplements.

She pulled out a calendar and blocked out dates for each action.

So much to think about, so much to do, what about the house, the bills? Should she ask a neighbor to keep an eye on things, or if she recommended Kate be promoted into her store, could she ask her to move in?

She worked herself into a frenzy, felt ready to burst.

She needed to share this with someone, so she reached for her cell and pressed speed dial.

"Kate, I did it. I signed."

"Holy cow." She heard Kate's excitement. "I'm so happy for you. Took courage, I know, but I'm proud of you, kiddo. What an adventure. Okay, so give me the timeline. Got to have your lists made, your priorities set. Probably have your bags packed, too."

"Come on, I'm not *that* organized." She snorted, relaxing for the first time this week. "I'm giving notice on Thursday and sharing a proposal with my regional, a list of who I recommend to take my store." After a brief pause, she asked, "How do you feel about being at the top of that list?"

She heard the sharp intake of breath, the long release as Kate blew it out.

"Wow. Are you sure you want a hard-ass like me taking over your store?" Kate snickered. "Aren't you worried your entire team might quit on my first day?" She said it playfully, but the truth in her words touched her. Their management styles differed.

"I know we're not the same, Kate, but you're good with talented people. My group is quite gifted. You think you're tough, but you're like a mother hen, doting on her chicks."

"Oh, geez."

"You know I'm right. No matter. In the end, it's my boss' decision. I just wanted to know if it interested you."

"Larger volume, Store of the Year times three, are you kidding? Of course, I'm interested. But let's not get too excited. As you said, it's your boss' final say, and he doesn't know me that well. I'm sure he's got his own 'to promote' list."

"Maybe, but I can plant a seed, can't I? If it takes root, would you move into my house while I'm away training?"

"It would give me a chance to look for my own place, but where are you going and how long will you be gone?"

"Madison's taking the team to Guam for the first five months of training—after that, I'm not sure where we'll be. Wherever the races take us, I imagine."

"Guam? What's in Guam? And P.S., where is it?"

"His best friend owns a resort there. It's a tiny island in the Pacific, near Japan, Northwest of New Zealand, above Australia. Tourism doesn't seem to be paying the bills right now, so he offered Nick a huge discount and total run of the place. Nick described it as the perfect terrain for training."

"How do you feel about it?" Kate understood CJ's fears and doubts better than anyone, and her concern came through in her tone. "Moving around the world is quite a change."

"I know, right? *Me* moving to a foreign land with strangers—men on top of that. Makes me wonder what I've gotten myself into."

"How many are hunks like your coach?"

Did she dare tell Kate about the kiss? No, smarter to bury that incident and never think of it again. Instead, she focused on her newer apprehensions.

"What if they don't accept me, Kate? Twelve guys may not like a girl invading their turf. And I don't think Madison's ever coached a woman before. Will he treat me with kid gloves or push me like one of the boys? What if I can't keep up?"

"Sounds like you'll face some challenges. But I know you. You'll push yourself. That need to prove yourself will carry you through. You'll be a stronger athlete, and who knows, maybe this will help you break that tie with your mom."

"She's not going to be pleased with my decision, but I'm doing this for me. I won't let her ruin this."

"Good girl."

"It's funny, Nick said two things that made me think differently about this chance. One, no matter what my decision, it had to be mine and mine alone. He didn't want me to regret my choice. And two, he described the triathlete community as a tribe. I've always felt a bond, but he said even with the pros, it's like a close-knit family, something I've always wanted. Maybe this is my destiny."

"Only time will tell, CJ. But no matter what, you're headed for a new adventure."

As Kate pointed out, no matter the results, she'd grow not only as an athlete, but also as a person. *New experiences, though scary, broadened one's horizons, right?*

"Can you get away the first weekend of April? Come up for a girls' weekend to celebrate?" No longer able to sit still, she dusted the furniture and rearranged the bookshelves.

"I'll bring the champagne."

"Cool. Can't wait." She hung up, allowing her friend to falsely believe she could care less what her mother thought. Childish maybe, but that deep-seated insecurity sat in her genetic makeup like a boulder. Could time on an island with macho men transform that?

* * *

On the drive to Atlanta, CJ hit a small rainstorm and pulled into a gas station to put the Jeep's top up. After that, one highway ran into the other with little change in scenery. She used the hours to ponder and project, to psych herself up. *CJ Fallon—professional athlete.*

When she gave notice the day before, her boss congratulated her on her golden opportunity. He even promised to track her results. He accepted her proposal but made no promises about yielding to her request. Then he stood by her side as she told her management team her news.

This morning, they held a storewide meeting to inform the employees, and the managers surprised her with a skit. They brought out a makeshift finishing chute and persuaded her to run through it, placing a huge medal around her neck. One her visual manager must have made.

It read "Number One Manager—Forever."

Her eyes filled, her throat constricted. These people cared. Over the past four years, she'd trained and built this team of incredible individuals, some hand-picked for their unique forward thinking, their abilities to solve problems and produce results. The ones she'd inherited with the store learned from her example, and within her first few months as general manager, she showed them how to invest in their own careers. All in all, she was very proud of her team, and she would miss them.

Hours later, the emotions still welled. She glided through Tifton, cut up through the middle of Atlanta and made it to Alpharetta, her parents' home, in time for dinner.

Grabbing her duffel bag from the floor of the Jeep, she lowered her feet to the concrete. Glancing up, she stared at the house she grew up in. Memories of perturbed exasperation permeated and held her prisoner as her gaze followed the roofline that speared the lead-gray sky. A storm brewed, both inside and out, but she pushed away the aches and willed herself to break through the wall of the past and take flight into the future.

Squaring her shoulders, she put one foot in front of the other and headed up the pebblestone walkway. There, under her right foot, was the gouge she'd created with the handlebar of her bike when she crashed at age ten. She'd scraped up her knee and elbow, had bruised her hip, but was her mother concerned about her injuries? No, she'd been red-faced as she scolded her for damaging the expensive stonework.

Looking at it now, CJ wondered if her mom left it there as a reminder.

She sucked in a breath when she reached the front door, rapped twice on the heavy wood before pressing the handle to release the latch.

"Hi. I'm home," she called out, stepping into the

foyer.

The sound of glass shattering in the kitchen greeted her.

She dropped her duffel in the hallway, along with her backpack and keys, and took a quick step toward the kitchen. Crossing the threshold, she reached to hug her mother.

"Be careful. You'll cut yourself." Her mother bent to pick up the larger pieces of the broken wine glass. "I didn't expect you for another hour. You must have been speeding in that thing you call a car." She looked up, disapproval in the form of a frown marring her face.

"It's a Jeep, Mom. And no, I didn't speed. I left work earlier than I thought I would." In one fluid motion, she knelt beside her mother to help clean up.

"You can help by bringing me the dust pan."

Her spirit plummeted, freefalling to her toes, but she fixed a smile to her lips. "Under the sink, right?" She got up to retrieve it and felt a fresh pinch when her mother grabbed it from her hands and shooed her away.

"Go freshen up and change. I do hope you brought something a bit more feminine, Cassandra." The look her mother threw at her army-green carpenter pants could have frosted the sun. "We're having guests, so do try to make a good impression."

Heat rose up her neck and she bit her lip to keep from responding. She would not allow the sharpness of her mother's tongue to cut too deeply. She stood taller, swallowed the hurt.

"For once, can't we have a quiet family dinner? I have some news to share."

"Well, Cassandra," avoiding eye contact, her mother turned to dump the shards in the trash, then went to the stove to stir something in one of the pots, "whatever it is will have to wait until after our guests have gone."

The blade twisted in her chest. She counted to ten in her head, accepting the fact that it would be a long night.

"I'll go change." She pressed a quick kiss to her mother's cheek, touched her shoulder. Her mother stiffened and a fresh wave of hurt settled under her heart.

The cold treatment she'd received her whole life puzzled her, for she witnessed first-hand the affection showered on Gordon instead. After all these years, it still hurt like hell to know that her own mother hated her, and damned if she knew why. She snatched her things from the hall and took the stairs two at a time. Inside the room, she leaned back against the closed door and blew out the ache in long, rusty breaths. The heat of unshed tears collected in her eyes. She brushed them away with impatience and scolded herself.

It was time for Ms. Full-time Athlete to buck-up.

She threw her bag on the bed and unzipped it.

The frilly guest room looked nothing like the room she grew up in. Mom redecorated two days after CJ moved out. The flowered bedspread and damask curtains displayed the exact opposite of her tom-boy style. Their cheerful colors only added to her gloom.

If she wore the sundress she brought, would that be giving in...again?

She went in the adjoining bathroom and scrubbed her face, then took time to apply a light coat of makeup. A guileless shield against what might come. Swiping mascara on her lashes, she bolstered herself for the masquerade they'd call dinner, and prepared herself for the worst, fearing what her announcement might unleash.

Mr. and Mrs. Bradford J Clark, new neighbors with a baby on the way, sat on either side of her mother. Cute, in a Barbie and Ken sort of way. The storm now in full swing outside did nothing to dampen their enthusiasm about their first child.

"We came straight here to share the news with your

mother."

That information punched CJ in the gut. She darted a glance at her brother Gordon, who seemed unaffected, before turning her attention to her mom.

"Wow, Mom, what an honor."

"Not really. Mrs. F is our mom away from home," the woman gushed. "Mine's in Dallas, Bradford's in Houston,"

Her mother smiled at the couple. "You're too sweet."

Thunder clapped outside the dining room window, and CJ took advantage of the silence in the room. "I wanted to let you know, I'm leaving Haley's to become a professional triathlete."

The temper of the storm seemed to intensify as each of her family members and their guests soaked in what she'd said. Assorted expressions greeted her, Gordon's reaction, the biggest surprise.

"No shit?" Gordon wrapped his arm around her shoulder. "How did that happen?"

Her mother's mouth pinched tight.

"A coach saw me race in New Zealand, recruited me for my talent. An ex-professional cyclist, Nick Madison. He thinks I have what it takes to win."

"Nick Madison? He crashed on the Col du Galibier," her father announced. His voice sounded strange; he hardly ever spoke. "I saw that crash. They didn't think he'd survive."

Her mother scowled, turning to stare at her husband. "Your daughter has toppled over the edge, Burton. Please don't encourage her with your trivial sports data."

The light she observed in her father's eyes flickered out. Or had it simply been a reflection of the lightning outside?

"You chose a management career. Now you're

going to throw it away to sweat like a boy? How unladylike. But that shouldn't surprise me." Her mother's face puckered as if she'd swallowed a lemon.

"There's more." CJ locked gazes with her mother, pinning her. "The team leaves for Guam in a few weeks. My twelve male teammates and I will be training there to get ready to race Wisconsin in September."

Her mother rose as if to leave the room, her way of dealing with most unpleasant things, but a comment from their female guest made her hesitate and sit back down.

"Guam sounds appalling." Angie's nose crinkled, but her eyes glistened as she giggled into her napkin. "But twelve male teammates—athletes on top of that, now that's appealing. Oh, CJ, maybe you'll find Mr. Right among them."

Her mother actually groaned.

Bradford nibbled at his food like a chipmunk, ignoring the conversation. He sipped his wine and went back to eating. Her father remained silent.

"I think it's cool. My sister, the athlete. Wow."

"You know what? I'm sorry...." She held her breath like a thin sheet of resilience, hoping her mother's more hurtful words would bounce off without penetrating. "I've got an early morning planned. I should turn in."

Her mother's emerald eyes darkened with fury like the sea about to erupt, but her voice remained lifeless. "You do what you have to, dear. Again, you always do." She fluttered her long, graceful fingers as if dismissing her, pushed away from the table, and crossed her legs with a refined flourish, her high-heeled sandals looking elegant against the expensive rug.

"Shall we have coffee in the living room?" Her mother smiled at her guests and put an end to the discussion.

Silence reigned and CJ once again felt the heat in

her face. Infuriated, she rose from her seat. How did she respond without sounding childish? "I'm sorry you don't see the lifetime opportunity here, Mom, but as a grown woman, I need to explore what's on the horizon. I'll never know what I'm capable of if I don't try. Dinner was fabulous, as usual. A pleasure to meet you both." She smiled and reached out to shake hands with the couple. "Night, Daddy, Gordon."

Something tugged at her, and she turned to hug her brother. "Thanks," she whispered into his ear. "Your support means more than you'll ever know."

Upstairs, under the covers, staring into the dark, she listened to the muted conversation as the party below continued. One silent tear slipped from the corner of her eye and burned a trail down her cheek.

Tomorrow—a new day. Even without her parents' support, CJ planned to sail into it.

She fell asleep praying not to sink.

* * *

Her mother's glacial stare at breakfast confirmed CJ's decision to leave after her doctor's appointment. *No need to stay in this polar climate.* Plus, her father's lack of backbone perplexed her. Why hadn't he said anything?

Gordon at least thought her brave and said so before going off to sell cars. His words warmed her insides and made her wonder if she couldn't begin a relationship with him.

Currently, the incessant *tap, tap, tap* of silver to china as her mother spooned fruit and yogurt into her mouth filled her ears, while her father eyed her over his wheat toast and egg-white omelet, a shadow in the room.

"I can't believe Dr. Taylor canceled a golf game to see me on a Saturday." Desperate to fill space, she spoke the first thing that came to mind. She hadn't touched anything on her plate, but that third cup of coffee assaulted her system. She waited, holding her breath, for one of them to respond.

An eternity passed, then in a whisper, her father said, "It's been ages since I saw James. Must be over a year since we played golf...." The last faded as he placed another forkful of egg in his mouth.

"Why are you seeing him, Cassandra? Are you concerned about your health?"

"Requirement for the team, Mom. And since we're going to a remote island, it's not a bad idea." Not knowing what else to say, she rinsed her mug in the sink then grabbed her things and went first to her father. She took his hand, squeezing it. "I love you." He nodded and looked down at his plate.

She moved to her mother. "I need to live my life without regrets, Mom. To feel good about the decisions I make, no matter the outcome." She bent to hug her and kissed her cheek. "It's important that you understand that."

Had she expected a response?

* * *

As she sat on the cold metal table in the examination room, CJ realized she expected nothing from her mother. At least, she'd given voice to her thoughts. Freedom to travel to the other side of the world with her mission stated, her goals spoken. Progress.

So why wouldn't the ache disappear?

After the nurse weighed her, took her blood pressure, and made her pee in a cup, CJ waited for the doctor to join her. She flipped through a magazine, but the words blurred.

"How's my favorite gal?" Doctor Taylor entered

the room, a warm smile melting his milk chocolate eyes. "Are you really turning pro? Will you be able to handle the press?" He chuckled under his breath as he scanned her file.

A nice looking, soft-spoken man in his late fifties, and the first doctor she ever knew. She remembered her first visit with him, how comfortable he made her feel. She broke her arm at age five, and he put it in a hot-pink cast then signed it. A few years later, when the measles kept her home, he gave her an intricate puzzle to do, and in her teenage years, he recommended a gynecologist. She liked his thoughtfulness, his gentleness.

"It's all new to me, Doc. I guess I'll deal with the press—if and when the time comes."

He nodded. "So, what's in Guam?"

"Training camp." She laughed. "Perfect conditions."

"Sounds tropical like Hawaii—without the glamorous name." He put her chart aside, lifted his stethoscope, but instead of using it, he bounced it in his large palm. "What are we looking to do today?"

"Just a physical. You need to sign off that I'm strong enough to tackle a professional racing career. No more once or twice a year hobby."

"Okay then, let's get started." He pulled the neck of the gown down and touched the cold stethoscope to her chest. "Deep breath. Let it out. Good." His gaze skimmed, latching on to her bare shin. "Hmm, what is that?" He pointed to a small bump that protruded.

He traced it with his thumb, lingering over it a moment. "Is it sore?"

"Not really." She pulled her leg back, rubbed it with her palm. "Once in a while, like after a long run, it feels bruised but nothing more. It doesn't...hurt."

"When did you race last?"

"Three weeks ago."

"Your body's probably recouping, but I'd like to x-ray it, just in case. Make sure it isn't a hairline fracture. We should do your blood work, too." He brushed at the spot again, his finger fluttering like a moth seeking a flame. "Could be a swollen tendon, but let's make sure, okay?"

He didn't wait for her answer. He called for a technician. "We need three angle x-rays of the right tibia and a full blood screen, pronto." As he helped her off the table, he squeezed her elbow. "Just a precaution, you understand?"

Upbeat and positive, his normal bedside manner. She felt fine, so why worry? He was just being thorough, attention she appreciated in her doctor.

After the x-rays, the tech led her back to the exam room.

"So...how are the parents?" Dr. Taylor asked as he looked in her ears, checked her reflexes. "It's been ages since I saw your dad. He needs a check-up."

"He said this morning that you guys haven't played golf in a while."

"Tell him to call me. We'll play a round and maybe I can talk him into having that checkup." He patted her on the back, noted something on her chart. "Everything seems fine. I'll call you once I've seen the film. In the meantime, good luck with your new adventure." He hugged her, kissed her on the forehead, then left her to change.

When he left the room, CJ rubbed at her shin. The bump felt like a small ridge of bone tucked tightly beneath her skin. Why hadn't she noticed it before?

In the scheme of what she did, she never thought anything of the small aches and pains. Wouldn't a swollen tendon be a common occurrence when a gal put her body through 140.6 grueling miles in one day?

Chapter 4

"How many of these things do you need?" Kate watched CJ place another running bottle, the kind with the colorful mesh handle, into her suitcase. It nestled between her fuel belt, the one with six small bottles, a container of tissue rejuvenator, and a case of GU, her preferred brand of energy gel.

"Several." CJ chuckled as she closed the lid. "I have a feeling Drill Sergeant Madison will have us hustling all day, which means late nights to wash out bottles and gear. I'm not getting caught short."

"Smart." Kate sat on the side of the bed watching, her expression thoughtful. "I can't believe you leave on Thursday."

"I know, I feel like I've been riding a carousel gone mad, waiting to be flung off." She moved the suitcase aside and sat next to Kate. "The truth is I'm better off busy. Otherwise, I'd overanalyze this whole deal."

"You? No."

"Oh, shush." CJ elbowed her friend as an a-ha dawned on her. She tapped her forehead. "Now, it makes sense."

"What?" Kate asked, a puzzled look replacing her pensive mood.

"My weird drawing." CJ separated the items she needed to add to her bike case as she explained. "When I called you to talk career, I doodled like I always do." She described the island, the broken tree, and the flames. "But above the branches, I sketched a ragdoll falling from the sky." She shook her head. "I know, sounds crazy, but it mirrors how I've been feeling."

"You have been in a spin for weeks. That's bound to bring your anxieties to the forefront." Kate stood up and walked across the room, fingered CJ's medals. "You put so much pressure on yourself, maybe your subconscious is telling you to ease up a bit. Relax."

"You've known me how long?"

"Long enough." Laughter bubbled up Kate's throat. "Come on, let's go walk on the beach. I'm dying to hear how the weekend with the family went."

They reminisced as they descended the steps from the deck, delving into the days when they shared their deep dark secrets, reconstructing their childhoods to better understand the adults they grew to be.

The barren, almost antiseptic, non-emotional world CJ knew had been filled with enough carping and blame that even an individual of sturdy stock might be driven to slit her own throat. It's a wonder she survived. They compared her non-existent *family* life with the fomented, emotional turmoil Kate experienced with three generations living under one roof. She knew love, yet she chose to break away from it to start a new crop in her life.

Her friend's small hands straightened the ball cap on her head, and CJ marveled at the power that oozed from this tiny woman. Kate raised a son on her own, a junior in college now, the boy's father never aware of his existence. She turned her back on her family to handle her own affairs. Hungry for adventure, she cast her net into the unknown.

Did Kate ever regret her choice?

Next year, would CJ look back and regret hers? She stopped by the edge of the water and stared at the undulating sea. The sun glistened upon the ripples caused by the light breeze, and her heart fluttered with fear.

She felt Kate's hand on her shoulder and turned to look at her friend. "You're taking a huge step, breaking away to follow your heart. Everything's going to be okay." Kate hugged her. "Now, tell me, how did the reveal to the family go?"

CJ moved a few feet back, then sat on the sand, motioning for Kate to join her.

"Gordon surprised me with his excitement. Dad lit up for a mille-second when I mentioned Madison, and Mom, well, you can imagine. She still coddles my brother and treats me like a disease, and now, she's playing mom to a young couple who moved in next door. It's bizarre."

"It hurts you, doesn't it?" Kate's lips pressed tight as if holding in more potent words.

"I don't understand how a parent can be so cold to her own flesh and blood."

"You have too big a heart, CJ. Your mother doesn't deserve your love."

"I wish I knew how to turn it off. My heart, I mean." CJ stood, brushed the sand off the back of her shorts. "Maybe the distance and fifteen hour time-change will help."

"Speaking of Guam," Kate linked arms and started them back toward the house, "tell me what the island's like." CJ smiled at the change in subject, comforted by her friend's company.

"The island is tiny. Take one-thousand square miles away from Rhode Island, stick it in the middle of the Pacific Ocean, and there you have Guam. It's two hundred and twelve square miles to be exact. Small, but very beautiful. I tagged some pictures online. I'll show you later. I even checked out the resort where we'll be staying—the one run by Nick's friend Mike.

They climbed the stairs and headed for the kitchen to pour two glasses of iced tea. With drinks in hand, they went back out and sat on the deck to enjoy the fresh air.

"I wonder what made Nick's friend want to live there. Must be an interesting story." Kate took a long, slow sip of her tea.

"I guess I'll find out when I get there," said CJ.

"Didn't you ask him?"

"No. We were a little preoccupied." She thought of the kiss then hit the delete key in her heart.

Not ready to talk about her confusing feelings for Nick, CJ changed the subject.

"How's Gregory doing?"

"He's doing great." Kate chuckled, reading CJ like an open book. "Raves about his architecture professor, says his teaching style is captivating. I don't understand what that means, but if my son pays attention and makes good grades, I'm happy." Kate set her glass on the table, crossing the fingers of her right hand, which meant she had a subject to broach.

"There's this trip the professor offers during summer break and it's all Gregory can talk about. They go to Berlin to study the works of Mies van der Rohe."

"Does the school pay for that?"

Kate shook her head. "The students pay their own way." She shrugged, making a funny face. "It's expensive, but it's a chance I wouldn't want him to miss. I'll scrape the money together somehow. I'm hoping to get your store with a substantial pay raise. Is that delusional?"

"Speaking of—is there any word on that?"

Kate's fingers uncrossed. "I'm interviewing with your boss next week."

"Ex-boss. When?"

"Wednesday, and I have a ton of questions to ask."

"Okay, shoot."

They spent the next hour discussing the regional's management style, his supportive yet independent nature. He did not micro-manage, but he expected partnership with larger issues. When he asked for opinions, he wanted them from the heart, not what one might think he wanted to hear. Overall, he made decisions for the good of the business. He cared about people and rewarded strong results. Beyond that, he loved to laugh, his sense of humor dry but witty.

"So...if you get the job, will you move in, watch the house?" CJ asked.

"Yes. Thanks for the offer. I promise I'll find a place before you get back." She sipped her tea. "Do you know when that will be?"

"No clue."

A few minutes later, they went inside to peruse the fridge for dinner fixings. CJ glanced at her friend, thinking about everything that had happened in the last month. Did her good fortune produce for Kate a domino-effect in play?

"Did you ever imagine us standing on the verge of new discoveries at the same time?" she asked as she prepared the salad and got the tilapia fillets ready for the oven.

"Never," Kate said as she joined her at the counter.

Did Kate marvel, too, that while standing on the shore of Lake Taupo only four weeks prior, Fate intervened in their lives? Fate in the guise of Nick Madison.

"So, tell me, how will you handle the attention you're bound to attract?"

Kate knew her well. CJ hated the spotlight.

"You've always diverted attention to someone else.

Have you thought about having cameras in your face, articles written about your life, questions asked, answers formulated—that some of those might be false?"

"Wasn't at the top of my list." Her stomach tightened and her mouth went dry. "I was so busy organizing and getting things ready, I hadn't thought about the press." She shrugged. "Like the rest of this adventure, it's unknown territory, but if I'm strong enough and fast enough to attract the attention, I'll have to buck up and handle it." She spoke the words with bravado, but inside she shook.

"I suppose." Kate studied her as if trying to gauge the level of bull. "I've never known you to do anything half-assed, so I'm sure you'll figure it out." In a whisper, she added, "But I worry. The other side of the world is so far away."

Her friend's concern brought a smile to her face. "I'll give it my all, even if it kills me. I'll make you proud." She laughed. "Unless of course the pressure, or one of my teammates, annihilates me first."

"I'm already proud of you. Look what you've accomplished so far in your life, and now, you're leaving that behind to start a new career." Kate reached out for her hand, squeezed. "No matter what happens, this adventure will shape the rest of your life."

"Thanks, Kate. You don't know how much that means to me."

She tucked Kate's words deep into her subconscious as a mantra for the future: new career, new adventure, new life. And then she said a silent prayer that stepping out of her comfort zone didn't plunge her off the edge of her brand new world.

* * *

Kate left Sunday morning with a set of house keys

in hand. Whether she got the promotion or not, she promised to check up on things. Sadness crept in as they said their final goodbyes, and CJ spent the rest of the day trying to stay busy.

She ran the beach, sprinting along the water's edge, reminding herself that phones and iPad's would minimize the distance for them. They'd stay in touch and get together once she was back in the States.

She went to bed with an emptiness in her stomach, and she woke with a hole in her heart. Loneliness crept in during the night, snuggling deep into her soul. Lying there staring at the ceiling, she tried to ignore the isolation, focusing on the fact that she'd soon have others to push her along. She'd never trained with anyone before. Used to her own quiet thoughts during workouts, would she adjust to the impact of twelve strong guys?

The phone rang and a small knot of hope unfurled in her belly. Did her parents call to say goodbye and wish her well? But when she said hello, her family doctor replied.

"CJ, I have some disturbing news, but I don't want you to overreact. I'd like you to see a colleague of mine for another opinion, some comprehensive testing."

"Disturbing news?"

"Yes, there are several dark spots on your tibia x-ray. They're the size of a robin's egg. They look like tumors, though your blood work came back fine, your PSI levels normal—no indication of cancer. Trauma from your endurance race last month is a possible explanation, but . . ."

Something shifted in her stomach.

"I'd like you to follow up with Dr. Hempstead as soon as possible. If it is cancer, we may have caught it early enough."

"How..." Disbelief snaked through her. She never got sick and her leg didn't hurt. "I leave for Houston day after tomorrow. I'm spending the night before meeting the team for a six a.m. flight to Honolulu the next morning. From there, we fly to Guam."

"You'll have to postpone your trip."

"Dr. Taylor, I can't do that. I'm under contract. This is my new job."

"I can't force you, CJ. But if you insist on going, I recommend you find a doctor for immediate testing. Have him call me for specifics."

They hung up and she sat motionless for a moment. If Nick got wind of this, he'd kick her off the team. She couldn't risk that. No, she would watch for symptoms, pay closer attention to her body—and if…oh, she didn't want to go there.

She spent the day fretting and finally took a long run on the beach in an attempt to exhaust herself. She focused on each step as she pushed off the hard-packed sand. Could she sense if something grew inside her?

Did she feel anything? Nothing, only the strength of her muscles as they carried her along the water's edge. She breathed a sigh of relief.

She pushed the doctor's words aside and gazed out at the Atlantic. The ocean calmed her. Over the past four years, it soothed her worries, cleansed her pain. It mirrored her inner struggles with its intense moods.

In just a few days, she would stand on a foreign shore and stare at an unfamiliar body of water. Would it, too, reflect her moods?

Chapter 5

Nick paid for the newspaper and magazines he chose and turned to leave the small store. As he pocketed his change, CJ walked by. In faded jeans and an Ironman polo, she had several heads turning in her direction. He stopped and watched, marveling at the fact she seemed oblivious to the men gaping at her. Several did an about-face to watch her from behind. One guy even removed his Stetson and held it to his chest, a lecherous grin spreading across his face.

Nick shook his head and followed her toward the gate. How could a woman be so blind? But hey, he, too, could enjoy the view. She pulled a small wheelie behind her. The oversized bag with the bulky sweater threaded through its straps bumped against her lean hips to the rhythm of her high-heeled boots tapping the floor.

When she got to the gate, she stopped and looked around as if searching for a familiar face. Her lips puckered then lifted in a smile of recognition. He picked up his pace as one of the guys jumped up from his chair to greet her.

Reed Parker, his named star for the year, reached out to take her bag, placing it in the empty seat beside him. An animated conversation ensued, followed by a quick hug and shared kisses. They knew each other? He couldn't fathom why it bothered him, because this would make it easier for her to fit in. She wouldn't be an island in a sea of strange men.

Still, he stifled a rush of possessiveness before he stepped up to say hello. Chiding himself, he joined them.

"Hey, I didn't realize you two knew each other."

"Well, we don't really," Reed answered. "But we ran together for a few miles in New Zealand. What a coincidence she's the girl you signed."

"Indeed." He turned as the others gathered. In the spurt of friends greeting each other with pats on the back and brisk hugs, CJ took a step back. Her stiff stance spoke volumes. He touched her arm, bringing her into the loop, and did a quick round of introductions.

The greetings varied among the team. A few shook her hand with cool indifference, and several grunted a hello. Hunter's laid-back style welcomed her, but his competitiveness took her measure. Kyle's genuine embrace showed pleasure at having a new teammate, and Uri, the blocky German, almost sent her tumbling with his slap on the back.

"Sorry," he said. "Sometimes I forget I am strong."

Laughter broke out, and with that, CJ's shoulders relaxed. Could throwing a girl into their mix be the catalyst needed to raise the bar?

She glanced at her watch. "I'm hitting the restroom before we board," she announced.

"Good idea," a few of the guys replied.

"Hey, Hunter, you're in the seat next to me, aren't you?" Reed asked. "Would you mind switching with CJ?"

"Reed, you weasel, what would Jenny say?"

"It's not like that." He rolled his eyes. "We shared a moment in New Zealand, and I just want her to feel comfortable. You dolts don't seem to care one way or the other."

"Wait," Nick interrupted. "I planned to bring her up to speed on our practices. She needs some instruction before I let her loose to kick your asses."

"Now, Coach." Hunter looked over his shoulder then turned back to Reed. "Okay, I'll switch. Seems me and Coach have some things to discuss. No worries though, Coach. You can brief her on the flight from Honolulu."

* * *

On Saturday at seven in the morning, CJ stood holding her bike in the outdoor lobby of *Mike's Resort*. They'd traveled for twenty hours on two flights, flying in business-class, which meant the free champagne flowed. The few glasses of bubbly she indulged in combined with the time difference from home made her feel sluggish. Her head ached.

The sun turned the sky a translucent powder blue while piercing her brain, and she now dreaded their first training ride. Puffy white clouds swept overhead as she thought of their first night on Guam. They'd arrived at five-thirty last night. Instructed by their tyrant of a coach to put their bikes together, unpack, and get the rest of their gear in order because training would be their number-one priority while on the island, she missed dinner.

She went to bed as soon as she finished with her equipment, hoping to change her body-clock with a full night's sleep, but her limbs hurt worse than her head.

Her teeth wore socks and her mouth tasted as if the white sandy beach rested on her tongue instead of behind her. The rustling of palm fronds grated on her nerves. She glanced around, taking in the expressions of her new teammates as Nick described the day ahead. The entire team looked bleary-eyed, and as she made eye contact with Reed, he pulled a face, rolling his sea-green—albeit bloodshot—eyes toward heaven. A giggle escaped her and shot an arrow of pain straight through her forehead.

"Today's more about flushing the jet lag out of our systems." Nick's forest greens pinned her, squelching her mirth.

"Not to mention the wine we consumed," Kyle blurted, making everyone laugh…then groan.

Nick's lips thinned, his displeasure apparent, though his movements remained fluid as he continued to address the group. "We'll ride steady, focus on spinning. And from now on, alcohol is off limits. I want to see discipline in my athletes. You know nutrition is as important as the physical training, so no more slacking."

In contrast to the group, Nick stood tall, exuberant energy oozing from his pores.

"We'll start with an easy ride up to Cetti Bay." His voice penetrated the fog in her brain. "Later, we'll take a long, slow swim in Tumon Bay." His grin flashed. "If none of you drown, we may end the afternoon with a run up near Two Lovers' Point."

A collective grumble echoed. Nick ignored it, making introductions for Mike.

"Our host volunteered to lead the way, so let's follow him. I'll warn you, Mike's ridden with me since we were twelve. He can ride most of you into the ground, and this morning, you've made it an easy option." Nick clipped into his pedal. "Ride regular pace line. Guys, you pull one minute, CJ, you pull thirty seconds." He let her roll by then merged in behind her.

So…he chose to start by treating her like a girl. Something she told him she would not allow. Anger rushed through her, beating off some of her fatigue. How could she bond with her teammates if the coach babied her? To gain their acceptance, she needed to earn their respect.

"Sorry, Coach, but I'll pull same as the boys," she flung over her shoulder. The click of her cleat catching followed. No reason in her mind why she couldn't pull the train for a full minute like her male counterparts. A strong athlete and competitive on top, she'd prove it.

Temper could even help push the pace.

Nick shrugged, but several of the guys whistled.

They rode south, riding parallel with the water, circling a roundabout with a statue in the middle of it, slipping through a few side streets, and merging onto the only main highway on Guam, Marine Drive. She'd never seen water so beautiful. Nothing like the ocean she left behind. How would she describe the color? Vivid turquoise like those ice mints for sale at the store, topped with thick, brilliant foam like a cappuccino's. Mesmerized by the hypnotic rush of each translucent wave rolling over the other, she shook her head. She needed to focus on the bike in front of her or end up splattered on the road. That would not impress this team.

With a slight tailwind, Uri picked up the pace, and she found it difficult to breathe. It irked that Nick, who rode behind her, might notice her struggle. She couldn't appear weak on her first day. Concentrating on pulling up with her quads, she imagined scraping dirt from the bottom of her shoes, and her breathing settled. By the time they reached the Chamorro Village, it was well under control. Pushing large quantities of air out her nostrils, she released the tension in her shoulders and got aero. She found her rhythm as escaping toxins beaded upon her skin.

The village seemed deserted, but that made sense at seven-thirty in the morning.

She'd read that it came to life each Wednesday evening. Local vendors sold everything from clothing to crafts, bananas to betel nut, island foods to carabaos rides. Today's schedule made her wonder if they'd have any time to experience the local customs and taste the local fare.

They approached the naval base, but Mike, who again led the pace line, turned left before reaching the gates. The team followed, once again riding with the water off to the right, so clear and vibrant, she swore thousands of jewel-colored fish flickered just below the surface.

Hundreds of boats docked at the Agat Marina came into view seconds before the road sloped upward. The thought of climbing that grade made her bones weep, and because climbing wasn't something one did in a pace line, she pulled out to let Nick and the others pass. Climbing was her weakness. She preferred the wind and the speed on the flats.

She shifted into an easier gear and spun, fighting to keep her heartrate under control. Sweat poured down her shins as she inhaled great quantities of air. The guys pulled farther away from her, though body language indicated they struggled, too. Everyone, that is, except Nick. He seemed to float up the mountain.

Mike dropped back and rode beside her. She wanted to tell him to go paddle an outrigger, but instead, she gritted her teeth and continued to breathe.

"You don't have to wait for me." She huffed. "I'm not a strong climber. Go ahead and I'll see you at the top."

He shook his head, and the fringes of blond hair peeking out from under his helmet danced. "I'm enjoying a day out in the sun. I'm in no hurry, and I'm certainly not competing." His easy-going charm placated her.

Side by side, they spun up the crest. When they reached the top, she sighed, only to realize that had been the first of two climbs, the second one much steeper.

She sucked in air, relaxed her shoulders and

continued to turn the pedals. Mike chatted, tried to make conversation, but she did not respond. She needed all of her breath to reach the top. When she did, a few of the guys glared at her. They ate their Accel gels, the team's favorite brand, but gazed at her like she didn't belong.

Hunter, known as Hammer to the group, strutted like a peacock with his tail fanned.

Zach, the one with the small scar next to his nose, twitched his lips.

"Good of you to join us, CJ." Nick's sarcastic barb sailed through the warm air.

"Not a strong climber, huh?" Val, the dark-haired European called.

"Give her a break, guys," Reed called from his perch on a nearby rock. "It's her first day training with us."

Whispers rippled, followed by roaring laughter.

She smiled in their direction, but without saying a word, she walked over to the edge of the vista. Her breath caught in her throat. Thousands of coconut palms framed the area that plummeted to a magnificent bay forming a deep curve against the backdrop of rugged mountains. Vibrant colors melded against the deep blue sky.

She turned and stared up at Mount Humuyong Manglo, known to the natives as Mount Lamlam. The highest point on the island looked like a fist of rock reaching for the heavens.

The sheer beauty of her surroundings invaded her system. The salty air, the warm, liquid sunshine mixed with the sweat from her working muscles to cleanse her of her cranky mood. Her tension melted.

She branded the beauty into her heart. No one could steal that from her.

No matter how hard Nick Madison pushed her or grated on her nerves, even if the majority of her team never accepted her, she planned to make the most of her time on Guam. She'd stepped into this adventure with her eyes wide open, and she would return home without regret.

* * *

CJ took a nap after the ride, and because she missed lunch, she now downed a Power Bar. Not a great idea ten minutes prior to meeting for their afternoon swim, but she needed the calories. The ride up Cetti Bay took more out of her than she realized.

Nick approached her as she crossed the sand. Half of the group stood around, laughing and cutting up, but they stopped when she neared.

"CJ, I want you to take it easy on the swim." He raised his hand when she started to react. "I'm not saying that because you're a woman. You raced a tough event five weeks ago. Your body is still healing. You must allow it to rebuild. That means rest, which I'm betting you've had very little of since meeting me. This first week is about repairing your muscles, and then we'll reacquaint them with the stress of endurance training. We'll pace the build so you can peak for Florida." He smiled...the one she associated with humor. The corners of his eyes crinkled and his lip twitched as if he knew a joke no one else did. "I know you're a tough cookie—no need to prove that to me. Just remember, if you push yourself too hard and don't listen to your coach, you'll peak too soon. And we wouldn't want that, would we?"

She debated responding to the innuendo, then thought better of it. Signing her contract flashed to mind along with his demand that she trust him.

"You're right on all counts." She nodded. The whirlwind of activity she'd experienced since he appeared—right; to the training know-how of the past—

also right. Had he not recruited her, she would have rested, started training again at the end of April for Kona.

"Things will settle. You'll see." He winked. "Just before I start to push."

She smiled, well aware of his demanding nature.

The rest of the group joined them. Hunter, Kyle, and Lars wore huge shark fins on their heads, giving the Japanese tourists a show. Cameras clicked at a dizzying rate. The boys tried to sneak up on Nick, but the expressions on Simon, Uri, and Zach's faces gave them away.

Nick turned, shaking his head.

CJ couldn't contain her laughter. *What a bunch of nutballs.* Some of the young Japanese girls giggled as well, their mouths hidden behind their fingertips. With chins tilted toward the sand, they stared up at these odd men. Little boys really—in the bodies of men.

"Okay. Goal is to swim from here to the Westin." Nick's seriousness cut the laughter. "This is not a race. I want you to focus on technique, stretch and roll, remember to glide. Think of pulling each stroke through the water. I'll follow in the kayak to analyze each of your strokes. When we're done, you have a choice; swim back to Mike's or walk the beach. Either is fine."

Heads bobbed as masks and goggles were secured.

"How 'bout I kayak back, Coach, and you swim?" Reed called out, just before diving into the surf, and his long, effortless strokes moved him away from the group.

Watching him, CJ understood why Nick tagged him as one of his stars. Each pull was symmetrical, so beautiful.

As the rest of them waded into the bay behind the Hilton Hotel, she once again marveled at the clarity of the water. Hundreds of tropical fish glistened beneath her feet, their colors bright and intense. Melon-orange coral waved in the gentle sway of light indigo water, which to her surprise was only chest deep. A giggle escaped, because if anyone experienced a problem from lack of sleep, they simply needed to stand up.

She read in one of her books that a reef protected the bay, but it seemed deceiving, because looking out, only ocean stretched to the horizon—that dotted by fishing and dive boats. Again, the beauty astounded her.

How unfathomable to think the Mariana's Trench sat just out there in the distance below the surface. What had the book said? The deepest point or highest elevation in the world? Taking the measurement from the bottom of the trench to the highest peak on Guam, Mount Lamlam exceeded the height of Mount Everest. She would never have known that.

With her first stroke, she headed north toward the Westin Hotel, a mile and a half away, the other anchor hotel on Tumon Bay. The first ten minutes, she relaxed, let her lead arm reach as far forward as possible, enjoying the natural aquarium below. Her breathing strong and unhurried.

Big, the only six-foot-five redhead on the team—in triathlon—slid by her. She watched in awe as two of his strokes took him a full body-length away. She pulled harder and jumped into his slipstream. Water from his kick fluttered against her face, but she benefited from his draft.

He must have sensed her merge behind him; he picked up speed. She worked harder, her stubborn nature pushing her to dig deeper, swim faster. She inched up on him. The tip of the kayak came into view as she took her next breath, and she darted a glance at Nick.

He looked pissed. She eased up, his earlier words echoing in her ear.

She seemed to have a knack for uncovering his cantankerous side, just as he seemed to understand how to irritate her. He floated beside her for a moment, an expression on his face she couldn't read, then paddled off to measure Pete's stroke. While up ahead, Dave, John, and Val Ekimov pace-lined as if on the bike, each taking a turn pulling at the front. She almost swallowed water watching them, and did when Nick broke them up with his paddle.

The sun beat down on her shoulders, the heat penetrating her skin. Below her an eel slithered beneath a rock. The sandy bottom gave way to a forest of dark brown weeds, which her fingertips tangled in, creeping her out. Feeling claustrophobic, she came up for air, treading water so as not to put her feet down. Who knew what waited down there?

Her heart skipped and she breast-stroked to settle her fear, then plunged her face back in the water and kept going, sprinting to clear the mass. Her anxiety fled as the weeds disappeared and the rocky-white bottom returned. Plum-colored starfish nestled in the sand, while two lemon-chiffon fish chased each other through and around sea fans as delicate as lace. Nothing would ever live up to this experience.

The Westin Hotel beach came into view, but she didn't want to leave the water. She paddled around, flipped on her back, and did the backstroke, letting the sun warm her face. Out of the corner of her eye, she caught the last two guys heading for shore. She dove, swimming beneath them to reach the sand first. Sprinting through the shallow water, she raced to Reed's side and plopped down on his left.

He gave her a friendly hug. "It's good to have you on the team, C. Changes the dynamics but in an interesting way." His gaze scanned the group, landing on Coach, and he nodded.

"Thanks, Reed. I wondered how you guys would feel about having a girl around. Some of the others don't seem thrilled." She brushed sand off her shin, then looked into his sea-green eyes. "I worry about keeping up, but don't tell Coach that, okay?"

"Zipped," he said, his thumb and index finger sealing his lips. A wink set off his smile. "You'll get strong with us. Whether some of them like it or not, it'll happen."

Uri joined them. "It is warm, the water. I think I will swim every day with no problem." His accent and broken English endeared him to her. "I swim back to camp."

"It's the most beautiful water I've ever seen. I tried to think of how to describe it to my friends back home, but it's indescribable. Hey, maybe we should buy snorkeling gear, so we can explore during our time off." The thought filled her with enthusiasm and made her smile.

"With Coach, no off time. Only work." Uri laughed, a sound so deep and strong, it rumbled in his chest. For some reason, she found it comforting.

"How long have you been with Coach?" she asked, curious. She wanted to learn about the individuals who made up this team. They were such an eclectic mix. From what she gathered so far, they created a mix of nationalities: German, Russian, Norwegian, and Polish— all part of this US team. It fascinated her because each individual carried a unique history, but they all came together because of one man. The same man who'd scouted her and changed the direction of her life.

"Since day one. Four years ago." His chest puffed out. "I was first to sign."

"How did you meet?"

"During time I train in North California. I stop at Starbucks one afternoon. He is there. He like my bike and begin ask questions." His large shoulders lifted in one huge shrug. "From there, we make history."

She turned back to Reed, who reminded her of a

tiger, all powerful with lean muscles and a graceful way of moving. "How about you?"

"He saw me race in Wisconsin two years ago." His fingers raked his chestnut hued hair, which now dried in soft waves. "I was an age-grouper, and he thought I had potential."

She nodded; just like her in New Zealand.

Nick called attention to the group, motioning everyone to gather round. He covered his assessment of each member in a concise thumbprint, two strengths, and one challenge.

When he got to her, he said, "CJ, you need to roll your body. You swim like a pencil, too rigid to gain the benefit of the glide, and it weakens your kick, too."

Hunter a.k.a. Hammer murmured, "Now that's an image."

Several of the guys snickered. A few gazed at her with rounded eyes.

Uri reached over and patted her thigh.

"You have a very nice pull," Nick continued, eyeing the group. "And strong breathing technique."

Dare she tell him that he made her nervous, therefore making her appear stiff and "pencil-like"? Heat crept to her face and she looked away.

He finished his last critique and looked at his watch.

"You've got the rest of the afternoon to explore, relax, whatever. Dinner's at seven. Tomorrow morning, we'll start the day with that run on Two Lovers'. Plan to meet in the parking lot of the Westin at six-thirty for an eight miler." He walked to the kayak, dragging it back into the water.

It didn't rock when he stepped into it. His biceps flexed as he dropped the paddle below the surface, the tips disappearing, reappearing in an easy motion, his shoulders rotating as the boat floated away.

She stood rooted, admiring his form. He did have a

nice body. One that matched that handsome face, the one that now tilted toward the sun, while his mahogany hair feathered in the breeze. She sighed, a warm sensation swimming through her.

He fit well in these surroundings, seemed very much at home.

"Hey, C. You walking back with us?" Reed called, as he and the others headed back.

"No. I think I'll swim." She pulled her attention from Nick and waved to them. "I'll see you back at the resort."

* * *

Nick let the sun warm his face, the breeze comb his hair. He paddled out about two hundred yards, then turned left in the direction of *Mike's Resort*. Mike's sat mid-way between the Hilton and the Westin, the only two-story unit on the beach. The other hotels were the high rises of the island. High rises Mike helped build— the reason he first came to Guam.

Tourists sprinkled the beach, but the masses quit visiting when the economy took a dive. Mike's business suffered. As a carefree spirit, he accepted it as part of the Universal Code. Nick sometimes wondered how they'd bonded and remained such tight friends. When his cycling career ended so abruptly nine years ago, he took refuge on the island, blaming Fate.

Mike had just started work on the resort and egged Nick into helping. Together, they pored over plans, modifying when necessary to keep it simple—what anyone would imagine a tropical island resort to look like, small and inviting, open and airy, with dining on the water and rooms that led directly to the beach. They even built a small gazebo as the bar.

Over the two-year project, Mike nursed Nick's ego,

his sunny attitude shedding light on Nick's darker moods. His friend put up with his temper, using his quiet persistence as a weapon to get Nick back on the bike. Something Nick believed would never happen.

For Nick's twenty-ninth birthday, the resort's grand opening day, Mike gave Nick an airline ticket back to the States. In the card, he wrote: *Mojo, the spirit of the island, speaks—Your body is strong, your spirit intact; go after your quest and return with the Golden Fleece.*

Midway through that Come-back Tour, Nick quit. Haunted by memories of his crash, the competitive edge missing, he gave up and came back to his second home. For two more years, he worked as handyman, assistant chef and occasional bartender, marveling at how easily his friend lived the island life. Having been smart with investments, he contemplated following his best friend's example.

He spent his off time running and biking every inch of the island. He swam every body of water. The workouts became his outlet, his time to ponder what he wanted from life.

Over time, he realized his passion morphed into a need for all three disciplines, his love for sports too strong to contemplate giving them up. So the task became defining how he could use his talent without competing. How could he share his passions and technical expertise without drowning in the world of European cycling?

That's when he decided to start coaching. He chose triathlon because of the three sports and because it did not cross into his former life.

His emotional state remained safe.

Now, he brought his team to train on the same ground that spawned his new goals. How odd that in four years of coaching, he never thought to bring them here. But now with a female on the team, he did. Coincidence?

Or something else?

Thinking of CJ, the spunky redhead with a definite edge, made his heartbeat spike. She played tough, wanting to stand on her own, to fit in, to please—all at the same time. Was that part of the attraction? Or did some of her vulnerabilities remind him of his mother— the woman he couldn't save, the woman who took her own life when he was ten.

As he paddled toward shore, he saw her, his newest protégé, standing in knee-deep water as she pulled off her mask, her tri-suit clinging to her body. Willowy yet strong, a natural beauty, so unaware of her own sensuality. The sun kissed the water beading against the freckled patterns of her creamy skin as she skipped to shore.

He paddled a bit faster then backstroked. There stood Mike, a towel stretched open for her, a huge smile on his face. He watched as she stepped forward, becoming enveloped by the colorful cotton and his friend's arms.

Nick turned the kayak, slapping the paddles against the water. Unfamiliar feelings surged through him, traveling the length of his arms, moving him at quite a clip atop the bay. He breathed harder than the effort required, churning internally. His strokes dug deeper, as if trying to scrape the sand from the bottom of the ocean with his paddles.

Maybe he'd been wrong to sign CJ. To bring her to an island halfway around the world, to train with twelve macho guys. To expose her to Mike. He cursed himself, because he'd been the one to place her in this predicament. What had he been thinking? Had he even contemplated all of the dynamics?

Suddenly, his paddles stilled.

His heart tightened. He knew. He didn't want her to get hurt, and Mike would hurt her. Not intentionally, of course, but nonetheless...

CJ covered her wilted self-image with such courage, but he glimpsed the truth. He knew how easily one's shell could shatter. Hadn't his mother's? She'd tried to put up a good front, too, but in the end, she hadn't been strong.

Not that the situations mirrored each other, but there were similarities. The vulnerability that flashed at times, he'd seen in both women. Had he been to blame for his mother's choice?

The harsh reality of the water engulfing him as the kayak flipped brought clarity and—damn it—he'd carry another burden if CJ got hurt.

* * *

When Nick approached the table, he noticed CJ standing off to the side as if waiting for the guys to take their places. Most of them wore surf shorts and t-shirts with flip flops on their feet, the unofficial dress-code on the island for both men and women. She had dressed in khaki shorts and a pear-green crop top, her hair spiked in an unorganized fashion.

He took a seat at the end of the table, greeting those already seated, doing his best to appear casual. She glanced at him once then looked away. Should he ask her to join him?

When most of the seats were taken, she moved, her bare feet carrying her to an empty chair at the opposite end of the table. She sat down, placing her napkin in her lap, never once looking his way.

Pete drew him into a conversation about his afternoon exploration adventure.

"I took one of the resort's kayaks to Talafofo Falls and paddled around the fingers of the river. Man, you should see the size of some of the spiders I saw hanging on the palms. They were bigger than my hand. Scared me shitless. Never seen anything so big."

Pete's voice droned in his ear as his gaze fastened on Mike, who slipped into the chair beside CJ. She looked so fresh in her sandal-less feet and cool green shirt, and Mike's intent gaze seemed to feast on her. He leaned in to whisper something in her ear, his lips almost brushing her hair, and her face lit up. Her eyes sparkled, the white of her teeth blinding, and she did nothing to remove Mike's hand, which now rested casually on her arm. *Damn.*

"Speaking of kayaks," Big said. "You missed a great show when Coach flipped his."

Dave joined in. "Had us laughing 'til we cried."

"Quite a sight," Zach agreed.

For those who'd witnessed his blunder, laughter came again. "I was hot, needed to cool off, is all," Nick said, causing a fresh wave of hooting, but he couldn't take his eyes off CJ and Mike.

"Yeah, right," Kyle added before his mouth snapped shut and his look followed in the direction of Nick's own stare.

Nick fumed.

Mike's past swirled in Nick's memory. By flirting, Mike messed with CJ's heart. She did not need a diversion like this right now. She had an aggressive racing season to focus on, and nothing distracted more than a brand new relationship. They'd only been on the island for twenty-five hours, for God's sake. Did Mike have to start a relationship with every woman he met?

The fact that Mike didn't do relationships but only casual flings was the crux of this problem. Nick would not have his lead athlete devastated. Though he didn't know CJ well at all, he didn't think her to be the casual-sex-kind of girl. So how would she handle this?

Would Mike be up front with her, honest about his

intentions? Of course not. That had never been his style. He didn't even think in those terms. Mike just liked to have fun. He never got hurt, and he was oblivious to the mountain of broken hearts in his wake.

Nick would have to put an end to this before it got too serious.

The staff served pepper-seared tuna, sliced thin with a side of soy. Mike transferred a piece from his chop sticks to CJ's mouth. Nick almost pounced. His look shot across the table like a dart, piercing Mike, his hand now poised to feed himself.

"What?" Mike mouthed.

In a straightforward expression, he warned, *Don't you mess with her.*

"Coach, when will we get our full schedule?" Hunter's question pulled Nick's attention. He watched as Hunter scooped red-rice onto his plate. When he took enough, he passed the bowl to the left. Next, he chose a crispy chicken breast from a platter, handing off that plate, too. And so the process of group meals began.

"I'll individualize schedules in a few weeks." Nick took one of the platters being passed and selected a piece of fish. "For now, I want group interaction as we learn the island." He glanced back at Mike, raising a brow to say, *We'll pick this up again later.*

"What's this stuff?" Reed asked, holding up a bowl. Looking at the shredded dish with uncertainty, he scrunched his nose. He sniffed it, waiting for an answer.

"That's Kelaguen," Mike responded. "It's a chopped, boiled chicken dish made with lemon juice, grated coconut, and hot peppers. Spicy, but not too hot."

Reed spooned a tiny mound onto his plate.

"For more of a pop, try the fiery finadene sauce on your rice or with your fish." Mike pointed at the bowl of brownish-liquid with finely chopped onions in it.

"What's it made of?" CJ asked.

"Soy sauce, vinegar, lemon juice, onions and hot peppers," Nick answered, the heat of his scowl floating in her direction.

CJ shot him an odd look.

"Is true what said about the brown snakes on island?" Uri asked, a look of revulsion rippling through his brawny body.

"Yeah, I just read they're trying to control them with poisoned mice. Are there that many? Pretty creepy, if you ask me," Pete jumped in.

That remark pulled her intense gaze away from his, but not before he recognized a flash of terror. Did she also have a fear of snakes?

"That's all hype." Mike laughed, reaching over to ease her obvious distress. He rubbed her hand, then took her fingers in his. "I've been here eighteen years, and I think I've seen two, both dead on the side of the road. Smashed like pancakes."

"I guess part of our adventure is learning about the island," CJ said, keeping her eyes on Mike. She seemed delighted with his flirting.

"I heard Guam is the number-one seller of Spam per capita," Zach threw out as he examined the small fried fish he picked off one of the dishes.

"It is," Mike answered. "As a matter of fact, they created Pika-Spam just for Guam. Notice the bottles of Tabasco sauce everywhere? They used that to influence the new flavor. You should see the Spam wall at Kmart. It's a hoot." He turned to CJ. "Our Kmart is the number one volume store in the US. Maybe I could take you to see it?"

Enough was enough.

"She won't have time," Nick launched. "We'll be too busy training, or have you all forgotten why we're here?"

Stunned silence answered him.

He made a mistake bringing a woman here…a big mistake. Maybe she didn't belong on his team, after all.

Chapter 6

She dreamed of the water—so incredibly blue and clear, so impossible to describe. The temperature of it so perfect even a person who was constantly cold, like herself, could easily get in. No more hesitation to fill in the log book on the swim schedule. CJ now looked forward to every workout.

As she dove below the surface to study a clown fish, the phone rang. *The phone?* The loud jarring sound yanked her from her dream world, from the warm light to absolute dark.

She sat up, shaken and confused, as it rang again. Fumbling, she reached to pick up her cell. "Hello."

"Cassandra Jade Fallon?"

"Yes," she replied, her voice still groggy with sleep.

"This is Dr. William Hempstead, the Third. Dr. Taylor sent over your file, and I wanted to follow up with you."

She tapped the button on the side of her watch to light the Indiglo: one thirteen in the morning. "Didn't Dr. Taylor tell you?" She stifled a yawn. "I'm currently living on Guam. Fifteen hours ahead of your time zone."

He sucked in his breath, and it made her feel good to think she shocked him. After all, he woke her in the middle of the night, resurfacing the uncertainty she put to bed weeks ago.

She hadn't felt anything unusual during or after her workouts, and until she did, it shouldn't concern her. She flicked on the bedside lamp, pulled the sheet over her lap, and rubbed at the small bump her family doctor had noticed.

"I'm sorry I woke you. I didn't realize you weren't in Florida. But the spots he mentioned to you are a concern, and we need to do some tests, a biopsy to determine what they are."

"Dr. Taylor also said my blood work was normal."

"Yes, your PSI levels are right where they should be. Normal levels indicate no cancer, but for an accurate diagnosis, we must drill a small hole in your bone and test for malignancy."

"I've embarked on a new career. It's impossible for me to return to the States right now."

"Then I suggest you get a bone scan and MRI done there. We need an explanation and a cause. Without them, we can't treat the problem."

She had checked into the local doctors when they arrived and found that most islanders traveled to Hawaii for medical issues, which shot her hope of following up here. "I'm afraid I can't. Only the naval doctors are well thought of, and I'm not qualified to see them."

"This is serious, Ms. Fallon." His tone chilled. "We can't leave this undiagnosed for long. Once you've explained, I'm sure your supervisor will understand your need to return home."

"He's my coach, and I can't tell him." Panic that she'd lose her contract squeezed the air from her lungs. "I left my career to race as a pro. I'm halfway around the world. Isn't it possible the spots are from the trauma of endurance racing? I've been racing long distances for six years."

"My responsibility is to be straightforward with you. The discoloration could be caused by many things, but as a bone cancer specialist, I must share the repercussions of my experience." He cleared his throat before continuing. "If they are tumors, you face a loss of limb...or life, but if we diagnose it early enough, we may succeed in beating this."

His voice resonated in the deafening silence, the darkness of the room closing in on her.

"Ms. Fallon, are you there?"

"Yes, I'm here." It came out in a whisper. His words flicked around her brain like gnats.

"Tell me, have you been experiencing any symptoms? Weight loss, nausea, pain? Anything out of the ordinary?"

"I'm an endurance athlete, doctor. Something I recently stepped up a level. I don't feel pain. I lose weight because of the miles I put in. I'm healthy and always have been." At least she believed so. "I rarely even get the sniffles."

"I see." The gravity in his voice made it hard to ignore him. "Does your shin bother you in any way?"

"No. Not at all, and I never noticed the bump." She chewed her bottom lip. "That is, until Dr. Taylor pointed it out. Since then, I've paid attention to my body, looking for any symptoms, but I've never felt stronger than I do right now."

"Well, until we get you in for those tests, which I suggest be sooner rather than later, I advise you to stop all weight-bearing activity."

"You can't be serious? I'm a triathlete. Running is a huge part of my life."

"I am, Ms. Fallon. I'm dead serious."

* * *

Reeling, CJ hung up the phone. *Loss of limb, loss of life,* the eerie echo of his words chased away all thought of sleep. Were those the challenges she now faced?

Instead of racing for glory, she ran from doom?

The silent minutes ticked by, her blood pulsing through her veins in thick, slow spurts. She placed her hand over her heart and felt the unsettled *thump, thump,* which oddly matched the throbbing in her temples.

"Stop all weight-bearing activity," he said. *Please.*

Panic closed in on her and the room shrank before her eyes, a pinpoint of light disappearing to black. She lay back on the bed and felt everything sway beneath her.

Her stomach pitched—*Oh, God.* She barely made it to the bathroom before the remnants of dinner shot from her throat.

With her stomach empty, she sat on the cool tile floor and let the tears come. She'd never felt so alone in her life. She couldn't call Kate. What would she say? Her parents, oh yeah, that would go well. She couldn't tell Nick...or her teammates, because then it would get back to Nick. She took a deep breath and tried to think.

Questions tumbled over themselves in her mind, but the answers came back to one thing. What could she do? *Nothing.*

She stumbled from her room, her feet carrying her to the small hut on the beach that served as a bar. Tiki torches blazed, cheerfully lighting the area, but it could have been squalling and it would have felt the same. Guests sipped colorful concoctions topped with tiny umbrellas, as the sea washed the shore, and the breeze sang through the trees. Her heart felt like stone.

"Hey, girl, what can I get you?" Mike stood behind the bar, wiping a glass dry with a pure white cloth. It almost glowed against his tanned fingers.

"Something strong." She slumped on a stool. Tears burned and she brushed at them with the back of her hand.

"Oh, no, what happened?" He put the glass aside and cupped her left hand with his right. "Did your coach say something stupid again?" He'd witnessed Nick's shortness with her several times, even mentioned that he hadn't seen that side of him in years. Should she pretend, cover up her real issue with Nick as an excuse? She shook her head. She couldn't do that.

"It's not Nick." She stared at the contrast of their skin as if in a daze, started to pull away.

"Then what? Did you get a visit from the taotaomona?"

"Taota—what?" She looked up at him; the confusion must have shown in her eyes.

"Ancient island spirits. It's said they visit newcomers." He grimaced, held firm to her fingers. "Never mind. Come on, tell me what's wrong."

Whatever words formed in her brain lodged in her throat, choking her. She swallowed and this time managed to pull away. She couldn't tell him. He'd tell Nick and her world would fall apart. Hadn't it already been turned upside down? She got up from the stool and turned to go.

"Oh no, you don't." He grabbed a bottle of something, two glasses, and without grunting, hopped over the counter, landing softly on his feet next to her. In one fluid motion, he pulled her to his side, signaled a waiter to take over, and guided her around the corner toward his room.

"CJ, you look like someone just dug your grave," he whispered, his back against the inside of the door, blocking her exit. "What's going on?"

Tears threatened again, and she turned so he wouldn't see.

He pushed her to sit on the couch, then he poured a generous amount of the dark liquid into one of the glasses, pressing it into her palm. "Take a sip of cognac. It will make you feel better." He urged her to sip. "What brought you out to my bar when you should be sleeping?"

She set the glass aside after taking a tiny sip. It burned going down, forcing fresh tears to her eyes. When she looked into his pale blue eyes and saw his questioning concern, she broke. The tears flooded and so did the words.

Wrapped in his embrace, she told him everything.

"Please. You can't tell Nick," she begged as more tears coursed down her cheeks. "He can't find out. It will ruin my chances with the team." She burrowed into his neck. "Oh, Mike, I'm so confused. And scared."

* * *

Like a large hand looming in the dark, a force pulled Nick from a sound sleep. His heart pounded like a wild bird caught in a cage. Panic seized him. Something that never happened to him. Maybe a quiet walk on the beach would help sort the unease, make the feeling of suffocation disappear? The fresh air, the salty spray, the sound of the ocean would lull him.

Pulling on a pair of jeans, he took the outside stairs two at a time as he zipped his fly. When he hit the last step, he faltered. CJ? Coming out of Mike's room?

He stood in the shadows and watched.

Mike stepped out behind her, his hand resting on her shoulder, a cozy scene from this vantage point. He flicked his watch: after three in the morning. Could this be a normal rendezvous? How often had this happened?

So far, her training had been solid. Would this little affair end up compromising her strength? Distract her from her purpose? And why did it inflame him? What burned in his gut? The continued urge to pound his friend senseless weighed on him.

He'd known Mike for twenty-three years and never felt animosity toward him. Irritation certainly, but never this. Since the day they arrived on the island, his annoyance with Mike had mounted. That Mike played with his star's emotions fed Nick's aggravation.

He remained out of sight but followed them when they moved.

Something pinched in his chest when Mike wrapped his arm around her, pulling her close to his side as he walked her back toward her room. Could it be that he hoped he'd been wrong about them? Would his spirits have lifted if she'd been alone, wandering because she, too, couldn't sleep?

Her attraction to Mike seemed transparent. The sunny, uncomplicated, buoyant personality that radiated from him was like a magnet, and she'd been drawn to it.

Had he expected her to resist? Deep in his bones, he admitted that he did. He estimated her to be different, believed she wouldn't be sucked in like all the other women. He worried that his friend would shatter her already fragile ego. For a triathlete, that wasn't good. For a girl with low self-esteem, that could be fatal.

He expelled a breath and wondered why he cared. But he knew. Admitting it hurt.

His body reacted to her. Even though he'd tried to distance himself, had in truth been rude to her on occasion, she captivated him. How could he be her coach and a love-sick bystander at the same time?

When they reached her door, Nick turned away, afraid to see what might happen. Would Mike kiss her? Would he go inside? Did they follow this routine each night to keep up appearances and allow CJ to wake in her own room?

The urge to interrupt them pulled, so Nick bolted.

His quiet walk on the beach turned into a full-fledged run. With heart pumping, his lungs screaming for air, he ran—away from the pain, away from the truth.

A grown woman could make her own decisions. That he didn't like what she decided made no difference. Now he had a new challenge. How could he coach her to win and keep his heart, his confused emotions, out of the mix?

* * *

The following week blurred like a cloud of dust swirling in her brain. CJ focused as best as she could on training. Her muscles strained as she went through the motions, but she couldn't stop her mind from drifting. She fought to push her body through the fog, to continue building respect with her team, but fear took a strong hold on her concentration.

Could Nick see her confusion? Had her team seen any digression? Had they talked to him? She swore he looked at her in a strange way. Had Mike spilled her secret after all?

The turmoil made her sick to her stomach, and she began to second-guess everything. On top of all the emotion, she now felt twinges she never felt before. Worry chipped at her confidence, chilling her even in the heat of the day. Dark circles appeared under her eyes, her cheekbones became more prominent, and she disliked looking in the mirror more than ever.

This morning on their bike loop, she almost crashed. Twice her front wheel got dangerously close to the back wheel in front of her. Without focus, she would end up with a broken collarbone, or worse. That she did not need.

Berating herself, she stared ahead and pedaled.

"Glass right," Simon called.

"Crap up," she heard Dave shout as her tire

crunched through debris. That dreaded *pttsss* followed and she groaned.

"Flat. I have a flat," she yelled, pulling over to the side of the road. "Darn!"

The train kept going. It would be a long, lonely ride back to camp. She shifted gears and got the wheel off. As she dug in her saddle bag for a new tube and tools, Reed and Uri pulled up, jumping off their bikes.

"Come, we help."

"You came back for me?" She gazed up at them, her eyes filling. She smiled so as not to cry. Her heart thumped in her chest with an unfamiliar feeling, because they came back for her.

"No man gets left behind," Reed answered.

"But we'll never catch up." Her mishap would cost them all.

"We strong like bull. Go like bullet." That made her laugh.

"Let's get this done, so we can bust a gut and reel them in like guppies."

She shook her head at their confidence, but sometimes determination was the ingredient necessary to close the gap. She would do her best to show them.

Uri changed the tube and checked the bead for any pinches while Reed got the CO_2 cartridge ready. She repacked her saddle bag. Once they inflated the tire and got the wheel in place, the three of them hopped back on their bikes.

Heads down and muscles pushing, they pace-lined and ramped up the speed. Her lungs pushed the breath up her throat, her heart pounding in her chest, but fifteen minutes later, she saw the caboose. They zeroed in, gave one gigantic effort. They were so close. Yet it still took another ten minutes before they hooked on.

Her chest swelled with pride when Big dropped back from his pull and noticed the three of them. She grinned at him.

"We've been snared," he called up the line. "They're back."

Several heads turned as if they didn't believe Big's announcement. She nodded with purpose, then thanked Uri and Reed for their support.

"We're family." Reed's unassuming shrug marked his statement. Her insides warmed.

* * *

Tonight, the exhaustion caught up with her, and she collapsed in her room. She gained a bit more respect with her team, but how long before they noticed the cracks? The façade of strength was wearing thin, and she feared they'd see.

She ignored the last two phone calls from Kate, letting them go to voicemail, answering her through email. She wrote stories describing the island and their busy schedule, cluing Kate in to the diverse personalities of the boys—"hunks" as Kate referred to them.

She feared Kate would hear something in her voice...and ask.

Spent, she slept, floating in a huge, dark space. Cold air wrapped around her like a blanket of ice. Suspended, she hung there, waiting for her sentence.

At two a.m., she awoke with a fright and found she couldn't go back to sleep.

She lay staring at the ceiling. Without rest, her training would suffer, and there'd be no hiding that from Nick.

Frustrated, she went out to the beach. She sat staring at the dark horizon, the rush of the ocean filling her ears. She hoped it would quiet the hysteria building within her. As she'd done countless times in Painter's Hill, she closed her eyes and concentrated on the sounds around her. She breathed in. The freshness offered by Mother Nature filled her lungs.

Another deep breath and she almost jumped out of her skin when a hand touched her.

"What are you doing up at this hour?" She half expected Mike's voice, but her body tightened when she heard Nick's. His nearness caused a reaction she didn't like to acknowledge. "You should be sleeping." He sat behind her, his hand lingering on her shoulder.

The heat of his palm burned through the thin material of her t-shirt. "I couldn't sleep," she whispered toward the sea. "I hoped the sounds of the ocean would lull me back to neverland."

"Maybe you need something more than the ocean." He massaged her shoulders, his strong hands working the tense muscles at the base of her neck. Without thinking, she let her head fall forward, let the magic of his kneading loosen the knots.

His fingers moved down her back, over, between, and under her shoulder blades. Like wax, the muscles melted beneath his strength. How she wished she could turn into his arms and share her angst, get it out in the open, but that was impossible.

"You've been preoccupied for days. Want to talk about what's bothering you?"

"Just feeling sorry for myself." She deflected reality. "Maybe questioning my decision..." She let her voice trail off, continued to enjoy his fingers on her skin. Tiny goosebumps rippled across her skin and she shivered.

"Are you cold?" He moved his hands to rub her arms from shoulders to wrists and her blood heated. A blush crept up her cheeks and she thanked the gods that he couldn't see.

"Your training's good, so why question your decision?" His words, like his fingers, probed. "Unless you're referring to something else. Yes?"

"No." The answer popped out of her mouth. As if electricity pumped through his fingertips, she jerked away, kicking up sand as she stood. She brushed sand off the back of her shorts while pasting a smile onto her face. "But it's good to know you think I'm doing well. It's tough when competing solely with men. Some of them think I'm soft. I guess that makes me second-guess myself."

He stood, too, stared at her for a long moment before responding, "Like I said, you're doing fine, gaining strength faster than a few of the guys even, which is probably why they're needling you. But whatever's distracting you could get in the way. You can't allow it to control you, CJ. Instead, you need to maintain power over it."

"Of course, you're right. I will," she replied mechanically, not at all sure what he referred to.

"CJ," he frowned as he continued to study her. "The team needs you, even if some of them don't think so. Don't let them—or me for that matter—down." He looked away as if embarrassed, and then turned and walked back toward the hotel.

She watched as he climbed the stairs, disappearing into the darkness. Alone, she fought back new tears. What if her destiny meant letting them all down? Could she live with herself?

Chapter 7

CJ's sore muscles made her groan as she hit the double climbs to Cetti Bay, but she stood up and put power to the pedal, leaning the bike from side to side as she motored up the crest. They were on their second loop of the island, and though not part of Nick's instructions, competition reared its pretty head.

If she hung with Reed and Kyle, she just might beat the rest of the team.

"Come on, C. Keep up the pace. You're doing great, and we're still pulling ahead." Reed understood her need to prove herself. Several times in the last month, he backed her, which pissed off the other guys. Now, he urged her on with his bright sunny smile.

"Relax on the descent. Lean forward into it and let gravity take you." Kyle came up behind her, tapped her on the back as he slipped by, glancing over his shoulder, his voice animated. "We dropped 'em like a prom dress. Woo-hoo!"

As usual in this section of the ride, her heart jumped to her throat. The steep descent created a perpetual alley of wind that made her feel like a piece of lint buffeted about. The bike shimmied beneath her, threatening to vibrate her right off the saddle. She swallowed her fear and clung to the drops as the three of them bulleted down into Umatac. She laughed as loud as she could, a form of war-cry escaping her.

Trying not to grab the brakes, which would cause her to endo—she'd seen experienced riders seize the front brake, velocity keeping the back end of the bike moving, up and over the front end, rider still attached—so she feathered them to scrub off some speed as they careened through a sharp turn before climbing out of Umatac. A quick steep climb, but they powered through it, while wild booney dogs waited at the side of the road to chase them and nip at their feet. The sight and sound of a pack of mangy mutts shot enough adrenaline through her and gave all of them reason to scurry up the grade without faltering.

CJ memorized the names of all of the villages and now clicked them off in her head as they made their way around the south tip of the island. Undulating and rounding into Merizo popped Coco's Island into view on the right. Tourists spent the day there sunning, jet skiing, and being pulled around on banana boats. Usually quite a sight, but at the pace they rode right now, she couldn't dally and watch.

They formed a tight pace-line, revving up the average speed. No letting up, because if the rest of the guys banded together and worked as a team, the three of them would be devoured in no time. They pushed to complete the hundred mile ride first.

They used the magic of a pace-line by taking short strong pulls—the front man busting a gut, allowing the two other riders to use less energy, conserving their strength until they had to pull. They encouraged each other with periodic shouts to drive their short train home and win.

It felt good to push, to exert such effort, forgetting—at least for the moment—the issues that plagued her.

The sweat rolled down her back as her heart pumped. She took advantage of the aero position and sliced through the wind, her companions sailing with her. They still had several tough climbs to conquer, but if they focused and stayed together, they could pull off this victory. Wouldn't that be sweet?

Up and over Talofofo Falls, dipping down into Ipan Beach. They whizzed by Jeff's Pirate Cove, a local bar and eatery—a great place for burgers and local fish. Her energy soared as they climbed the next vista, Pago Bay. Sky and water merged in vibrant blue, cut only by a slash of dark green vegetation. Zigzagging back down out of Pago Bay, they cranked up the speed. Just a notch to keep the edge. They motored.

Turning on to Route 4, they headed northwest, cutting across the middle of the island to reconnect with Marine Drive and head home. Would the team catch them?

When the Statue of Archbishop Flores, which stood in the roundabout, came into view, they kicked it into overdrive.

"May the strongest man win," Kyle cried as he sprinted.

A race for the finish. She pounded on the pedals. Wheezing, she stood up and threw every ounce of energy into her sprint.

They kept jockeying for position and the last two hundred yards became their race to win. Who would take it?

Nick stood at the side of the road with a look of astonishment on his face as the three of them came barreling down on him. Stopwatch up, he screamed for CJ to pour it on.

"Show those guys what you're made of."

Like a sprint finish at the Tour de France, she edged

by the boys and finished first. She raised her fists in the air and cheered with gusto. *"Hafa Adai!"*

Pronounced like half-a-day, it meant *good day* or *welcome.*

"Great job," Nick shouted, and her chest puffed with pride.

Did he happen to catch her finishing stunt?

After learning about Nick's pro career, CJ bought several race DVD's and watched them over and over. She studied his form, counted his pedal strokes, and practiced the winning pose for just such an occasion.

In each clip, he looked so happy zipping his jersey for the photo op, just before pumping his fists in the air. His youthful cockiness had filled her screen more times than she could count. She memorized every curve, every nuance, every line on his face as he radiated pleasure.

"Did I get it right, Coach?" she asked as she pulled the bike around to stop next to him.

"You did." His eyes remained fastened to the watch, no doubt waiting for the rest of the team to show. "Fabulous ride." He grinned but still watched for the others.

"I don't see them. Did they get lost?" She peered down the road, not yet seeing anyone approach. "They couldn't have fallen that far behind."

"What did you guys do, take a short cut?" he asked. "Let me see your odometer."

"We would never cheat." She feigned shock. "Go ahead, have a look. The three of us worked together, dropped their butts." She pushed the button on her computer to prove her point.

"That's right, Coach, to prove we're the best," Kyle added as he got off his bike.

"You think our team's in for a win this year?"

"Several." Reed joined them. "Incredible ride, Irongirl." He turned to hug her, praising her spunk.

"You're a winner."

"Thanks," she said, but whispered in his ear, "for letting me win." She'd seen him ease up at the last second to let her take the glory. "You're a cool guy."

He answered with a huge puppy-dog smile.

Two minutes later, a blur of color appeared at the end of the road. The freight train approached, a long thin line worming toward them. About a hundred meters from where the four of them stood, the line spread. Riders vied for position, rolling shoulder to shoulder, blocking the entire width of the street.

Uri pushed and skimmed by Val Ekimov, crossing the finish line a fraction of an inch before the others rolled by, the *swoosh* of their wheels deafening.

Uri circled around and called out to her, "You go, Irongirl." He saluted her with both thumbs up to endorse her accomplishment.

Several cheered while a few grumbled that she'd never have pulled that off without Reed and Kyle to help.

"Stuff it, boys," Nick groaned, staring at the two culprits. "They just proved three could beat ten. Focus and teamwork. It's a lesson you could learn from."

A thunderous debate started with pushing and shoving. CJ stood in the fray, looking around for a way to escape. The noise level rose and she cupped her hands over her ears.

She noticed Mike rush out from the lobby. He interrupted the spat, pulling her from the rowdy group.

"Your brother called—six times. He sounded upset, but he wouldn't tell me why. Give me your bike, go to the office and call him. Now!"

CJ dialed Gordon's cell. What could her brother want?

The phone rang twice before he answered.

"CJ." He sounded out of breath. "You have to come home. Dad, he's in the hospital. Dr. Taylor said he may not make it."

"Oh, my God, what happened?" Her knees went weak, and she sank into a chair. "Was he in an accident?"

"No. He collapsed out in the yard. They think heart attack, but they're running tests, while we go crazy in the waiting room. Mom's a mess. Here...talk to her."

"No, wait. I'm the last person who can help her. You know that." A chill passed over her skin. "Gordon, you're her golden child. If you can't calm her down, I certainly can't. I'll only make it worse." She tried to reason. "Can't you have a nurse check her, maybe get her a sedative?"

"I tried that, but she's ranting, won't let anyone get near her. She's said such terrible things, called Dad a bastard, blamed him for doing this on purpose. I've never seen her like this. It's freaking me out."

The reality of distance hit her. She couldn't get there to help, and by the time she did get home, it could be too late. Her gut twisted, thinking of the last time she'd seen her parents, that morning in their kitchen.

She had to believe he'd be fine. She had to believe she'd see her father again.

"Gordon, I'm on the other side of the world. I can't do anything from here. Pull yourself together and support Mom. She's upset, that's understandable. She needs you."

"Come home. Please," he begged. "You're the strong one."

Glancing at her watch, she calculated. "Even if I got the first flight out, I wouldn't get there until Saturday morning, eleven o'clock Atlanta time."

"I can't do this alone, CJ."

Her pulse moved like molasses, thick and slow. What could she do from here but soothe? "Listen to me, okay? Dad is going to pull through. He's young, he's never been sick. Maybe this is a warning for him to slow down. I don't know, but you have to believe he's going to survive."

The office door opened and Mike and Nick slipped in, sat across from her with questioning expressions on their faces.

"But..." Gordon started, and then his voice changed, as if it came from far away. "No, no. You've made a mistake. Please tell me it's not true."

"Gordon? What is it?" No reply. Had he hung up on her? "Gordon. Gordon?" She depressed the button to get a dial tone. Her hand shook as she hit redial.

The hair on the back of her neck raised; she knew before Gordon spoke.

Her father was dead.

"C-J," it came out as two long sounds, slurred and almost incoherent. "Dad's gone. They couldn't save him."

Her eyes flooded as pain stabbed her heart. "Please, no," she whispered. But the eerie sound she heard in the background confirmed it, her mother, the anguish in her cries announcing that life ended in a flash.

"Gordon, tell her I'm coming home."

Through her tears, she saw Nick move, felt him take the phone out of her hand.

She turned into his arms, buried her face against his chest, and murmured, "Dad died. I have to go."

* * *

For the next hour, Mike and Nick fussed over her, helping make the arrangements. With airline tickets bought, CJ threw some things in a duffel bag, fighting the tears that burned.

"Not even fifty years old, how could such a quiet man die of a heart attack?" She said it out loud, but not as a question to either of them.

Nick came over and wrapped her in a hug. "No one can ever explain something like this."

"Just know we're here for you," Mike added as he hugged her from the other side.

Sandwiched between these two strong men, she realized she still wore her crusty, salt-covered skin suit from this morning's ride. She needed a shower.

"I've got to clean up, change into dry clothes. Look at me, I'm a mess." She pushed at both of them. "I appreciate everything you've done, but I think I need some space."

"Can we get you anything?"

"Don't want to leave you like this."

They both spoke at once as they reluctantly backed toward the door, each looking at the other for reassurance.

"Please, just give me time. It's sinking in and I need to deal with it. Alone." Firmly, she pushed them out the door and locked it.

She drew the curtains to close out the sunshine, to encase herself in darkness, creating a shroud against what might swamp her when she stopped long enough for emotion to catch up.

In the shower, as the deluge of hot water cascaded over her, emptiness crept into her heart. She shivered and turned the knob to hotter. Steam filled the bathroom.

Her father had been a stranger to her. She never knew his dreams. He never shared his passions. That small hole in her heart opened, spreading until the numbness disappeared and sheer anguish took over. Sliding down the wall of the shower, sitting on the floor in a ball, she let the tears come. She wept for the father she would never truly know, the man she wished could have seen the real her. She cried that he never knew she threw herself into sports because of a comment he made when she was five. Her mother called her hefty and he joked that no, she was built like an athlete. It was the first and only time he ever supported her.

Track, the swim team, volleyball, soccer, she tried everything to give him a reason to love her. Oh, the dreams of family, the wishes of youth. How many kids grew to adulthood never having theirs realized? Why did it hurt so much?

Wrapped in a thick terry-cloth robe, she curled in the center of the king-sized bed, tiny and insignificant in this vast world of unanswered hope. Alone.

She hugged herself, wished she had someone in her life who'd hold her. She drifted to sleep with Nick and his earlier hugs on her mind, the drying tears tightening her skin.

In her dreams, flashes of childhood memories battled with unknown scenes of the future. Doctors and nurses in hospital greens, prodding and poking, sticking needles the size of spears into her leg mixed with the image of a teenager, hiding in the dark corner of her closet, checking clothing labels with a flashlight to ensure she was not fat. Her mother's criticism blended with her own words as she relived the moment in the kitchen when she told her father she loved him.

The finality woke her. She was encased in the darkness, not sure how long she slept, the chaos of her dreams fuzzy. Then she realized she heard knocking. She glanced at the clock: eight-thirty at night; she'd been out for over five hours.

Another knock sounded at her door.

She opened it, surprised to find her entire team standing there staring at her. They held plates of food and came abuzz as soon as the door gapped.

"We were worried when you didn't show for dinner." Simon walked in, carrying a platter covered with a cloth.

"You must eat. You need strength," Val bullied.

"We're here for you, CJ." Reed hugged her, smoothing her hair. "You can lean on us."

"Were you close to your dad?" Zach asked as he placed a case of water on the small table near the window.

"No." She shook her head, sat on the edge of the bed, new tears threatening. Embarrassed, she burrowed into the robe. "It makes it worse, really, because now I won't ever have the chance. Death is so final."

"Tell us about him." This from Lars, the Norwegian who looked like a blond-haired Elvis. "Make you feel better, no?"

His bright blue eyes and devilish grin brought a smile to her face. "He was such a quiet man. Never said much about anything." She turned to face Nick and added, "Though he knew about your cycling career, the crash. That surprised me, because I never saw him watch the sport. There's so much I don't know, now..."

"He could have read about me in the papers." Nick sat in the corner armchair, watching.

"Why do you think he was so quiet?" John prompted.

She shrugged her shoulders, not knowing the answer. "He never argued, never yelled. I used to think he avoided conflict and let my mother run the household, but maybe not. Maybe he simply held things in. What if holding everything inside killed him?" She wiped at another tear. Wasn't she, too, holding something in? "I guess I'll never know."

"What did he do for a living?"

"CFO of one of the larger companies in Atlanta." She needn't go into what company. At this point, it didn't really matter, and it made her sadder to remember that when she was young, he spent more time at work than at home.

"Don't be sad." Dave pressed a basket of muffins upon her.

"You just lost your father. It's okay to let it out." Lars took the basket back and made a face at Dave.

"I have a big shoulder for you to cry on." Big slid over and pulled her against his side. She fit beneath his armpit, which made the group snicker.

"I hope you showered after our ride," Zach said, which totally undid them.

"Come, I have broad shoulder, too. Much better fit, yes?" Uri sat on the other side of her and wrapped her in a hug.

"Hey, you're not the only jerks who care. I want a hug, too." Pete pushed at Uri, tried to muscle his way in.

A new emotion stung her throat. Men she barely knew—who shared her grief, her turmoil, her uncertainty—cared. They showed that as they attempted to cheer her up.

Coach included.

Her gaze came to rest on him, the man who'd created this team, added her to it. Something uncurled in her belly—a soft, mushy feeling that swam down to her toes.

Their eyes met and held, locked together in a private moment. She took comfort in the sympathy there, drew it in, then turned back to Pete. There'd been something raw in Nick's expression, a flash like a kindred spirit. Afraid she might do something stupid in front of the whole group, she deflected the attention.

"Pete, who is Serge Carter?" She knew Pete's last name as Carter, but the team roster listed Serge not Pete.

"Me." He blushed. "When I was born, my father brought a good friend over to see me."

"Yeah, so where did Pete come from?" Kyle asked.

"My dad's friend hated the name Serge, so he renamed me Pete. It stuck with my family—they never called me anything else. Unless my mom got pissed at me, then the full name came out—Serge Gregory Carter, she'd yell." He shrugged, but his cheeks turned pink.

She didn't know what else to do, so she hugged him.

They held briefly then broke apart, an odd pulse in the room like the invisible force that pulled them all together as a unit. She glanced from one face to the next. The levels of sympathy registered as salty tears trailed down her face. They accepted her into their club. Whether they openly competed with her or not, she belonged to their tribe.

"It's ten o'clock." Nick stood after looking at his watch, prompting her to do the same. "She needs rest. She's got an early morning, has to be up and out by four."

Each of her teammates took a moment to touch or hug her.

It amazed her that each contact varied in strength. Some she described as the slow pulse of waking, others the intense beating of a hard workout, still others a soft imprint against the skin. But when Nick held her, electricity sizzled in the air. It crackled like power lines on a stormy night, so strong, she marveled that the others didn't sense it.

Did he? Could that be why he jumped away so fast?

"I'll see you at four." Nick stepped toward the door, motioning for the guys to move.

"We're all meeting in the lobby at four, right?" Zach asked, grabbing a bottle of water as he passed the table.

"There's no need," Nick responded. "I'll drive her."

"We were planning to go with you," they clamored.

"We want to be there to say goodbye." Reed spoke above the commotion, "Coach, we need to do this. Besides, it'll just give us an early start on our training."

"Yeah, can't argue with that. Can you, Coach?"

"I could just as easily take a cab," CJ volunteered.

A cacophony of retorts hit her.

"It's settled then. Lobby at four." Nick shoved the last one out the door, shaking his head. From the doorway, he turned back to her. "Sleep tight, CJ. If you need anything, call."

"I will."

The warmth from his gaze lingered long after the door closed.

Chapter 8

CJ's loneliness dissipated as she boarded the plane after fourteen guys, new friends, wished her well, stating they'd miss her and would wait with breaths held for her return.

"Would that be considered killing off the competition?" Her smile faltered as she pecked each cheek. "Please promise me you'll breathe."

After a spatter of laughter, Mike hugged her, lifting her so her toes left the ground. "Come home soon."

He continued to keep her secret. He hadn't betrayed her.

Nick cleared his throat. "Don't ever forget you're an Irongirl." He cupped her face with a gentle touch and kissed her nose. "Stay tough. We'll be right here when you get back."

Something inside her loosened, and the heaviness of the last thirteen hours lifted from her shoulders. In an emotional time, these men stood beside her. Even the ones who disliked having a girl on their team pushed those feelings aside to comfort her. Walking down the jet way, she sensed that a Divine Being accompanied her

Acceptance, a gift she would treasure, but it came because of a loss. For each new turn in her life, would she discard something from the old? Could this be the Universal Balance of life?

On the plane, she refused a mimosa and stared out the window.

She flew home to bury her father, but she also made appointments for those tests. At the moment, fear crowded the sadness. She immersed herself in music, her favorite artists, to avoid thinking about what waited at home.

As the plane carried her above the vast ocean and across the International Date Line, her thoughts reentered her old life. The power of familiar uncertainty climbed onto her back and she shuddered at its obstinate hold.

In Honolulu, she walked the terminal to stretch her legs, bought a Starbucks' latté. Savoring it, she meandered back to the gate and thought about her mom. How would losing her husband affect her? Would she soften from this tragedy or would it serve to harden her more?

On the next two flights, she tried to read but couldn't concentrate. Again, she listened to music to block her thoughts. When she stepped off the plane in Atlanta, she saw Kate waiting just outside of security.

"What a pleasant surprise. I expected Gordon."

"I told him I'd get you on the way in." The look on her friend's face undid her, and fresh tears pooled. They hugged to right the off-kilter world.

"I'm so sorry, CJ." Kate took CJ's bag, walked toward the south parking garage. "Will your mother mind that I drove up?"

"As my friend, you'll be welcomed with open arms. She has no problem with 'outsiders'—it's family she can't handle."

Kate nodded her understanding.

Sitting in the car as Kate drove, CJ finally told her friend about her leg. She described the spots as Dr.

Taylor had and filled her in on the conversation she had in the middle of the night with Dr. Hempstead. She tried to sound clinical, to keep the fear out of her voice.

"Why didn't you tell me?" Kate's annoyance showed. "I thought we were best friends."

"You are my best friend, but what could you have done for me except worry?" CJ blew out a small breath and continued, "I'm telling you now, because I made appointments for a bone-scan and a biopsy. I wanted to know if you'll go with me?"

"Of course, I will." Kate reached out and took her hand.

"Thanks. And Kate, please don't mention this to anyone. No one else needs to know."

The odd expression on Kate's face voiced her concern—she thought it a mistake to keep this quiet. But CJ had no choice. That the guys finally accepted her intensified her need to stay on the team, to produce a win for them.

* * *

Hundreds of people crowded the small chapel at the funeral home. Flowers of every color imaginable spilled from arrangements. Candles flickered and soft organ music soared as dozens more tried to find a spot to sit. Many simply stood at the back, hands folded, heads bowed.

CJ whispered into Kate's ear, "I never realized my dad was so popular."

Her mother leaned forward in her seat and glared at her.

The catholic priest stood and opened the service with a prayer. Why her mother commissioned a catholic priest mystified her. Dad grew up Baptist and requested years ago a simple memorial and cremation. Mom might have been from catholic descent, but she rarely attended church. It made her wonder, did one burn in hell for staging a funeral not acceptable to the dead person?

CJ remembered his request for cremation because he said he hated the thought of rotting in the ground. Plagued by nightmares for weeks after that, she couldn't get the visual image out of her head. Now as an adult, could she blame her mom for cringing at the idea of burning flesh?

She shivered when she gazed at the elaborate casket perched on the altar. Her father's lifeless body lay within. The ache in the center of her chest pulsed and fresh tears filled her eyes. Kate reached over and took her hand.

Gordon, his lips trembling, sat between her and Mom, whose expression remained empty, her eyes dry. How did she do it? How could she control an emotion that in CJ erupted unchecked? Didn't she feel the finality?

When the service ended, Kate helped steer the crowd toward the door. CJ, Gordon, and her mom stood off to the side accepting condolences, practiced words to soothe and support coupled with handshakes and hugs. Through it all, her mother stood strong.

The burial followed and as hard as CJ tried, she couldn't rein in her emotions. It embarrassed her, and the looks her mother darted her way didn't help. She smoothed the skirt of her simple black dress and dabbed at the ever-constant flow of tears. How many soggy tissues now filled her purse?

Gordon slipped his arm around her shoulder, squeezed. "I'm glad you're home."

"Me too," she whispered, trying to smile, but a sob broke through instead. "Why, Dad, why now? So sudden with no warning at all. It hurts so much."

Tears flooded his eyes as he hugged her harder.

Sharing that moment with her brother made her feel less alone, though the silent ride home in the limousine stretched her nerves.

At the house, they busied themselves with the guests, circulating with platters of food then again empty handed. More than once, someone's comment about her father flabbergasted her. How many spoke of a man she didn't recognize?

"More than a CFO, Burt was a true business partner."

"He always kept clients' needs high on his list."

"The life of the party. He sang and danced for the joy of it. Told jokes to keep everyone laughing."

"He volunteered for all of the benefit drives, because he believed in them. Coordinating the committees put a sparkle in his eye."

"Definitely, *the* man."

Her brows drew together, a puzzled expression taking hold. They spoke of an imaginary being who masqueraded as the man she grew up with. As they stood in the kitchen refilling some of the platters, she turned to Kate. "I didn't even know my own father."

Kate's lips tightened, and she shook her head. "How sad that he hid his true identity from his immediate family."

Choked up, CJ turned away, busied herself by filling a basket with hot rolls.

"We're out of canapés." Her mother floated in. Her hand stilled as her eyes raked CJ's face. "Please, pull yourself together before you ruin what's left of your makeup. Your constant tears show your weakness. We must remain strong in front of these people. Cry later when they've all gone home."

"Will you?" CJ asked with a snap. "Other than the single tear that slipped down your cheek when you threw the rose on the casket, your eyes remain dry. How do you do it, Mom? How do you hide something so awful?"

Anger sparked in her mother's deep green eyes, but only for a second. "Think of something pleasant; that usually helps." Her mother handed the plate she held to Kate, patted her hand. "Be a dear and get some fresh hors d'oeuvres, would you?" When she faced CJ again, all emotion vanished. "Go upstairs and wash your face. Put on some fresh makeup."

"Okay," she agreed. Had they just shared a moment? Catching a glimpse of that slight crack in her mother's ice-queen façade made her almost seem human. Could the death of her father be a new link in the broken chain of their relationship?

* * *

Dave Southwood, her father's attorney, sat behind the huge mahogany desk in the family study, his files and papers spread before him as if someone grand left this world to enter one much more important. He looked around the room twice and cleared his throat.

She and Kate exchanged glances, trying not to display their disbelief. Gordon slouched in a chair in the corner while Mom perched on the edge of the seat adjacent to Dave. She clutched a lace handkerchief in her left hand, and though she had yet to shed another tear in their presence, the puffiness around her eyes indicated otherwise.

"Are we all ready?" the attorney asked as he once again glanced around the room.

With a flourish, Dave began reading—the standard garble of the beginning of any will.

CJ tuned out, thinking instead of her appointment with the hospital, her bone-scan scheduled for tomorrow at seven a.m. More resigned to the obligation of discovering the mysteries of her own body than scared, she lied to herself. The echo of the doctor's warnings vibrated in her brain, but she rejected them due to the lack of physical evidence. It could not be cancer; she'd feel something. Other than the heartache over her father, she'd never felt stronger.

When the attorney got to the specifics, her ears tuned in, but she marveled that the rush of anticipation never morphed. A ball of dread did.

"The remaining money will be distributed in thirds," the attorney stated after detailing the arrangements for Mom's financial security. He then wheeled away from the desk, reaching beneath it, and brought out three odd shaped boxes. Placing them on top of his papers, his gaze once again scanned the room. He stared at her for one long moment.

"Burton stipulated that each of you keep this gift private." He handed the purple box to CJ, the blue one to Gordon, and the pink one to her mother. "You are to open them while alone and share the contents with no one." He turned to stare at Kate.

"You needn't worry. We'll abide by my father's wishes." Since they ignored his earlier wishes for a small simple service, this they would do. "Right, Mom? Gordon?"

The small knot in her stomach coiled. She didn't want her father's hard-earned money, his personal possessions, or his present. No, what she wanted, she now knew, was out of reach.

All she ever wanted was his love. His unconditional love.

But how could she get that from a dead man?

Chapter 9

Sitting in the waiting room at the hospital proved to be oppressive. Surrounded by sick people, CJ looked the vision of health. An Irongirl, an athlete—strong with wiry muscles—yet something inside could be devouring her. She tried to keep the bubble of panic contained.

"Is it easier to discuss the possibilities of what you're facing or better to chat about everyday life?" Kate's unease reflected in her blue eyes.

"Better to avoid the issue." She mustered a smile. "Tell me about Gregory. How's school? Is he dating anyone?"

"Dating many, but none seem to be special. He's more charged about his studies than girls at the moment, which isn't a bad thing. I have a feeling when the right one moseys along, my boy is going to fall like a rock." The blue of her eyes intensified, deepening with love as she spoke of her son. "But I guess that's all a mother can hope for, right?"

"You think?"

Knowing CJ's mother, they both laughed.

"Have you ever been in love, Kate?" An attractive woman, one of class and sophistication, she sat there wearing black jeans, a royal blue cotton shirt with the collar turned up, and a cropped jacket, her signature piece.

"Can't say that I have." Kate's fingers flicked through her spiky do, reshuffling the fine layers. "You?"

"Had a crush on the tuba player in high school, but that doesn't classify as love. Besides, he never knew I existed."

"With your eyes and that hair? CJ, you piss me off when you put yourself down." Kate glared at her. "He was probably intimidated by your looks."

"Oh, yeah that's it—too stunning for him." She rolled her eyes, revisiting all the times her mother implied differently. Not worth going there. "During the reading of the will yesterday, I had this thought."

"You fell in love with your father's attorney?"

"Oh, yes, stuffy Dave stole my heart. Funny, Kate." She pursed her lips and decided to blurt it out. "I want to fund Gregory's trip to Berlin."

"No." Kate popped out of her chair, her shoulders rigid, stubbornness taking hold. Her lips firmed as she crossed her arms over her chest.

"Look, I know you tried to figure out how to send him, and I don't think taking over my store helped. Bonus next year might, but that won't help this year."

Kate stepped back, putting space between them. "You've already done enough—the gift basket as congratulations, the wine of the month. I appreciate the thought, but I'll manage."

"Kate, why strap yourself when I just inherited money I don't want?" She stood, taking Kate's elbow and drawing her back to the chair. "I wanted his love, not his money. Please? Swallow your pride and accept it as a gift from my father and me."

"That's too generous." Embarrassment colored her cheeks, so she lowered her head. "Gregory will be floored. Thank you."

"It makes me happy." She hugged her friend. "See, we support each other."

They settled back, waiting for CJ's name to be called by one of the nurses in the pale pink outfits. No one seemed in a hurry, which seemed interesting since they dealt with life-threatening diseases. Shouldn't there be some urgency?

"How did you decide on Gregory's name? And why is it I've never heard you call him Greg?" She crossed her legs and absently rubbed the front of her shin.

"It's always been Gregory," Kate answered wistfully. "Don't laugh, but I used to play with this medallion my granny Annalise wore on a chain around her neck. Some of my first memories as a child were of holding it in my fingers, feeling the textures. It fascinated me. When Grandpa Sven died, his wedding ring joined it. When I turned ten, I asked about it.

"Saint Gregory, she told me, was the first monk to ever become Pope. He was born in 540, and he not only saved the Church, but also founded what we know today as Western Civilization. He saved his people and the whole of Christendom by renouncing his immense wealth and consecrating himself to God. I felt a surge of strength, absolute power when she told me the story."

CJ nodded, engrossed.

"It reminded me of her will. After Grandpa died, she stood alone, yet she became the family savior. Still is. When I got pregnant, I knew—boy, Gregory; girl, Annalise."

"Amazing how impressionable kids can be. A charm and a story shaped your future." She grinned, thinking of her father's one lone comment. "I want to meet this woman."

"She's incredible. And talk about love, you should have seen her and Grandpa. How they moved together like a dance. How they communicated, sometimes without words, like poetry. The looks that passed between them when they were in the same space." Kate smiled, "I always wanted to find that kind of love. Said I'd never settle for less."

With a sigh, CJ agreed. "Me, too."

"CJ Fallon." The nurse with the clipboard in her hand motioned for her to step through the door to the left.

"I'll be back soon." CJ followed the woman.

Ninety minutes later, she reentered the waiting area, holding a huge manila envelope.

"What is that?" Kate stood and stretched, putting her book and glasses in her bag.

"My bone-scan film. I'm to give it to Dr. Hempstead when I see him tomorrow."

Kate's eyes went wide in disbelief. "Do they think you won't look at it?"

CJ shrugged, heading out the door. When they were in the hall with the door closed, she turned to her friend. "Of course, we'll look at it. We'll wait until we get to the car though. I'm too scared right now to see it."

"Maybe you shouldn't look."

"Not an option." She pursed her lips. "Hey, am I glowing?"

"What?"

"They shot florescent dye in my blood for the scan. I wondered if I resembled a neon sign."

"Nope." Kate stopped her, a nervous laugh escaping. It eased the tension, the uncertainty surrounding them. She lifted her lids then peered into her ears and made her stick out her tongue. "I'll keep my eye on you, though, just in case."

In the car, CJ grabbed Kate's keys and used one to slice open the envelope flap. With great care, she slid the film from its sleeve. Holding it up to the windshield to let the light shine through, she swallowed—the bone from knee to ankle glowed bright green.

* * *

"Where are you girls headed this morning?" Her mother sat in the wing-backed chair in the piano room, sipping tea from a Limoges cup. "Do you plan to leave me alone all day?"

"Just a few hours." CJ tried to sound nonchalant. "Several errands to run including a trip to the grocery store."

Her mother set her cup aside and stood to scrutinize her face. "Pale skin, dark circles under your eyes, why would you leave the house looking like that?"

As always, her mother's words bruised her self-esteem. "Mom, I need to keep busy. Otherwise, my emotions take control. I'm not like you." She gave her a quick hug, ignoring the stiffness of the woman's shoulders. "Can we bring you anything?"

"No, I'm fine." Her mother looked away, then sent them off with a wave of her hand.

Dismissed. Once again, CJ felt the familiar twinge as they left the room. Her mother had a way of darkening the sky even on a sunny day.

Kate touched her arm, a gesture of comfort, but CJ masked her hurt. "We'd better go. I don't want to be late," she said as they stepped outside.

When they neared the car, Kate turned to her and growled through clenched teeth, "How do you put up with her? She's mean spirited and I want to strangle her."

CJ patted her friend's arm. "She's my mom."

"Yeah, I know." Kate threw the car in gear and pulled out of the driveway. "But I'm your friend and she pisses me off."

"Tell me how you really feel." CJ laughed.

"You don't want to know what I'm wishing right

now," Kate answered.

An awkward silence descended for the rest of the drive to Resurgens Orthopedics.

Dr. William Hempstead III was a distinguished-looking older man with silver fanning through his otherwise dark hair. His kind blue eyes twinkled. His eyebrows looked like pewter wings that seemed to sweep down toward his nose. The deep timbre of his voice followed the rhythm of a strong and steady heartbeat. It soothed her a little.

He took her hand between his cool ones and urged her to sit down on the edge of the examining table while he viewed the film she brought him. Thinking of the green glow ramped up her nerves again.

Kate sat in the corner, her discomfort apparent in the slant of her shoulders. CJ smiled at her friend to reassure her, even though fear now pumped through her system like wildfire.

He secured the film against the lighted panel and drew in his breath. His hand shot up, his ring finger and middle finger creating a vee beneath his nose. He rubbed up and down a few times as if scrubbing something distasteful from his face.

"Well, I don't like the looks of this." He spoke to both of them. "I want a new set of x-rays, both legs, and an MRI of the right before we do the biopsy." He turned, kneeling in front of her, and placed his palm against her right shin. In a slow sweep, he moved his hand over the area then held it there. Heat pulsed beneath his hand. "CJ, this hot sensation indicates the body's need to heal a problem. I intend to find out what it is."

She nodded, though she suspected he recognized the worry in her eyes. Then he did something that shocked the heck out of her. He turned his face and laid his cheek against her leg. The heat intensified, felt twice as hot as before.

"Wow." Her voice sounded small in the bright room. "What makes it pulse like that?"

"It's the blood flow as your body attacks the problem." He straightened to his full height; she guessed he was just over six feet. Quite a presence in a small space. "Kate, why don't you wait in the outer room? The nurse will bring you back in once CJ's prepped for surgery. Right now, we have some pictures to take."

"Yes, sir." Kate left the room after giving CJ a quick squeeze on the shoulder for support.

In a small room down the hall, the tech took several images of her legs, then led her to a large machine, where he scanned her right leg from her toes all the way up to her hip.

Back in the examination room, CJ waited for the doctor to return. She shivered, dread icing her skin. She picked up the hoodie she brought and put it on. Not that it did much good. The chill came from inside her body.

Fifteen minutes later, the door opened and Dr. Hempstead reentered, sliding two more films under the clip of the lighted panel.

"Let me show you something." He motioned for her to join him. "See this? This is a perfect bone. Your left tibia." He pointed to one of the x-rays, tracing his finger along the length of bone. The image looked like something an artist might have drawn, straight, solid, and strong.

"And this is your right one." He moved his hand over the other film. It was a curvy, light gray version of the other tibia with five black spots nesting within it. It looked murky, like white paint swirled into gray. She wasn't sure which looked worse, this image or the solid green one.

"Do you know what this is?" Again using his finger, he traced three solid white lines just outside the shape of bone.

She shook her head. She had no clue.

"You've created new bone. Like a splint to protect itself against a break. It's amazing. I've never seen anything like it." His fingers caressed his chin, playing with the small indent at the tip. "Come, let's go drill a few holes in your bone. See if we can't determine the problem."

* * *

Kate entered the small prep room and found CJ in a washed-out blue hospital gown five sizes too big for her. She looked tiny. And the large leather recliner she sat in only added to the illusion. Her head rested against the back of it, her eyes closed. On her left shin, inked in black magic marker, the word NO with a smiley face drawn beneath it.

"Are you nervous?" Kate asked as she took a seat in the small folding chair to the right.

"Scared to death." CJ blew out a breath, her shoulders sagging. "I swallowed two pills the nurse said should relax me prior to the IV, but they're not working."

"I wish I knew what to say."

"Just sit with me." CJ reached out a hand. "Thanks for coming with me."

A middle-aged nurse came in, her smile wide and filled with kindness. She checked CJ's pulse before moving to the tray of instruments set up by the side of the recliner. She picked up a needle, and Kate looked away. "Well, love, are we ready?"

"And if I said no?"

"It wouldn't much matter, now would it?" The nurse laughed and rubbed CJ's shoulders. "Take a deep breath and relax."

Kate left the room, but she overheard the nurse

whisper, "You'll see your friend soon."

Just outside the double doors, another nurse approached her. The woman's dark brown eyes reminded her of ground coffee. They gleamed, warm with concern. "Are you with Ms. Cassandra Jade Fallon?"

"Yes," Kate replied.

"Come, I'll take you to the proper waiting room. The doctor will want to speak with you after the procedure." She led her to a small room filled with light purple chairs.

Kate settled into one and pulled out the book she brought, but when she opened to the page, she couldn't read. The words swam before her as she once again pictured the film of CJ's leg. A bright green stamp that screamed disease.

She bent her head and said a silent prayer.

Why CJ? Why at this juncture of her life? She took a huge chance walking away from her career, but it seemed bad followed in the wake of good. How would CJ handle this, knowing it could change all of her dreams?

Kate shook her head and vowed to remain strong for her friend. She would do whatever was necessary to support her through this. No matter what the outcome.

People slipped in and out of the room, but she barely noticed, her thoughts centered on CJ—on what she would learn from the doctor. How many times had she opened her book and closed it? Waiting sucked.

An hour and twenty minutes later, she looked up and saw him walking into the waiting room.

The doctor strode toward her, a grim look on his handsome face. His surgical gown swung as he walked. His mask bounced against his neck. She rose from her chair, but he motioned for her to sit back down.

He sat next to her, took her hand. His touch was so gentle, his smile warm. "Everything went well. We took five samples. They're on their way to the Mayo Clinic. I medicated the areas and stitched her up. They're self-dissolving and don't look like much, but it's still surgery, so CJ should stay off her feet for a few days."

"That's a difficult request." She made a face. He had no clue. "You don't know CJ."

"Athletes are always tough, but as her friend, you'll have some influence." He stood. "I've prescribed pain medication, which she may feel she doesn't need. She doesn't have to take it, but just in case. And an antibiotic that she must take and finish. Remind her, no impact sports until I say differently. The nurse should be out soon to get you. You'll be the first person CJ sees when she wakes up." He shook her hand and turned to go.

"Doctor?"

"Yes?" he stopped mid-stride, turning back to face her.

"When will we know?"

"About two weeks. We're running several involved tests." He raked his long, thin fingers through his thick hair. "They don't appear to be tumors. Though the sticky mass we extracted worries me. I've never seen anything like it. We'll have to wait for the results—I can't even begin to guess what it is."

"Will she be all right?"

"I wish I could promise. But I've seen too much in my career to make those kinds of statements. Tell CJ I'll call her as soon as I know."

She nodded as he walked away.

She stood and watched his broad back recede down the hall. In his profession, he must carry the weight of the world on those shoulders. How did he deal with death on a daily basis and still retain that handsome smile or the tenderness of touch? How did he manage to show compassion on a continual basis? Did he have enough successes to balance the destructive darkness of the losses? She could only hope.

"Ms. Brooks." The nurse with the big brown eyes stepped forward as Kate sat. "I'll take you in to stay with Ms. Fallon, if you'd like. She should be stirring in about ten minutes. Once she's awake, we'll gauge how she feels before we let you take her home."

Kate sat quietly amid the activity in the recovery room. People came and went—doctors, nurses, family members. Cups of juice, wet compresses, and bags filled with IV fluid floated by as if the person carrying them moved in slow motion. It was like being in a foreign country, unable to understand the language. She focused on the bodies instead, much easier to read—sadness, hope, despair. A minor victory for a small child. It was all there, surrounding her.

She watched as a little girl of about three was wheeled by, bandages on her head, wondering—then CJ moaned. Her attention shifted. She stared as her friend's eyelids fluttered and she licked at dry lips.

"Nick?"

Kate sat back in surprise. Had her friend just asked for her coach? Was there more to the relationship than CJ let on? He was gorgeous; she knew that first hand. But CJ hadn't mentioned anything out of the ordinary. *Hmm, interesting.*

"Do you need some water?" she whispered.

"Kate?" CJ's eyes opened, a drugged dreaminess in their amber depths. "You're here."

"I'm here, but were you hoping for Nick?" Her voice remained soft, but it made CJ sit up.

"Excuse me?" She sagged back against the pillow.

"You just asked for him?"

"No. Really? Oh." The words tumbled in confusion. CJ's eyes appeared unfocused, sleepy looking. She shook her head. "I guess I'm just worried he'll find out about this."

Kate cocked one brow. "You're going to have to tell him sometime."

If it was cancer, there would be no hiding it from him.

"I'm praying that I get to race at least once as a pro."

Kate couldn't believe her ears.

"CJ, you're lying in a recovery room. How can you think of racing at a time like this? Didn't you hear your doctor say this is serious? What if you can't race at all?"

CJ closed her eyes, a gesture that confirmed the magnitude of her quest. It went beyond the simple need for her parents' acceptance. This was an all-out cry for love. CJ's delusional view that perfection drew real love flapped like a flag at full mast. Would she ever have a chance to learn that the opposite was true: love accepted faults and failures as well as celebrated victories? It broke Kate's heart, and yet what could she say?

Silently, she wondered what Nick's reaction would be when he found out the truth.

* * *

The rest of the week crept along, quietly and unhurried. CJ kept her feet up as much as possible and grieved in silence. Kate cooked every night, comfort foods that warmed the belly and soothed the ache in her heart. Mom remained polite yet distant, grieving in her own fashion.

They watched movies, but her mother stayed only for the beginning of the first. When CJ noticed her eyes misting, her mom made excuses and left the room.

Gordon popped in only to change out of his work clothes before heading back out to party, though last night, he lingered to say goodbye. Their relationship shifted, the death of their father bringing them a bit closer. Too bad it hadn't worked that way with her mom. Or had it?

When she went into her mother's room to say goodbye, her mother feigned sleep rather than face farewells. But CJ stood firm, giving her mother a light shake. "Take care of yourself, Mom. I'll call you when I get back to the island."

Her mother nodded and, in haste, pecked her right cheek. Hope sparked in CJ's heart, making her smile. As tenuous as it was, it was something. "Bye, Mom. I love you."

Due to the early hour, the roads remained clear. CJ sat in the passenger seat of Kate's car, enveloped in sadness. She wanted to get back to plunge herself into activity, but at the same time, she wanted to stay. She would miss her friend and the frail bond she started to build with her mom. But her new friends waited on the island, along with her coach who counted on her.

"What are you thinking about?" Kate asked.

"Everything," CJ answered, turning her focus to her friend as she drove. Kate's fingers squeezed the wheel, her knuckles turning white, her complexion ashen, worry tugging at the edges of her mouth. "How I'm going to remain strong mentally and physically. How to buy time so I can race. I know you think I'm foolish, but this is my chance. I walked away from my career to find out if I could win. I'm not ready to give up yet."

"I know." Kate glanced her way then returned her attention to the road ahead. "I want you to know I'll be here for you...no matter what."

"I appreciate that. I promise to keep you in the loop. You're the only one I can talk to about this." She couldn't take back telling Mike. She only hoped he wouldn't ask questions upon her return.

"What?" Kate must have caught her pause.

"I didn't mention..." She went on to tell Kate about

Mike being there the night the doctor called. "I was so upset and he listened. What else could I do? I hope he kept his promise."

"I wish you'd reconsider telling Nick. I know he's your coach, but he's also an athlete, so he'll understand what you're facing. More so because of his own past."

"I can't." Her statement punched the air. "I don't want him to know. I have to function as if everything is normal, at least until we know what we're dealing with. Remember, I have no symptoms, and the routine of each day is the only way I'll survive. Please try to understand."

"I'm trying," Kate said with a solemn nod. "But what about your doctor's orders? No weight-bearing activity until he says otherwise. Are you going to ignore his warnings?"

"I don't have a choice. I need to prove my abilities as a pro. I can't do that unless I race."

"I wish I could say I understand."

"You should. You left your family to start a life of your own. This is my purpose. I can't give up without trying."

"Leaving my family did not put my life in danger."

What could she say to that? Pressing her lips together, she crossed her arms over her chest and stared out the window.

"I'm sorry." Kate's tone softened. "I'm worried."

"You think I'm not?"

Kate's right hand left the wheel to squeeze CJ's shoulder. A lengthy silence followed.

When they pulled up to the curb at the airport, the look of remorse on Kate's face brought tears to her eyes. CJ leaned over and hugged her friend. "Please stay strong for me."

"I will." As if the emotion were too much for her, Kate pulled away. "Hey, by the way, did you open your father's box? I didn't want to pry, but..."

"I needed time." CJ shook her head as she grabbed her bag. "I thought I'd open it on the plane, though I'm not sure I want to know what's in it." Her father's box filled her with curiosity, but it also created dread. What could possibly be inside? Everything in her life seemed murky at the moment. A mystery.

She hugged Kate one last time and headed into the terminal.

Through security and sitting at the gate, CJ touched the purple box but resisted opening it. Why were the contents a secret? Did each box hold a sacred truth? Or a piece of the past?

What did the future hold?

Her team awaited her return to the island, and she couldn't wait to get back to them, to the intense workouts in the warm sun. To immerse herself in a routine that would help her forget the pain of her loss and the uncertainty of her situation. She held tight to the knowledge that she had felt so much support on the island—more than she'd ever felt in her entire life.

Chapter 10

On the plane from Hawaii, CJ settled into her seat. She tucked her headset and iPod Nano into the seat pocket in front of her along with a magazine, her book, and the letter she extracted from her father's box.

She'd been too emotional after looking through the contents of the box to read it on the prior flight. She held the creamy linen envelope to her heart, fresh tears spilling down her cheeks. She needed to pull herself together before opening it to discover what other surprises he had in store for her.

The box was his declaration of love. It said everything he hadn't when he was alive. In it, she found all of the school awards she earned. Her sports ribbons and medals as well as her scholastic achievements. He made a scrapbook with little notes next to each entry, some humorous notes with little drawings that showed how proud he was of her and her accomplishments. Had he planned to share it with her at some point? Other than after his death?

The last page held the article from *Triathlete* magazine about her signing with Team Fear US. Next to it, he wrote, *CJ follows her dream. May she find all that life has to offer.*

He didn't know how to share his feelings, so he remained silent. But this said so much. What had he done for Gordon and her mom? She wasn't likely to find out. He requested the gifts remain private, and her family held secrets well.

She could only hope they were as thoughtful as hers.

When they were airborne, and the cabin lights dimmed, she reached for the letter. Sealed with her father's initials in wax, BMF, it seemed very official. Somehow that made it harder to open. Adrenaline kicked in her blood stream. Her throat tightened, but she slipped her finger beneath the seal and popped it open.

Unfolding the three pieces of crisp stationery, she read.

Dear Cassandra Jade,

I always loved your full name, though CJ better fit your spunk. And spunky you were. Even as a small child, you always followed your own path, though I suspect you never realized that. I know you were trying to garner approval, in your way, trying to please. But even with that forlorn look in your golden eyes, you went in your own direction. I never told you how much I admired that about you. I'm sorry. I was too afraid of upsetting your mother.

If you're reading this, it's because I'm not around to tell you the things I should have. I'm ashamed that I didn't have the courage to tell you while I was alive. That I couldn't look into your eyes as I revealed the things you are about to learn.

Maybe it will help you understand the bitterness trapped in your mother's heart. Maybe it will shed light on the way she treats you—not that it makes it acceptable, because it doesn't, but just maybe, it will free you to follow your heart. Lift the weight that has surely held you down.

When I met your mother, she was a beautiful young girl with aspirations far from the norm. I lived next door and worshiped her from afar. We became friends in junior high school, and I felt honored to be included in her life. I made myself available to help her with homework. Told her I was there for her if she ever wanted to talk. I never deluded myself that she might fall in love with me. I only hoped to be close.

During high school, she blossomed into a gorgeous young lady with a promising modeling career ahead of her. She made a few commercials and did some print work and the camera loved her, as I secretly did.

She had a lust for life, for the finer things in it, and she had a laugh that sparkled. She talked about her dreams, and what she would do with the wealth she acquired. She always looked ahead, planning her future.

Until that Christmas Day, when she discovered she was pregnant. The boy she'd been seeing wanted nothing to do with her or the baby. He walked out of her life and never looked back. It crushed her. I think the only reason she kept the baby was to hold on to a piece of him.

CJ, I saw the opportunity and with stars in my eyes went for it. I asked her to marry me—to let me raise the child as my own. I wanted to hold her and tell her everything would work out. We wed on Valentine's Day. Gordon may not be my blood, but I've loved him as my son.

She put her dreams on hold for Gordon. And when she felt he was old enough, she pursued them again. That's when you came along. You were my whole world, my little girl, my creation. Your mother resented that. She hated that you took extra years from her success. I'm sorry, baby, that's the truth.

When she did try again, they considered her too old. She hadn't made a name for herself early enough, so she competed against the fresh-faced sixteen-year-olds. Rejected time and time again—her spirit died. I watched as the light in her eyes diminished.

I couldn't fight her; I felt responsible. The sadness inside her, I couldn't change, but I worked hard to build the kind of life she dreamed of. Over time, the spark of her laughter fizzled and turned into an evil streak. She used her tongue as a weapon, for she would never have laid a hand on either of you. She sliced through life to avoid the truth, to cover her regrets, smiling only for the outside world, a mask to hide her despair.

I tried every day to make it up to her.

My dearest, CJ, you can't, as I couldn't, make her happy. But I pray you can understand her and love her for who she is and who she might have been. She did the best she could under her circumstances. Am I asking you to forgive her for the grief she caused you? No, not at all. Am I asking you to forgive me, for I am just as guilty? Again, no. I simply want to free you to follow your heart, to go after your dreams—which you have by signing with that coach. I'm so proud.

You are bright and talented and so full of life. I want you to find true happiness. You deserve that!

You are the apple of my eye and always will be. I want you to live your life without regrets, as you said on the morning you left. No matter where your journey takes you, I want love to sing in your heart and for you to feel loved by someone special. Go forward and seek—good things shall come to you.

I wish that more than anything. And I hope that I am smiling down upon you from heaven, watching you reach for your stars. Who knows, maybe I'll be there to hand you one.

I love you.
With all my heart and soul,
Your father.

Oh, my God. Hot tears coursed down her cheeks, and her heart clenched as if someone held it in his fist, squeezing at irregular intervals. No wonder she and Gordon were so different. No wonder her mother pampered him. Did she still love the boy who left her, still pine for him after all these years?

Her thoughts shifted. Had Dad revealed this secret in Gordon's box? He said he loved him as his own. He couldn't have, knowing the devastation it would cause. Loving her the way he did, could he do that to her mother? So, if not, what had he put in their boxes? Why had he specified they keep the contents private, other than to reveal the secret only to her?

The date stamped on the letter: the day after she told the family about her decision. That flash she saw in his eyes must have spurred him to do this. Fire caught in her lungs, her breath ragged. He loved her after all. Knowing did nothing to ease her pain. Instead, it intensified it.

They wasted so much. Time and energy and love— wasted to protect her mother. A bitter, unemotional woman.

Now what? What was she supposed to do now that she knew? The questions were endless. They circled her brain like a renegade merry-go-round. Faster, more furious, they spun, leaving her dizzy and light-headed.

Shock dried her tears and numbness spread through her system. The loss of her father, now this, combined with Dr. Hempstead's words, swirled like a cloud of dust through her mind. Truth dimmed and faded into the corners of her mind. The pressure in the cabin buzzed in her ears, as panic threatened to overcome her.

Was everyone's life a lie?

Drained, she finally slept. Weird dreams flitted at the edges of her consciousness but never materialized.

She hovered in a state of confusion and hurt, the bruises deep in her bones.

Dad loved her, but he protected the woman he loved more. How could she blame him?

Didn't she have her own secrets to keep?

* * *

Nick left the boys playing pool in the rec room. CJ was due back in a few hours, and his mind wandered from the game. No, his thoughts centered on her. He missed her. All week, the urge to comfort her strengthened, and he hoped she would let him hold her.

She lost her father, he reasoned. Of course, he'd want to console her.

During training, the guys teased him because his concentration blurred. They accused him of losing his edge. Did they know why? That something about her made him go soft inside?

He smiled, because he wasn't the only one affected. In varying degrees, the entire group felt something. Even the ones who complained about her softened after witnessing her reaction to the news of her father.

Earlier, Reed suggested they decorate her room with flowers and balloons to cheer her up. But the group took it beyond that. Their competitiveness made Nick laugh. Each guy wanted to add his own personal stamp to the decorations. Hunter left a hammer on the dresser, and Uri wrapped an extra inner tube with a note: *In case of flat tire, open.* Kyle painted the team motto, *No Pukin',* on a poster, and Big collected a dozen red hibiscus, placing them in a hat on her pillow.

It seemed each day he learned something new about his athletes. They were a great bunch, but bringing a girl into the mix brought out new characteristics. A thoughtfulness that went beyond simple team dynamics.

Would she be surprised? Touched?

It made him think. What made CJ happy? What melted her heart? His chest tightened, and he wondered what drew her to Mike. Why, if she liked Mike, did he feel that odd electrical current when she stepped near? Why did he sometimes feel her watching him?

Like that night when her father died. He looked across the room to find her eyes on him, and when their gazes met, the rest of the world seemed to disappear. She stirred his emotions, blurring the line of his professionalism. *Shit.*

Shaking his head, he turned the corner to take the stairs to his room and froze. Anger scorched his blood. Mike stood there flirting with a pretty Asian tourist.

She giggled. Seemed almost shy with her hands held in front of her lips, but her gaze encouraged more attention. Nick stood watching and moved only when Mike guided the girl toward his room. He intercepted them at the door.

"Can I have a word with you?" he ground out through his teeth.

Mike shrugged his shoulders, motioned for the girl to wait, and stepped a few feet away. His expression came off as an unconcerned "what?"

"What the hell are you doing?" Fire flashed in his eyes. Anger ripped through his words.

"I'm taking this little hottie to my room for a drink." Mike winked. "You want me to find out if she has a friend?"

"Are you out of your mind? Have you forgotten that CJ returns tonight?"

"No, but so what?" Mike's puzzled look sent fury skidding through Nick's system.

"You're a son of a bitch. How can you do this to her?" He grabbed the front of Mike's t-shirt. "How can you fool around with a stranger when you supposedly care for someone else?" His disgust vibrated through his fingertips, but he dropped his hand, letting go before he struck his so-called friend. "I don't get it. I don't get you." He raked a shaky hand through his hair and turned away.

"Wait." A long pause settled before pulling Nick's gaze back to Mike. His friend stood there scratching his head, then his eyes brightened as if a light switched on in his brain. "You think I'm cheating on CJ?" Mike smiled, which infuriated him.

How could he be so bloody insensitive? Yeah, he was a laid-back guy, but come on? "What the hell would you call it?"

"You better hold your tongue." Disbelief flickered over Mike's face, his sunny smile gone. "You're making accusations you know nothing about."

"I know what I see." He swung his pointed stare toward the girl waiting by the door. She seemed to shrink against the wall.

"You don't know shit." Though Mike didn't raise his voice, the tone bit.

"I know I saw this same scene over three weeks ago, but it was CJ coming out of your room." Nick once again fanned his fingers through his hair. They itched to pound his friend's face. "What was that? A little two a.m. romp?"

"You're pushing your luck here, Nick. Shut up, and go back to your room, before someone gets hurt." Mike took a step back.

"The only one I see getting hurt in this mess is CJ, and I won't let that happen."

"If she gets hurt, it won't be because of me."

"And how do you figure that?"

"Go pushin' the wrong buttons, Nick, and something's liable to blow up in your face."

"What are you talking about?"

"You've got a lot to learn about your athletes, Coach. Particularly with CJ. Why don't you ask her?" Without another word, Mike turned and left him standing in the twilight.

The sun dropped quickly, the sky a stunning orange. Frustration moved him, and he stood at the water's edge as the ball of fire sank into the sea. A flash of green sucked the orange from the sky, leaving behind a fuchsia as intense as the emotions surging through him.

What did Mike mean, go ask CJ?

* * *

Nick stood waiting for CJ as she exited Customs. He opened his arms to her, and she nestled there for a minute, absorbing his strength. How she needed it right now. Fighting embarrassment, she rested her cheek against his chest and counted his heart beats. One-two-three, the steadiness of them grounded her, and she breathed in. His sexy scent filled her nostrils.

With regret, she stepped away, his fresh scent lingering.

Nick cleared his throat. "How are you doing?" he asked as he took her bag.

"I don't know," she said. "I think I'm numb."

"I can understand that." Warmth softened the green of his eyes. "I lost my mom when I was ten. Though it fades with time, the emptiness never goes away."

"I'm sorry," she said, grateful that she could focus on him for a while. "She must have been young. What happened?"

"I'll tell you over dinner. My bet is you didn't eat on the plane."

They got in the car, and he drove to the Santa Fe Grille, a cute little place only a few minutes from the airport, not that anything was far on this island. They found an empty table by the water. Flames from the Tiki torches danced in the breeze. The aroma of grilled steak spiced the air. Soft music played while a gecko darted across the wall.

A waitress brought over a basket of chips, some salsa and two menus, which she set at the edge of the table. "Can I start you off with a drink?"

She wasn't hungry, so she ordered a mango-melon bubble tea. She had yet to try one since arriving on Guam. Nick ordered the same but also looked at the menu.

"Did you eat?" he asked. "Won't you share a little something with me?"

"I'm really not hungry, but you go ahead." She gazed out at the water and recognized the lighted party boat that went out for the night. In a minute, *YMCA* would be blaring.

Their teas arrived and the waitress took his order. Once they were alone again, she turned to face him. "You mentioned once that you were raised by your aunt and uncle. Was your mother's death the reason for that?"

"Yes." Indecision seemed to veil his expression. Did he not want to share this?

"Nick, it's okay. We don't have to get into it."

He reached across the table and took her hand. "You're hurting. I've been there. I understand. I do want to share."

He sipped his tea, his lips pressing together as he swallowed. Would she ever be able to look at that mouth without thinking of the night she signed her contract? How many emotions had she felt in the last seven weeks?

"My mother committed suicide." The look in his eyes hardened, but his voice remained soft, just like his touch. "I found her."

"Oh, God." Shocked, she moved her hand to his

forearm and squeezed, her fingers lingering. "You were ten?"

"Yes. My mother's mental health had been declining for years before that. She was paranoid, delusional. She seemed to become frailer each year. When I turned nine, she started pulling out her hair, exposing small patches of skin. It scared me, but I didn't know what to do to help her."

"Oh, Nick."

"She had this look in her eyes like someone was after her. She seemed afraid of my father, was always looking over her shoulder." He shook his head. "I think he liked the power he wielded over her. Once, I saw him whisper something in her ear and her whole body folded in. She stared at the floor, her tiny form quivering as if she waited for him to strike her."

"Did he?"

"No. I never saw him raise a hand to her, though that day I thought my presence might have stopped him. Anyway, one month after my tenth birthday, I came home from school and found her sleeping in her room. I called to her, but she didn't move. It was April 1st, and I thought she'd pulled one of her stunts to freak me out. April Fools, you know. When I finally shook her and realized she wasn't playing, I couldn't breathe. I sat on the floor, found an empty pill bottle and a near-empty bottle of vodka just under the bed. In a panic, I called 911, but they couldn't save her. I was too late."

"Oh, Nick, I'm so sorry. I can't even imagine." She looked away, afraid of what might show in her eyes. Her heart clenched for the second time, but this time for the pain he must have felt. He'd been so young. How did he grow to be so strong?

"The cops called my father and sat with me until he came home. It seemed like hours passed before he walked through the front door. He answered the cops' questions. But when they left, he glared at me, told me to go live with my uncle Ed, my mother's brother."

She understood lack of emotion, but how could a father send his child away?

"His last words devastated me. 'I never wanted you.' He said it with such a sinister laugh. Something died inside me, and I never wanted to see him again."

She sucked in a breath, tears welling. The need to wrap her arms around him and hold him blossomed in her belly. She fought that urge but did not remove her hand from his arm.

"I moved in with Uncle Ed, Aunt Millie, and my cousin Shayne the next day. I stayed angry for months. My own father abandoned me. But years later, I realized I got the better deal. My aunt and uncle loved me. Shayne, who's only a year older than me, became my big brother." He shrugged though the edge remained in his voice. "Had I stayed with my father, I would not be the man I am today."

"You are so strong."

He wiped the tears that fell from her eyes with his thumb, the gentleness of his touch unleashing more. He stood then and gathered her into his arms. All of the emotions from the last week poured from her as she clung to him. His hand glided over her hair, resting on her neck, and the warmth from his palm seeped in. Her breath hitched again, and she reached for a paper napkin to blow her nose, noticing the waitress hovering nearby. She seemed to hesitate, not wanting to interrupt the moment, but stepped forward and set down Nick's order.

He turned then, breaking away, and motioned for the woman to bring an extra plate. As they took their seats, she considered telling him what she learned. A need to share burned in her, because right now, she felt connected to him, her coach, and it bore more than the previous electrical current. This thread drew their hearts together, which made it difficult to catch her breath. The air felt thin and her lungs heaved. She paused for two seconds.

"What is it?" Could he read her mind? "There is more than sadness in that look."

"I learned a family secret today, and I don't know how to handle it." Torn by her need to open up to Nick and her loyalty to her father, she stalled.

"Let me help?" Something—relief or compassion—glimmered in his eyes.

Needing a minute to think, she took her first sip of tea. She grimaced. The flavor was sweet, but the small tapioca ball that came up through the straw made her gag. It rolled on her tongue, its texture reminding her of a fish's eyeball. She spit it into the napkin she clutched and pushed the glass aside. Nick chuckled. She wiped her mouth with a fresh napkin.

"Is it considered betrayal to reveal a family secret?"

"Depends." One corner of his mouth tipped up. "If it helps you process and goes no further, I don't see it as a sellout." He transferred a portion of his grilled fish and salad to the plate the waitress brought and placed it in front of her. His eyes, dark green pools surrounded by impossibly long lashes, never left hers. "Do you trust me to keep it to myself?"

She nodded, her fingers playing with an uneaten chip.

She did trust him. She told him first about the box and its contents then went into the details of the letter. The tiny flutter of panic she expected for letting the secret out never happened, and his gaze remained steady as he listened. His expression spoke of devotion, not betrayal, which warmed her insides like melted butter.

"It's my turn to say I'm sorry," he said when she finished. "I didn't realize what your family life was like. This explains some of your earlier concerns, but now you can put them to rest. I know what it's like to love but not have that returned by a parent, although, unlike you, I was lucky enough to have substitutes. It's unfortunate that your father couldn't demonstrate his feelings, because that would have eased some of your burden as a child." He sighed. "Regret can do such horrible things to people. Take what he gave you as a gift, a means to understand your past, and a way to determine your future." His grip was fierce as he once again took her hand. "Never give up on your dreams, CJ, no matter what happens. Your true friends will stand beside you and support you through thick and thin."

She sat there in the glow of his speech and realized that her father had given her more than one gift.

* * *

Nick walked her to her room, let her put the key in the slot. He stood back, waiting for her to go inside, but he got a surprise, too. Not only were the decorations there, but the entire team sat around, grinning like monkeys at the zoo.

"Oh!" She laughed. "What are you all doing here?"

"We wanted to welcome you home." Reed got up from the corner chair and hugged her. "How are you holding up?" He ruffled her hair like a big brother might.

"As well as can be expected," she answered as she hugged him back. Then she stepped away, turning in one huge circle, her arms spread out, an incredible smile lighting up her face. It made Nick beam with pleasure. His heart did a somersault in his chest.

"We wanted you to come home to something festive." Big unfolded himself from his position on the edge of the bed. "I hope we didn't overdo it."

"No, Big, it's wonderful. Are those from you?" She pointed to the hibiscus.

His cheeks flushed, making his freckles stand out, and she laughed.

Joy swept her face, making Nick's heart pump faster. That the guys called this home and included her in their family made this moment so much sweeter. She needed this more than they knew. His earlier reservation about signing her flew out the window. She did belong here.

With this kind of support, she would grow not only as an athlete, but as a person as well, and that pleased him. He'd coach her to win and watch her confidence soar.

They'd shared parts of their lives this evening, common threads that bound them. Yet there was still the question of Mike. Could he compete with his friend for her heart? Would he be smarter to wait for the relationship to fizzle, to be there to catch her when it did?

Or was he better off letting her continue her infatuation with Mike while he focused on being her coach?

Chapter 11

The team got back to a regular routine of workouts, early rides, afternoon swims, and evening runs. The camaraderie grew with each day. Nick tried hard to focus on each of his team member's abilities, but CJ found ways to distract him. Like now, what was she up to?

He watched her mount her bike and tried to head her off.

She waved. "I'm off to explore the local stores."

But something in her expression suggested she did not intend to shop. She pedaled as if trying to escape him. Had their evening of confessions driven a wedge of awkwardness between them? Did she just need space to grieve or had she found another type of solace?

Would he find her in Mike's arms? Not considering his reaction if that were the case, he grabbed one of the resort scooters to follow her. He caught a glimpse of her coming back from the direction of the Cetti Bay climb, so he ducked the scooter into the Agat Marina parking lot, pulling in behind a dive van. He watched, astonished, as she u-turned and headed again toward the climb. No Mike in sight, just CJ and her bike.

Five times she climbed and came back. On her sixth round, he zipped past her, cutting her off, signaling her to pull to the side of the road. Color flooded her already exertion-reddened cheeks as she stopped and unclipped.

"Coach." Her breath came hard and ragged. "You following me?"

"Needed to see what you were up to." He pinched his lips together while he searched for the correct way to approach this. With the guys, he never thought about how to phrase things, he just spoke the truth. She wanted to be treated like the others, so he said, "CJ, I appreciate your dedication, but I'm afraid you might sabotage your strength. You're losing too much weight, getting boney. That concerns me."

"I'm building strength, not undermining it."

"Ever consider the extra work could backfire?" He parked the scooter, getting off to stand beside her. "How many days have you snuck out? Are you running extra miles, as well?"

"Just the bike—climbs only." She stared at the ground.

"Look at me," he snapped.

When she did, he regretted his tone, unshed tears glistened in her amber eyes.

"Why, CJ?" He softened his voice. How many extra hours had she put in these last two weeks? "Don't you realize I built your plan to benefit you? Do you realize the injuries you could suffer by deviating like this?"

"I'm not a strong climber. To keep up with the guys, I have to work harder. I thought..." The tears spilled, her bottom lip quivering as her nostrils flared.

He ached to reach out and tweak that pretty little nose of hers, but would that serve to make her more uncomfortable? He stepped back to give them both some space.

"Work with me, not against me. There is a reason you call me 'Coach.'" He grinned, trying to ease the visible strain in her shoulders. "I do know the drill."

That made her grin.

He drew her toward the scooter, threw his leg over the seat. "Hop on. Hold the center of your stem, and I'll get us back. You've pedaled enough today."

He concentrated on getting them home in one piece, trying to ignore the sensation of her arm around his waist, her body pressed against his back. Sweat popped out on his brow.

Eyes focused on the road, he kept his hands steady—the only shot to get them to the resort without dumping them into a ditch or crushing her bike. Each time she moved, he winced and fought his reactions to keep them upright.

Every day, his feelings for her grew. His heart took the plunge the day he met her, and he crossed a fine line allowing emotions in the night they shared secrets, but he couldn't erase that line with physical involvement, no matter how much of a temptation she presented. Their relationship must remain professional. As her coach, he owed her that—a truth that became difficult to adhere to when she sat so close.

Pulling into the lot, he slowed. She jumped off as soon as he stopped and he released the breath he hadn't realized he held. He watched her walk away as his lungs resumed the in and out of normal breathing and his heart settled down.

Later that night, he found her sitting in a lounge chair by the pool. He approached her about her training. "I thought about your climbing abilities. We'll start weight training tomorrow. Build strength without risking injury. I am worried about the amount of weight you've lost since returning." He sat in the chair next to hers. "I understand you're emotionally drained, but we're fifteen weeks out from Wisconsin. You can't afford to drop much more. You need to increase your calorie intake. CJ, you have to eat."

She didn't respond.

"Is it the extra training? The emotional drain? Or something else?" He needed to broach the Mike issue.

The shocked look on her face puzzled him.

When she said nothing, he pushed. "Has your relationship with Mike robbed you of your appetite?" Her expression changed, a confused smile cresting her lips, but when he pressed about the two in the morning rendezvous, she got angry.

"I can't believe it." Spots of color burst to her cheeks. "You've been spying on me."

"Not spying; something woke me, and I headed to the beach for a walk. That's when I saw you with him." The reflection from the overhead lights played in her hair, while sparks shot from her eyes. "Besides, I'm not blind. I watch how he touches you, whispers in your ear. Like when he wraps you in a towel after our swims. He gets that surfer-dude dreamy look. It makes me sick."

Even in his own ears, he sounded like a jealous boyfriend. He jumped up, moved away, needing a bit of space. "You don't seem to mind the attention."

"So sue me. It's flattering." She skimmed her fingers through her hair, tucked her feet beneath her, and raised her chin just a hair. "It's heady to capture someone's attention for once."

"Oh, come on. Who are you foolin'?" Nick's blood headed south. "I bet men have danced at your feet for years?"

"You have no idea, Nick," she stood up and glared at him, "how very wrong you are."

She turned her back and stalked away.

* * *

He infuriated her. Sometimes she hated the man. What did he know about her and her love life? CJ slammed the door to her room and threw herself on the bed. Did he really think men fawned over her? And if he did, why did that bother her? So what if he thought she slept with Mike? She knew better. Why should she care?

Her anger dwindled, confusion replacing it.

She sat up, drew her knees to her chin. What Nick Madison thought, not only about her training—but about her values, as well—mattered. It made a difference.

It hurt that he thought she jumped into bed with Mike because of the attention he paid her. She wasn't that type of girl. But Nick had no way of knowing that, and what he saw that night—the night the doctor called—must have looked like.... Oh, she didn't want to go there.

Muddled emotions pushed her off the bed. She paced beside it. How could one man provoke so many feelings in her? From electrical currents to irritation, sympathy to anger, hatred to lust. What was it about *him* that made her heart tumble, beat twice as fast as normal?

He made her head spin, yet he still held the power to aggravate her. None of the other guys affected her like that. Not even Mike, with his cute charm. What was it about Nick, this man who entered her life like a ferocious Florida storm?

She could not ignore that her body reacted to his, like when he kissed her that night that now seemed so long ago. Though she pretended to be upset, her insides had turned to mush. And today, when he made her get on the scooter behind him, her pulse quickened from the feel of their bodies touching. Even at the airport, when he hugged her to console her, a surge of adrenaline kicked through her.

Oh, and when he looked at her with those gorgeous eyes, her resolve melted.

She wanted him more than anything, but she couldn't risk heartbreak. She darted a glance at the mirror and shook her head. No man had ever thought her beautiful. Why would he? But this feeling in her belly.... Was it disappointment? Regret? Or the simple yearning to find true love?

Like the intense sun after a blinding storm, clarity struck. Her feet stilled. She stared at her reflection, her hand flying to cover her mouth. She wasn't just smitten, she'd actually fallen in love with her coach.

Chapter 12

The next week tortured CJ. The more time Nick spent with her, focusing on her strength training, the more difficult it became to ignore the feelings his nearness stirred.

During team workouts, he popped up beside her and her heartrate soared. He gave instructions and her pulse skipped. More and more often, she got light-headed, and not from strenuous efforts.

Earlier, he'd watched her swim, and a chill erupted along her skin, even though the ocean felt like bathwater. And now, during one of their weight-training sessions, he stood by to spot her and her chest tightened.

"You have to breathe, CJ." He looked down at her. "Deep one in. Push it out as you lift the weight. Good."

His hand brushed hers and she almost bobbled the bar. He caught it, steadied the weight of it, then helped ease it back down. "Come on…one more," he coaxed.

Each guy had a partner, and she had Nick. Could he not sense her distress? Like a bow pulled taut, she waited for the string to break, for something to happen to announce to the world that she'd fallen for her coach like an idiot schoolgirl.

She needed a break.

"I've got to use the restroom. Give me a minute." Inside the stall, she expelled the pent up energy. If only she could find a way to steer it toward her workouts. Ignore him and focus on the task—*Yeah, right. Easier said than done.*

She moved, stood at the sink, gripping the edges for support. She felt a tightness in her chest and a sharp twinge in her shin. They'd become more prominent—the twinges—but she ignored them, because she refused to believe her body betrayed her, as her heart already had. It was bad enough that she admitted she had feelings for Nick, but to think she might let him down.

She couldn't go there.

* * *

Nick watched as CJ came out of the bathroom, a different expression on her face—a look that said *I'm back, let's get this kicked into gear.* Her shoulders were squared, her mouth set in a serious line as she marched over with purpose.

He liked her spunk and knew if he could channel it, the team might have a winner.

"What's next, Coach?" She grinned and her shoulders relaxed a tad.

"Squats and lunges, let's build those quads."

"Power muscles to climb," Uri called from across the room, and the boys hooted.

"Hey, we want to be powerhouses, too." Reed stepped over, pulling Hunter with him. "She can't have all of your attention."

Hunter shot her a challenging look, but spoke to Nick. "Yeah, how about focusing on your top guys for a change?"

"You sound like jealous children." Nick shook his head but laughed. "You want attention? Fine. Start with

1.5 times your body weight. Come on, do the math, then give me five squats."

They both stared at him with rounded eyes.

"You asked for it." CJ giggled. "You should know better than to challenge Coach."

"Thanks a lot, bud." Hunter punched Reed in the arm.

Reed reacted by swinging his foot under Hunter's legs, taking him down. Hunter retaliated with a scissor kick, knocking Reed over, and their struggles turned into a wrestling match, which brought the rest of the team over. They cheered and clapped as they huddled around to watch.

Nick let the boys go at it, hoping their horseplay would release a bit more competitiveness. These guys needed to step up to the plate, to have winning on their minds.

Winded, Reed called time, sitting up to push the hair out of his face. "I'm glad I'm headed to Madison tomorrow." He bumped Hunter with his shoulder. "Maybe Coach will team you up with CJ for the week I'm gone."

Nick raised his eyebrow at the absurd suggestion. "No way. I'll split my time between the two of them."

"It would make more sense to partner us," CJ interjected. "That way you could focus on the rest of the team."

"Coach doesn't like to share." Kyle snickered, elbowed Big in the abdomen, and the others burst out laughing.

"You are too funny." Nick rolled his eyes. "Look, we've lost our edge. We'll pick this up tomorrow after our ride. Reed, you're not going home just to celebrate your son's first birthday; you need to keep training, too."

"Yes, sir." Reed put his hand out, and CJ was the first to reach out and help him up.

Nick waved them off. "See you at dinner." He straightened up, putting the weights back where they belonged, and watched with curiosity as Reed wrapped his arm around CJ and led her toward the door. He bent his head close to hers and whispered something in her ear. She beamed, and Nick felt jealousy surge through him. He wanted to know what they were talking about but knew that he shouldn't. He turned back to putting the weights away, trying to shake off his feelings. It wasn't his business what they were discussing. He was her coach, not her boyfriend.

Did the others think he was too possessive of CJ? Or did they believe that he focused on her because he was grooming her to be one of their stars? Did he believe it himself?

* * *

Reed led her outside, whispering how cute it was that she had Coach wrapped around her little finger.

"He is not," she replied. "He's just not used to coaching a woman."

"Yeah, that's it." Reed made a face. "Believe what you want, but as possessive as he is of you, he may not stand up and protect you if some of the bigger egos try to intimidate you while I'm gone. You have to show them you're tough, that you can take the barbs as well as any of the guys. Most of the guys respect you and your abilities, but there are a few who like to push your buttons."

"Let me guess." She laughed, holding up a couple of fingers, but her insides tingled that this God-send cared enough to warn her.

"Give them a run for their money, CJ. Show them who's boss." Reed stopped and touched her arm. "That would light up Coach for sure."

"How did I get so lucky to have you in my life?"

"There is a reason we ran together in New Zealand, that Coach signed you." He smiled that calming smile of his. "Remember, I'll only be gone a week, so hang tough and show them how cool you are. If you need someone, stick close to Kyle."

"Oh, Reed, I'm going to miss you." She gave him a quick hug. "You're more of a big brother than my own flesh and blood."

"Glad to be of service." He hugged her back. "Now, let's go shower up and grab some grub. I don't know about you, but I'm starving."

She floated back to her room, feeling for the first time what a family bond felt like.

* * *

Pride in her efforts to zero-in on the task and semi-ignore Nick these last several days made CJ smile. That she received brief moments of peace while Nick spotted one of her teammates didn't dim the glow.

Reed was spending a week in Wisconsin. Nick was forced to split his time between her and Hunter. She tried again to suggest that he pair her with Hunter for the remainder of Reed's absence, but he reacted with an odd look—probably due to Hunter's macho-competitiveness. Not a wimp, hence his nickname, Hammer.

However short the respite, she thanked the Lord for the moments she escaped Nick's touch.

This morning, running late for their first ride of the day, she reminded herself to focus on her technique, count her RPM's, anything to keep her mind occupied.

She entered the lobby in her bare feet, her shoes and socks in the bag with her helmet and bottles. The group sat, Nick in the middle of them. An unusual hush hovered over them, their carefree banter and loud laughter missing.

She slowed and scanned the room, searching for a reason, but saw only stillness. Her eyes settled on Nick. The look on his face—something was terribly, terribly wrong.

Drawn to him by a strange pull she didn't understand, and at the moment made no attempt to, she moved. Dropping her bag, she knelt before him. Her eyes locked with his. In one slow motion, she removed the cell phone from his grasp and set it aside on the floor.

"What happened, Nick?" When she spoke, it seemed loud even though she whispered. "What's wrong?"

"It's Reed. He's dead." His voice broke. "He went for an afternoon run, got killed by a sixteen-year-old driving while high on drugs."

She jumped back as if some force punched her in the chest. She stood staring at him as disbelief rippled through her body. No, it couldn't be. Reed went home to celebrate his son's first birthday, to share that joy with his wife, Jenny.

"I don't believe it. I won't believe it." She covered her face with her hands, not to see the truth written on his face, in the expressions of her teammates. Her throat closed, burned with an intensity that grew with each breath she drew in. "No. It's not true." She shook her head, a sob fighting to escape.

Nick's arms enveloped her, pulling her in. Her hands were trapped against his chest. Another pair of arms, another body closed around them. Soon, the entire team stood clustered, her body smothered beneath them all. They stood sandwiched, a cloud of grief weighing on them as a whole. But even in the closeness, she shook, her body quivering with denial.

From somewhere behind her, a teammate cleared his throat, and the group splintered. Several coughed and sputtered as if the comfort they'd just shared turned to fire.

Big stepped forward and laid a gentle hand on her shoulder, but he looked at Nick as he spoke. "Coach, why don't you walk CJ back to her room? You can fill in the details for her. This is such a shock for all of us, and right now, I need to move. I can't stand here and think...." He turned away in an abrupt motion, tears flooding his eyes.

"I'm thinking of getting drunk." Kyle's lips trembled, his face a pool of misery. "He was my best friend."

Kyle was too disciplined an athlete to ever do that, but nobody batted an eyelash at his comment, even at seven in the morning. He stalked away, an action that spurred several of the guys to move, some clamoring to join him, varying degrees of pain and shock visible in their expressions. The others scattered, muttering that they wanted to be alone, to digest this tragic news and find their own emotional outlet.

When Nick took her hand, something new passed between them, traveling clear to her heart. It spread through her like maple syrup on warm French toast, melting her earlier skittishness. This was soft; this was shared comfort. They walked to her room in silence, a peculiar stillness engulfing them, like being in a vacuum, only with the wind and the ocean sighing at their backs.

In her room, Nick sat on the edge of her bed. She stared into his eyes, his pain so clear. The color drained from his face. Even his lips were pale. Tears hovered on his lashes but stayed in place. How did one comfort a grown man?

Not sure what made her do it, she crawled into his lap, wrapped her legs around his waist and curled her body into his. Not lust, but the simple need to be close, to share all that moved through them. She felt his heartbeat under her skin and reeled that it kept time to hers.

She pulled back, her teary gaze scanning his face. "Nick, how could this happen?" Emotions once again swelled in her chest, but this connection kept them stifled, at least for now.

"It's always a possibility in this sport. But it's usually a cyclist who gets hit by an angry motorist or an elderly person who can't judge the distance of a person on a bike coming at twenty-five to thirty miles per hour." His eyes blazed, the sheen of tears deepening the green. "But this is even more tragic. The kid ran. He drove away from the scene, leaving Reed on the side of the road."

"What?" Disbelief stabbed beneath her ribcage.

"The kid would have gotten away, too, had Reed not just passed two other runners going in the opposite direction."

Nick went on to tell her that the couple had witnessed the car speed by, then heard the gut-wrenching screech and the loud bang. Tires squealed and, as they turned to look, the car sped away. They ran to help. The woman leapt into action and went to Reed. She dialed 911 on her cell, while her husband raced after the car. The kid turned into a cornfield, thinking he could escape. Instead, he got stuck. The husband pulled him out of the car and held him down until the police arrived.

"Reed was already dead," Nick whispered brokenly. "The impact killed him instantly."

She watched Nick's jaw pulse, felt the anger heat his skin. When he closed his eyes and rested his forehead against hers, the tears came. "He never knew what hit him."

She drew him closer, if that were possible. She seemed embedded in his skin. She couldn't deny the sharp blade that sliced her heart, but she couldn't imagine Nick's pain. She rocked and let her own tears mingle with his. Together they cried, their hurt erupting.

She cried for Reed Parker, her teammate and friend for a few short, wonderful months, and the injustice of it all. She cried for his wife Jenny, her heart breaking for the woman who would never see or touch her man again. She cried for his kids, Kimberly, age four, and Kevin, who would turn one tomorrow. They would no longer feel their father's hugs. None of them would ever again hear Reed say I love you.

She held tight to the living, breathing man in her arms and sobbed until there was nothing left. The ache in her chest pulsed with the thought that a life could vanish in an instant.

"I feel like someone's squeezing the air from my lungs," she whispered into his neck. "It's so unfair. Why him? Why now? He was so young, had his whole life ahead of him." Reed…their star this year…expected to be a winner, but in a flash, gone.

Nick soothed her though she knew he hurt, too. His arms tightened around her—together, they comforted each other, held each other, feeling less alone in this crazy world.

* * *

CJ came out of the bathroom after washing her face. She cleansed away the crusty tears, but the ache lingered. Nick sat in the chair, watching her. Their world shifted yet again. In a blink, one event influenced another. Was that Karma?

She looked at him, the towel dangling from her fingers, and a fresh surge of emotion caught in her throat. Walking over, she touched his cheek, her fingertip tracing the patterned streaks left by his tears. A watery smile lingered on his lips, and she traced that, too.

His gaze locked with hers and her insides liquefied.

Too strong a pull to ignore, she once again crawled into his lap, wrapping her legs around him, but this time the air seemed to thicken as their bodies touched.

Her heart thudded in time to his, a powerful tempo that made everything around them fade. With all of the conditioning of her childhood, her brain screamed, *This is wrong. This is wrong.* But for the first time in her life, what she did felt so right. With each breath, each pulse of her blood, she knew. She belonged right here.

His hands slid around her back, their bodies a perfect fit. He inched forward, pushing her back, and took one long, slow breath. With the next, his mouth came closer. So close, her breath met his. And when his lips brushed hers, softly—just a whisper of a touch—her bare toes curled around his hips, drawing him closer.

They were still clothed, but the connection sizzled, a feeling so potent her breath caught.

As their lips met again, their hearts pumped in unison. No matter what, no matter where, as long as she had Nick, she was home.

The kiss deepened, and their souls entwined.

He stood and carried her toward the bed, settling her against the mattress. He ran his fingers through her hair, skimming her neck, his palm coming to rest in that now familiar spot. He shifted, his fingers moving to cover her heart.

He kissed her; she kissed him back, and they came together, body and soul, reaching out to each other in grief…and love.

* * *

She and Nick spent the rest of the afternoon in her room. They discussed whether tragedies happened for a reason, and if so, why were innocent people allowed to die? They opened their hearts to each other, then made love again. Bittersweet, unhurried, introspective love.

CJ's cell phone beeped several times, voice messages or texts, but she ignored them. Whether her mother or the doctor with results, she needed neither right now. They could wait. Nick was more important. She stared at the man sleeping beside her and thought about life—precious yet fragile, something that could be extinguished in a blink.

Acknowledging that grief brought them together made her insides ache, but at the same time, her heart soared. This new sensation fluttered in her stomach when she gazed at his face.

Her coach was now her lover.

Nick opened his eyes and looked at her, a sad smile floating into place. "Hey, you." He pulled her into his arms and hugged her tight. "I'm glad you're here."

Twisting, he lay on his back with her on top of him, the side of her face resting against his chest. One hand cupped her head, the other the curve of her hip, eliminating any space between them. She felt whole for the first time in her life.

She inhaled his scent, let her hand roam over his muscles, marveling that they rippled beneath her touch. She wanted to stay like this forever, but what about the rest of the team? They suffered the loss, too. Shouldn't she and Nick support them?

"We should find the guys. If I feel like this, I can't imagine how devastated they must be. They need you, Nick, and I bet you need them, too." She touched his beloved face, the face etched in her mind since March.

"Part of me wants to be selfish and stay here with you." He got up. "But you're right. We're a team. We should support each other. None of us should bear this alone." He pressed a soft kiss to her lips, sighed, and began to dress.

"You want to check your messages before we go?"

he asked, as he pulled on his bike shorts and jersey. "I have to swing by my room for regular clothes."

"It's probably my mother. I don't think I can handle her right now." She shook her head as she zipped her jeans and opened the drawer to find a t-shirt. "Besides it's four in the morning in Atlanta."

After Nick changed, they walked together, their bond strong, and found the team sitting at the dinner table, pushing food around on their plates, no one eating, their need for support palpable. Nick held her hand and coughed to gain their attention.

Every face turned up, varying degrees of upset still visible in their expressions. Anger, sadness, disbelief flickered like lightning bugs in the dark.

They sat down, Nick slipping his arm behind her back. She rested her head on his shoulder, but wondered how the team would react. Would they sense the change in their relationship? The quiet hum of loss fused the group, creating a new tie.

They shared a moment of silence.

"It is plenty time you two admit feelings." Leave it to Uri to break the silence, dispelling the gloom with his statement. "We watch for months the dance you do—with hold breath."

"Now, we exhale," Val added and every one of the guys blew air from their lungs. One collective release.

"Too bad it took this to remove your blinders," Hunter said as he pushed aside his plate.

"Yeah," Zach added, "this sucks." His eyes widened. Stammering, he said, "I didn't mean you. I'm happy you figured it out. We've waited for one of you to explode."

"Or implode." Pete laughed, the sound jarring in the otherwise soundless space.

Had they been that transparent, CJ wondered, yet oblivious?

Clearly shocked by the teams' comments, the face Nick made sparked another snicker. CJ bit her lip, opened her eyes wide, her shoulders lifting in question, which truly undid them.

The guys roared, some of them with tears slipping down their cheeks. Tears of humor mixed with those of mourning. Out of the corner of her eye, she caught the look Mike sent Nick's way. His brow raised, his head cocked, he looked like a bratty kid announcing he knew something no one else did. She almost expected him to crinkle his nose and poke out his tongue.

"Reed would hate that we're all moping like this," Simon said. "It's good we laugh."

"He's applauding right now," Hunter snapped as he gathered plates. "He recognized the spark the first day."

"Shouldn't we do something?" Dave asked.

"A memorial service," Big volunteered. "It's the least we can do." His large fist slammed the table, making plates and glasses jump. "What a senseless fucking thing to happen." He dropped his face into his hands. "I'm sorry, but I'm so angry."

Lars, her blond-haired Elvis, reached over and placed his hand on Big's shoulder. "We're all upset. It's not wrong to show it. Strength has nothing to do with hiding feelings."

"Nobody can take this back." Big's shoulders dropped then shook as new tears surged. He made no attempt to stop them. "Reed's not coming home like CJ did."

The reality hit hard, and CJ fought her own tears as they all struggled with the truth that faced them. They were minus one member.

She never knew death before, but now it came in waves. Two within one month—age not a determining factor.

Heat shot through her tibia, a reminder that she too

could face death. Was this a sign to share her secret, or did this make it impossible? How could she burden her teammates, her coach, who was now her lover?

"A tradition on the island is to have a fiesta to honor the life of someone who has passed." Mike took the plates from Hunter, pressed him to sit down. "We'll do one on the beach at sunset tomorrow. I'll take care of the arrangements. Why don't you each come up with something to share about Reed?"

"I like the idea of doing it at sunset, the end of a day." Nick drew CJ closer to his side. "It's symbolic."

Like a stone cast over still water, a ripple of agreement fanned the table. In time, the hurt would fade, but at this moment, nothing else mattered. A tranquil hush descended.

* * *

"I have to get my gear." CJ slipped from Nick's bed. She kissed him. "I'll meet you in the lobby."

As she made her way to her room, she paused on the landing of the stairwell. The sun's fingers painted the edge of the morning a glorious pink, the color so rich, tears of wonder welled and burned. With as many tears as she'd recently shed, shouldn't the pool be dry?

Her cell phone waited just where she left it, on the nightstand. Three new messages. Perching on the bed, she went to her voicemail. The first one was Dr. Hempstead.

"Cassandra, I'm sorry it's taken so long to get back to you, but I had them run your tests three times. Please call me ASAP to discuss the prognosis."

She wrote down the two numbers he left, glancing at her watch. It was afternoon yesterday for him, he'd still be in the office. She waited for the next message to play.

Her mother. "Cassandra, you must stop this charade. Don't you understand? You broke your father's heart by leaving your job to move around the world with strange men. Is that part of the income arrangement?" She skipped forward and hit delete.

Next, Kate, sounding breathless. "I got your message. Oh, CJ, I am so sorry, first your father, now this? I don't have words..." After a lengthy pause, Kate's tone changed. "Hey, where are you? It's late. You should be sleeping. Call me."

She deleted it and texted Kate that she ran late for the team's workout; she'd call her later. After taking a deep breath, CJ willed herself to dial the first of the numbers the doctor left. Cold sweat erupted on her skin as she waited for someone to answer. By the time she heard the doctor's voice, she felt ready to pass out.

"Cassandra, let me begin by saying we are not dealing with cancer." She sprang from the bed, her fist up in the air. "But we can't celebrate yet. The spots are actually holes, referred to as pseudo-tumors. The reports indicate the mass we extracted is bone marrow. Your body is trying to heal itself, but it's still quite serious."

"I'm listening." Her toes dug into the carpet, holding her from pacing.

"We've discovered two rare diseases that resemble your diagnosis, though not exactly. Osteogenesis Imperfecta is known as 'brittle bone disease.' It mirrors the small fractures or cracks we saw in your x-ray, but your bone density is strong, unlike most reported cases which involve bones that are weak and prone to multiple fractures. Osteomyelitis is a form of bone inflammation caused by bacteria, usually due to an infection in another part of the body that is transported through the bloodstream to a bone in a distant location. We believe the holes were caused by blood seeping into the tibia, pooling and eating through, if you will. In your blood work, we were able to identify three specific bacteria, flu-type, that you may have been fighting off. I remember you said you haven't been ill in the last year."

"That's correct." CJ sank down on the bed, a chill racing over her. "In fact, since I've been racing, I've been healthy and strong. No pain, other than normal muscle aches from long, strenuous workouts." She waited for him to say more.

"Now, you haven't been stressing the leg, have you?"

"No," she lied. "Why?"

"This case is unusual. I've deliberated with many colleagues—another reason for the delay in calling you. Nothing like this has been reported in the United States, but with the knowledge of the two diseases I spoke of, we have options to consider. Since your body seems to be healing itself, we can monitor the growth and density of your bone with routine MRI's. That would necessitate monthly trips to my office." There was a pause. "But if you are on the island training, as I suspect, we move to option two. Surgically, we place a titanium rod in your leg. The bone mass rebuilds itself, thicker and stronger than before. The rod prevents you from taxing the bone to the point of fracture. Total rehab time approximately eighteen to twenty-four months, at which time we remove the rod and you continue on with life."

"But..." The blood drained from her face. Horrible images danced though her mind. "If it is healing itself as you said, do I really risk a fracture? Must a rod be inserted?"

"Don't kid yourself, Cassandra. You happen to be a remarkable patient, but the bone is still weak. If just one of the holes fails to heal, it could continue to deteriorate, and if you are running on it, it could easily snap in two. A clean break would call for a cast and rehabilitation, but if the bone shatters, you could lose the leg. And if it fragments, pieces of bone could travel to your heart and kill you."

* * *

Reed's death shrouded the team, the mood a thick haze obscuring the beauty of another tropical day. The brilliant sun heated the slight breeze, but CJ paid no mind as they plowed ahead in a pace-line now minus one engine.

She forced herself to focus on her pedal strokes rather than Dr. Hempstead's words. Sweat beaded her skin as she breathed the salty air.

Today's training plan called for a brick—right off the bike, a quick change of shoes, and straight into the run. This acclimated the different muscle groups and helped build a faster, stronger transition.

She pushed up the steep grade to Two Lovers' Point. As they ran the dirt trails through the tall jungle grass on one of the cliffs that bordered Tumon Bay, CJ called to mind the story that made this place famous. It kept her thoughts occupied, away from death and the invisible strain she might put on her shin.

She slowed her pace, letting the boys run ahead of her, and thought of the island's version of Romeo and Juliet. Legend stated a beautiful young girl whose father was Spanish, her mother Chamorro, fell in love with a handsome boy from a modest Chamorro family. This displeased the girl's father, who promised her hand in marriage to an arrogant Spanish captain. But on the morning of the engagement announcement, she ran away from home to meet her lover on the high cliffs above Tumon Bay.

A search party led by her father went after her. On horseback, they climbed the steep grade and found the young lovers by the edge of the cliff. Her father, the captain, and several soldiers advanced, knowing they had trapped the couple. As they continued to close the distance, the couple tied the ends of their long hair together and plunged into the raging surf below. Shocked, the men watched in disbelief.

In anguish, the girl's father slid from his horse, staring down the sheer drop into the swirling waters. He saw only their hair floating among the rocks and waves of blood. Legend stated at that moment he understood the symbolic meaning of their act. He would never question that true love came from the entwining of two souls, true to one another in life and in death. He went home to his wife with a new surge of love.

Since then, the spot had become a favorite place for weddings. The islanders built a small white wood and glass chapel only a few yards from the statue erected in the young lovers' memory, a replica of the two tangled in their calf-length hair as they tumbled to the rocky ocean below. Large stone storyboards, carved to illustrate the details, bordered the statue.

At present, visitors stood at the edge of the 378-foot cliff and enjoyed the splendid view of gleaming white beaches and lush hillsides along the Philippine Sea.

The entwining of two souls. She smiled, thinking of her and Nick. The feelings they discovered yesterday, the ease with which they slept last night, their limbs tangled in the sheets, their hearts meshed as one. Admitting their passion for one another made it more difficult for her to ever consider revealing her secret. She hadn't wanted to let him down before. Now, she couldn't even imagine it.

A tightening in her throat restricted the airflow to her lungs. How could she not continue on this journey? She could not and would not give up on this dream. She had to race as a pro under Nick's guidance, not only to prove her abilities but to gain recognition for him as a coach.

She told her mom that morning that she wanted to live life without regrets and she intended to do just that. Ignoring her doctor's orders weighed less heavily than if she chose the other option: to quit and return to her old life.

Her focus shifted to her leg and she examined every foot strike—did she feel anything? Were there any sensations she didn't feel in the past? No, both legs felt strong and capable of handling the distance, but she forced herself to remain light on her feet, not to pound the hard-packed dirt beneath her shoes. She listened for the soft *swoosh* of her feet kissing the ground, but that got drowned out by rustling in the bushes off to her right.

Startled, she turned her head in that direction.

A wild boar jumped out in front of her, ran across her path, barely missing her toes. Her heart bounced off the walls of her chest. She froze...then sprinted ahead as fast as she could in case it turned to chase her.

She raced after her teammates, catching sight of one of them. Using his back as a target, she increased the speed of her turnover and rushed past him. He laughed, but she kept going. One by one, she picked them off until, winded, she blazed down the path to the mock finish line.

There stood Nick, stopwatch in hand, a grin splitting his face. He called out her winning time as she shot by. She stopped, straining to breathe, and realized fear could be a tremendous motivator.

Chapter 13

CJ wore her best island outfit, a mint green sundress paired with strappy white sandals. The guys, too, took care with their wardrobe. Pressed shorts and buttoned Hawaiian shirts, hair combed as if they attended church.

Tables laden with island fare and lush flowers flanked the small area of beach cordoned off for the ceremony. Tiki torches flamed at each corner and on either side of the platform in the center space. Two rows of chairs, surrounded by colorful bouquets, faced the small elevated riser. Soft music played while Mike stood off to the side and motioned for one of them to get the ceremony started.

"I'll go first." Big stood and turned so his back faced the water. "I stand here in the heat of this evening with goose bumps covering my body. They rush over my skin, leaving an icy trail of disbelief. Reed Parker, so full of life, a spark in a sometimes dark world, is gone, snuffed out by a punk who won't admit responsibility. It burns me but leaves me cold. I look among us and realize how much I need to see his smile or hear his laughter, just one more time, so I'll never forget his magic. May his memory be branded in our minds, so we can carry him in our hearts."

As he stepped down from the rostrum, he took the long tapered candle from Mike's hand, lit it from one of the torches, and moved off to the side, head bowed, silent tears of anger dripping from his powerful jaw.

"The senseless death of a teammate, a friend to all, can't be explained." Hunter's eyes glistened, his gaze coming to rest on her. "He knew how to make outsiders feel welcomed. He never questioned, as some of us did. He simply accepted. That he will never be with us again, never race beside us, echoes like a song badly out of tune. I want to right the wrong. I want to bring him back, but the weight of reality crushes me and I realize we must learn from his wisdom. Though he is gone, he left behind a powerful force. The ability to embrace what others shun can no longer be ignored."

Nick's fingers tightened around hers and she looked away, trying to curb the tears that hovered. One more barrier came down, but like the others, wouldn't she rather have Reed here?

"We must remember his laughter, the boyish way he played jokes on us, for Reed would not want us to cry. Sadness was not a part of his makeup." Simon cocked his head as if listening to the sea. "He found the sunshine on the stormiest of days, and we must do the same. He was a beacon to many. Carry his memory with you and let him light your way."

"I need to wake from this nightmare. Wish it was a cruel joke we could laugh about, but no, reality is—my best friend was taken from this world far earlier than was his time. I pray the pain fades and his memory remains strong." Kyle's lips trembled, the trail of tears grazing his cheeks. "I don't know what else to say. Nothing will ever fill this hole." He shook his head, stepped forward, his misery heart-wrenching.

"I will remember his grace. The power he slice in water with. Never have I see body so tuned for speed."

Uri looked up at the sky, raised his hands. He stood for a second, eyes closed, then he whispered, "Share your strength. Give wisdom." He glanced down, paused, then tapped the center of his chest with his large palm. "Race with us in here. Give to us your energy. We honor you, my friend."

He, too, bowed his head after lighting the candle Mike handed him. He stood shoulder to shoulder with the others, as another seat next to her and Nick emptied. CJ gripped Nick's hand as each teammate took his turn.

After each one spoke, another flame fluttered against the dusky sky. Reed touched so many people, and she would hold that close to her heart. She would treasure the brief moment in New Zealand and the ease with which he accepted her on the team. His special qualities would remain with her, a reminder—his gentleness could not be stolen.

Nick squeezed her fingers, signaling her turn. She stood, but before she faced the group, she leaned down and kissed his lips, let his strength feed her. She stepped up, and as the last of the sun slipped through the clouds behind her, she gazed at the men in front of her.

"Close your eyes and listen with me." She closed her eyes, folding her hands in front of her. "Can you hear Reed's voice? I can—in the sweep of the ocean, the whisper of the palms. That distant chirp of a bird as he sings a lullaby to the sun while it sets into the sea. The sigh of the clouds and the flutter of a butterfly. They all deliver a part of his being to us through Nature's voice. Let us remember that, so we can listen for him each and every day." She wiped a tear, took her candle, and joined the group. How she wanted to sob, but she held firm, and looked at the man she gave her heart to last night.

Nick took his place. He angled his body to face them, all the chairs now vacant—another symbol. Sucking in a small breath, he twitched his lips into that now familiar pucker, before his voice, sweet as honey, reached them.

"Each individual is brought to this earth for a purpose. Reed's was to touch as many souls as possible in a genuine and hypnotic way. He touched us all differently, but in a way that will not be forgotten. We must be thankful for the time we had with him. Though it was much too short, we must cherish that we were allowed to know him. The Lord felt we were special enough to share in the life of this incredible man.

"We will continue to weep for the injustice. We will feel pain and anger, but we must also hold in our hearts the knowledge that we'll share his company again one day."

That did it. Her sob broke free, fresh tears wetting her cheeks. When she glanced up at her teammates, she saw they couldn't contain their tears either. Nick joined them, and they stood together in the darkness, their candles illuminating the sand, while the Hawaiian version of *Over the Rainbow* played.

The music stopped and they stood as a unit, sharing one more moment of silence in Reed's honor.

* * *

"Mike, you did an awesome job with the Fiesta." Nick hugged his friend before giving him a brotherly punch in the arm. "The setting, the food, the candlelit vigil—the thoughtfulness of closing the day with Reed's memory—spoke volumes."

CJ joined them, kissing Mike's cheek. "It was lovely," she said, as she slipped her fingers through Nick's. "Thanks for pulling it all together."

"Reed was a good guy. He deserved something special." Mike's sun-bleached hair toppled over his forehead. "I'm going to miss him, too. Usually, I believe in taking what comes, but man, this blows."

"It sucks." Nick nodded in agreement. He put his free hand on Mike's shoulder. "But you made it easy to honor him." Lifting CJ's hand, he kissed her fingertips. "Would you mind giving us a moment?"

"Not at all." She waved over her shoulder, blowing him an air kiss, and went in search of her teammates.

"Could you please tell me what went on the night I saw you with CJ?" Nick said it under his breath, his gaze following CJ's backside.

"I can't. Please don't ask me to." Mike shifted, stepping out of one flip-flop to dig his toes into the sand.

"But I really need to know."

"Ask her." Mike seemed uncomfortable with the topic. "She needs to tell you."

"Why can't you?"

"Look, sometimes tending bar makes you the resident psychiatrist; you know that. People talk, get things off their chests. That night, I was available. And not in the way you thought. I represented an open set of ears, which she needed." Casually, he crossed his arms over his chest.

"CJ needed to talk?" He scratched his head. "About what?"

Mike shrugged, palms turned up in the air, lips pressed tight. He remained silent.

"Okay, but why talk to you and not one of the guys? There were a few personality clashes in the beginning, but for the most part, they accepted her. Reed and Kyle protected her. Why wouldn't she lean on one of them?" He angled his head closer to his friend but kept his eyes on CJ, who in the distance took a seat on a lounge chair. He ignored, or tried to at any rate, the fact that Zach zeroed in and joined her in the same chair.

"Nick, we've been friends for way too long. I'd risk my life for you, but I won't get between you and your girl. Trust me, it was not what you thought. You two were oblivious to your feelings for each other, but the rest of us read and recognized the signals. The tension built from the first morning until we felt it hum in the air. Give her some time. When she's ready, I'm sure she'll share what's on her mind." Mike patted him on the back.

Nick didn't understand his feelings for CJ yet, and he struggled with them. He worried they'd interfere with his focus on the team. Would knowing she had secrets make it worse?

He never let emotion rule his decisions. He always stood aside and supported from afar. But looking at the group now, all clustered around her, he faltered.

Could he lead the team to victory now that his heart was involved? Or would his compassion soften the edge of his coaching style and result in his biggest fear. Would letting CJ in ultimately lose him the team?

* * *

CJ sat on the lounge chair with Zach, but her attention zeroed in on Nick and Mike, their heads bent close, their conversation intense. What were they discussing that put that small frown on Nick's face? She wanted to go kiss it off.

He'd told her they met at age twelve, doing odd jobs at his uncle's construction firm, but what drew two opposite souls like them together? Mike was the sun, bright and optimistic; Nick was dark, moody, almost sullen at times. Yet Mike was shallow, Nick was deep. Where Mike wore his emotions for all to see, Nick's demeanor built layers of complexity. His thoughtfulness ran through the depths of his marrow, his determination a second skin. Were he and Mike like her and Kate? Did they complement each other?

His touch carried the volts of a lightning bolt, and

his lips seared their mark, which made it understandable that his dark side drew her in like a magnet. She experimented with sex in her first years of college but never enjoyed it. She figured her partners were not the real deal; therefore, the acts seemed awkward, stilted, anything but appetizing. But with Nick, she craved more.

He made her want, tickled her to delirium. With one stroke of his fingertips, he could send her over the top. A secret smile edged its way to her lips, because she could do the same to him. She held the power to buckle his knees in her hands.

"Hold on, girl." Zach's voice cut the cord. "Coach and Mike have something to finish. Get a handle, Sweetheart. Sit still."

"W-w-what?" she sputtered. "I wasn't moving."

"Yeah, you were. I felt the pounce from here." His hand circled her wrist. "You guys fit. We all recognized that months ago, but you've got to know when to slow things down. No need to rush a beautiful thing. Pace yourself. Savor it a while."

"You're right." She relaxed, her limbs loosening. "How did this happen?" She let her shoulder rest against his. "He irritated the crap out of me in the beginning. Now, I can't get him out of my mind. For other reasons."

"Too much information. Don't need the details." He held up his hand, a smile curving his lips. Laughing, he wrapped his arm around her shoulder and pulled her close, whispering in her ear, "A few of the guys wanted to make a play for you, then it became apparent Coach wanted you. That halted them in their tracks."

"But why?"

"Are you kidding? Compete with Coach? He can still kick our asses."

"No. I mean why would any of them, including Nick, be interested in me?"

"You're for real, aren't you?" He scooted away, his

eyes wide in the light of the torches. "Good God, CJ, have you looked in a mirror lately?" He placed his fingers below her chin, lifted, turned her face side to side to study her. "Oh, wait, you're the girl who turns when a guy yells, 'hey, ugly' but keeps walking if someone whistles, right?"

Heat rose to her cheeks.

"CJ, you are beautiful, athletic, strong. You have this streak of, I don't know, fire that flashes in your eyes. It's so cool." He shifted, so he sat facing her. "You push yourself to keep up with us. You're one of the guys, yet you are so feminine. It's quite an exotic combination."

"I don't know what to say." Compliments embarrassed her, so she kept from looking at him. What she saw in mirrors, when she had to look in them, did not match his description.

"Don't say anything. But believe me when I tell you what we see. Your self-image got muddied by someone or something, and it irks me, because it is so wrong." He shook his head, a protective big brother. "Maybe Coach can clear away the muck."

"Don't you two look cozy?" Dave leaned over them from behind the lounge chair. "You trying to piss off Coach? Bet he makes you swim extra laps."

"No, he make Zach ride *tree* loop." Uri stepped up beside them, a smirk cresting his lip. "CJ, he spank."

"Who's spanking CJ?" Kyle dragged Lars with him. "Can we help?"

"You better watch what you say. You're all asking for double workouts." John joined the group, Pete and Val in tow. "Haven't any of you noticed the laser stare aimed this way?"

"Look, no one is spanking anyone. Thank you very much," she scolded as she glanced in Nick's direction.

"What's going on?" The other three wandered over. "Sounds like y'all are having too much fun. You gonna clue us in?"

"Was about to share with CJ the topic we discussed earlier," Lars said, his gaze sweeping each face before landing on Nick. Was he worried Nick would overhear?

"What are you talking about?" She cocked her head, puzzled by the mood change.

"We took a vote," Simon volunteered. "We think you should accompany Coach to the funeral. He really shouldn't go alone."

"I agree, but one of you should go. After all, you knew Reed better than I did."

"We may have known him longer, but the two of you bonded in a special way."

"Besides, we'd look pretty funny holding Coach's hand," Pete added with a laugh.

"Yeah, you're the only one who can pull that off." Big lifted her feet, slid to sit under them, and resettled them on his lap, her strappy sandals now resting against his massive thighs. "Not to mention consoling him when he cries."

"Coach acts tough, but this hit him hard. He needs you, CJ. Emotionally, he's torn up."

"He's softer than he wants us to believe." Hunter nodded in agreement. "Majority ruled. You're it. If he fusses, we're prepared to push, because in the end, we think he'll surrender."

"We just wanted to warn you before we broach the subject," Lars rounded out the conversation.

"I appreciate that." She rolled her eyes, not sure how she felt about the focused attention on her and Nick. Once the emotion of Reed's loss wore off, would this strain the relationships she'd built with her team? Would it change how she and Nick interacted on a daily basis?

Dave's hand crept to her shoulder. "It's a time of adjustment for all of us, but we'll learn to deal." He seemed to have read her mind. "Coach needs someone in his life who challenges him, keeps him on his toes. He's dealt with us lugs way too long, and besides you bring a freshness to his style. It's a nice change."

"Yeah, when he's not acting like a bear. Don't get all weird on us, okay?"

"I think is love," Uri said, never mincing words, although his dialect sometimes did that for him.

"Whoa. Please don't go there." She felt trapped by these men, their bodies surrounding her so she couldn't move. "This is all so new and, under the circumstances, I don't think we understand the depths of what we feel. Let's not rush things." She winked at Zach.

"Yes, but the looks you give are..." Uri didn't finish.

"Hot," Simon completed.

Laughter erupted then turned into coughs and sputters.

"Get your hands off her." Emerald sparks shot from Nick's eyes, as he scanned the group. "Why are you all huddled around CJ, manhandling her? Stop that." His look pierced Dave before zapping Zach.

As if a grenade dropped in the center of the group, the guys sprang apart. Big and Zach vacated the chair they shared with her, almost toppling it. Once the chair settled, she sat still and took it all in. Could Nick be jealous? That thought warmed her insides.

"Nick, it's okay." She smiled at him to ease his worry. "We were discussing Reed's funeral. Someone should go with you." Her voice remained calm in the chaos. "We just wondered who."

She took the burden off the others' shoulders, and they thanked her with huge grins.

"Most of us concluded that CJ should go," Dave said. "It's the only logical option."

"Why is that?" Nick replied, his expression blank.

"As a couple, you'll draw less attention. Can you

imagine how odd two grown men bawling like babies would look?" Kyle's voice whispered in the darkness. "The two of you can support each other in a natural way."

"That's true." Nick planted himself next to her, folding her into the crook of his arm. "But let's get one thing straight, from now on, no one touches CJ. Got that?"

A collective intake of air delayed the answers.

"She's our teammate," Lars stammered. "When we train…"

"Geez, Coach, I never pictured you to be possessive," Pete spoke from the left. "But the green monster has reared his head. You're jealous."

The group remained silent, waiting for Nick's reply.

"I guess I am—both." Nick raked his hand through his hair. "Until I saw you messing with her, I didn't know that. But yes, I've realized I'll castrate anyone who lays a hand on her."

Their eyes widened, color draining from a few of their faces.

Only when Nick laughed that deep throaty laugh did they all relax.

Chapter 14

Like a beacon flashing a warning in her brain, CJ's mortality stared her in the face. Within weeks, she'd lost two people close to her, both much too young to die. Her father hadn't reached fifty. Reed's death came one month shy of his twenty-ninth birthday.

In eight weeks, she would turn twenty-eight, and it seemed—Death did not discriminate against age. Every day she ran from the possibilities, the insanities vibrating in her ear. She poured her energy into her speed, the hours needed to build strength. She cycled to forget her own fears, swam to escape the pressure. She focused on nutrition and did everything in her power to remain strong.

On the good days, she soared like the birds that skimmed the surface of the water. Her muscles moved as if with little effort, parts of a well-oiled machine, carrying her to faster splits and higher averages. On those days, she beat all but a few of her teammates, and Nick looked upon her with pride.

But when the doctor's words crept in, finding any crack in her constitution, or she thought about the two deaths, it was all she could do to keep moving. Then, she wanted to do nothing but curl into a tiny ball and hide from the world.

The two sides of her brain battled: One screamed for her to keep pedaling, to continue forging ahead, to break through the madness and prove her strength. The other coated her insides with worry, drew pictures of horrible outcomes and ground her power to a snail's pace. That's when Nick showed concern, his expression puzzled but frustrated, as well.

She now categorized her training days as hot and cold.

Today, she lagged behind the rest of the team. She struggled against the need to quit, and with tears in her eyes, she finished long after the others had gone back to their rooms to shower. Nick looked pissed.

"Damn it, CJ. What is wrong with you?" Nick's fury snapped in each syllable. "By far your worst performance—you're not focused." He turned away from her, his head down as if he needed to gather himself, but the disappointment seeped from his pores, indecision bouncing off of him. "We need to fix this."

"Coach, I bonked." She tried to steady the quiver in her voice. "Maybe it's emotion. Maybe I didn't eat enough this morning. Everybody suffers a bad day once in a while."

He looked at her, the fire in his eyes intense. "You've had more than one. Is our..." he turned away without finishing his statement. Then he turned back. "Yesterday, you left the guys in the dust. Today, they couldn't drag you in. These highs and lows you're experiencing in your performance are not normal. Maybe I'm the distraction and you—no, we, the team, can't afford that." His jaw tensed as he clamped his lips together, waiting.

"It's not you." Fear snapped through her blood. They'd been inseparable since the funeral, but today she felt his distance. That he questioned their relationship, blamed himself for her poor performance, made her wonder. Would he, like everyone else in her life, break her heart?

She removed her running cap, fanned her fingers through her hair and walked away, afraid to hear the truth. She vowed not to let him down. But how could she convince him of that without revealing the real issue?

Keeping this secret from him hounded her, pulling the weight from her bones, as would any serious illness. How could he not notice? And now, the added worry of him getting fed up and breaking off their relationship pressed on her. She couldn't breathe, yet she couldn't tell him.

"CJ, every night you toss and turn. You think I don't feel it?" He came up behind her. "Something's eating at you? What is it?"

She turned toward him but hung her head.

"CJ, talk to me. Let me help." His tone softened as he reached under her chin, forcing her to look at him.

She sighed at his touch, the ache for him strong. The look of pleading on his face pierced her heart. She wanted to fold, to tell him everything. Instead, she sat on the sand and covered her face with her hands.

"Maybe I'm not cut out for this." The words came out in a squeak. "I'm a lone vessel drifting on a sea of doubt."

"Bullshit." He dropped down next to her, the aggravation back in his voice. "You're not a quitter. Or you didn't strike me as one when I first met you."

"No. I'm not." The muscle in her jaw pulsed, but her temper slowed, because the disappointment she saw in his eyes stung. "But the pressure…"

"Goes with the territory," he finished. "You knew that when you signed on."

"I'm exhausted, Nick." Her head dropped, her fingers tracing small patterns in the sand.

She sounded pitiful, she knew. And when he looked at her that way, she sighed.

Nick wrapped his arm around her and pulled her close. "Babe, listen to me." He kissed the top of her head, whispered into her hair. "A lot's happened. You're wrung out with emotion, but you can't let that rob you of your physical strength. You need rest to rebuild your torn down muscles. Stay focused and turn the emotions into power. Use the pain as fuel for your next workout."

"There is something else." With an exhalation of air, she cracked open one of the many windows encasing her. They shared stuff, right, so he had a right to know— no matter how hard she tried not to let it, it affected her. "My mother keeps calling. Can you believe she thinks I killed my father? She says by moving away, I broke his heart!"

"What?" Damp air touched her skin when he pulled away. "That's insane."

The look that moved over his face said he didn't believe anyone could go that far. Or were the shadows, flickering in his emerald depths, something else? It made her wonder about his relationship with his father.

"You've been there, haven't you?" She needed to know.

He nodded, his lips pursed, his brows drawn together, creating a small crease above his nose. "My dad blamed me for my mother's suicide."

Another similarity, one more thread that bound them. How could parents be so cruel?

She stood up and reached out. The need to comfort him nestled deep within her. "I'm so sorry, Nick."

When his fingers closed around hers, she pulled and moved into his arms. They stood there at the edge of the water, bound by their parents' selfishness. Her arms tightened around his waist, her cheek resting against his chest. "How did you get through it?"

"I had my aunt and uncle." He cupped the back of her head, his fingers slipping between the layers of her hair. "You have me."

She sighed with relief; he planned to stay. The thought of losing him scared her more than the thought of losing her life.

They walked the beach, let tranquility settle over them. Then they went back to her room and made love. Lost in the passion, she forgot about the past—at least for the moment.

Afterward, she fell asleep in his arms, relaxation seeping through her bones like a drug. She stirred only when she felt him move. She watched him slip out of bed and studied his body as he got dressed.

"Mmm." The sound rolled off her tongue. She yawned as she stretched her muscles, still enjoying the view. "Where are you going?"

"You need rest." He moved toward the door. "We don't need a repeat of today, so I'm removing myself from the equation for now. No more distractions." He came back, planted one hot kiss on her before adding, "Promise me you'll think about one thing as you go back to sleep."

"What's that?" She drifted a bit, her eyelids heavy.

"I won't stay in a relationship without trust and honesty." His lips pressed together. Then he whispered, "Ball's in your court, sweetheart."

He left. And sleep lost its appeal.

* * *

The morning ride started as usual, each member taking a turn at the front, but because emotion churned in CJ, when it was her turn, she pushed the pace. Nick said he wouldn't stay in a relationship without trust and honesty. Hadn't she shared her father's news and the fact that her mother blamed her for her father's death? Did he know she held something else inside?

She'd never had a serious relationship and she feared she'd ruin this one. What could she do? How could she convey trust without sharing her turmoil?

Reed's voice slithered into her thoughts, *Hang tough, show them who's boss.* She had to stay strong. To prove her place on this team—with her teammates and with her coach. She devoured the road, her thoughts spinning.

Dave pulled up next to her, his face red with exertion. "You've ridden half the team off your wheel. Who are you pissed at?"

"Myself more than anyone." She shot him a smile, easing up a fraction. "I'm on a mission, that's all."

"Well, yeah, we all are." He sat up. "But you're going to pop a blood vessel if you attack every workout like this."

"I need to get stronger and faster."

"By trying to kill yourself?"

"The group's back together," Simon called. "CJ, pull off, let someone else take the lead."

She did, and Dave came with her. They dropped in behind Uri, and she tried to relax her arms and relish his draft. His broad shoulders cut the wind. She forced herself to breathe, to hide what might leak through.

Nick saw the cracks in her façade, guessed at her self-doubt, but could her teammates read her as well? She needed to distance herself, reclaim her own space, and not bring more attention to her situation.

Her hands rested on the drops as she continued pedaling, her brave-face back, even though emotions bubbled below the surface, and it felt like a hot steel blade jabbed her shin bone.

She found her rhythm just as a loud curse barked from up ahead. Sitting up, she grabbed her brakes.

The speed altered and the line bowed, wheels almost touching. Her heart clenched, and she pulled out of the line to avoid a crash. Her gaze raked the front of the group to see what caused the problem.

Three of the guys were stopped on the side of the road. One extended his hand as Pete climbed from the ditch. He reached down for his bike as he rubbed dirt from his shoulder.

Big chased a car, swearing at the top of his lungs, his fist pumping in the air.

"Holy crap," Dave shouted. "Old man almost mowed them down. He could have killed them. Big's about to murder him."

"You need to have your license revoked," Big yelled as the car pulled away.

Shaken, they regrouped in a nearby driveway. Tempers cooled and they finished their ride with less gusto. When the guys rushed to tell Nick about the event, she slipped away and went to her room.

With drapes drawn, she sat in the semi-dark, shaken by what happened. Since embarking on this journey, she learned a hard lesson, the biggest and hardest to swallow: Life could end in a nano-second.

* * *

The next two months went by in a blur, the countdown to Wisconsin etched in her brain. Like her teammates, CJ focused on getting stronger and faster, listening to Nick as he guided them through each workout. He hadn't broached the trust issue again, and she attributed their less frequent sleepovers to race preparation.

As their coach, it was his job to focus on each of their performances, to home in on the special needs of each member. She'd be selfish to believe she deserved one hundred percent of his attention, even though she craved it. There were other potential winners that needed him too.

Knowing he watched her, supported her, believed in her abilities was enough.

Her birthday came and went—celebrated with a group of hunky men, which fueled her determination to win. More than ever she wanted to prove she belonged, that Nick signed her for the right reason.

She pushed herself through each workout, trying not to think of the twinges and aches, the heat that radiated up her leg.

Nick and her teammates seemed excited by her progress, and though she appeared strong on the outside, she felt like a ticking time-bomb, the uncertainty of the future weighing on her shoulders. No one knew what the future would bring—look what happened to her dad, to Reed.

Chapter 15

When CJ envisioned Wisconsin, vast fields, flat and dusty farmlands came to mind, but what greeted them as they drove from the airport to their hotel bore lush sweeping hills, and a city much like a miniature Washington DC. The magnificent lakes bordered the strip of land that connected downtown to the more rural areas, where the heavy odor of manure hung in the air.

Early September boasted dark green vegetation that stretched as far as the eye could see, and she imagined how majestic it would look when fall turned the leaves to bright reds, oranges, and yellows. Though they were on a taper—a decrease in mileage, so the body could recover and the muscles could strengthen until race day, nine days from now—she yearned to run long and hard across those fields.

The day before yesterday, they said a tearful goodbye to Mike, who offered his resort as an annual training ground, making them promise to come back. Would she see the island again? A pang echoed in her heart that she might have experienced her once-in-a-lifetime adventure, but she shook her head, banning such negative reflection.

She took in a breath, and a feeling of calm settled

around her.

After they checked in and assembled their gear, the team drove the two-loop, fifty-six mile bike course. She squeezed Nick's hand and thanked him for making her climb so much in Guam. The relentless rolling hills proved to be challenging.

Headhunter Hill, tagged the most aggressive climb on the profile map, made the mini-van tremble. The motor coughed and sputtered as Nick accelerated up the incline.

"Holy crap," Dave whistled, "that's worse than Cetti Bay."

"What's it going to feel like the second time around?" CJ groaned.

"It never lets up," Hammer called from the last row. "Damn hard to get in a rhythm."

"Have you all raced Wisconsin?" she asked the group.

"Simon, Lars, and Dave join you as virgins." Nick kissed her fingertips. "You're prepared, so relax."

When they got back to town, the group toured Monona Terrace, the elaborate center that would house the transition area on race day. The building had been designed by Frank Lloyd Wright, the final plans signed off in 1959. The actual building didn't gain support to be built until 1992, when Madison voters approved the idea and sought funding. Construction began in 1994 with the Terrace opening its doors to the public in 1997.

She stood at the ledge, looked down at Lake Monona, and imagined over two thousand athletes swimming a rectangular pattern. Closing her eyes, she tilted her face to the sun and took in a long, slow breath. It calmed the nerves bubbling in the pit of her stomach.

"Are you ready for your interview tomorrow?" Kyle came up beside her and wrapped his arm around her shoulder.

She nodded. "I practiced with Nick on the flight in, focused on remaining calm. He said to use short, concise answers to show I'm ready, but without masking my enthusiasm as a rookie."

"Tell us, how will it feel to race as a first-time pro versus an age-grouper?" He took on the tone of an aggressive newscaster.

With a gentle laugh, she answered him, "I'm excited and ready, but we'll find out next Sunday, won't we?"

* * *

After a practice swim in the lake and a bike ride to test equipment and map the run course, the team went into town. It bustled with high-strung athletes. CJ checked out the competition as they waded through the sea of lean muscle mass. A ripple of fear tickled her spine.

Nick must have sensed something, because he took her hand, squeezed.

"Who is that?" She pointed to a lean but buff-looking girl.

"Sophie Kessler," Nick answered. "She's one of the top female pros."

"Look, she check you out." Uri smiled. "Bet you beat her."

The girl waved and shot CJ a thumbs-up. She returned the gesture, awed by the interaction.

Nick stopped at a small shop in the middle of the block, opened the door and urged her in—Uri, Zach, and John close behind.

As if on a mission, Nick strode to the corner of the store and picked up a small wooden statue, placed it in her hand.

She looked at a bald man sitting Indian style, his

face in his hands, which rested in his lap.

"Yogi, he'll help keep you calm before each race." Nick paid for it and motioned them out of the store. Out on the sidewalk, he kissed her. "So you can race in your zone."

"Thank you, Nick, that's sweet."

"You've gone soft on us, man." John pulled a face before sipping from his bottle of Gatorade. The others laughed.

"Heart is happy to see you together." Uri smiled, tapping the center of his chest.

Someone wanted ice cream, another wanted pizza. So they split up to spend the rest of the day relaxing. All athletes dealt with pre-race days in their own fashion. Some found quiet places to sit and reflect; others stayed busy so they wouldn't have to think. CJ's nerves hummed and butterflies flitted in her stomach, but having Nick by her side kept her grounded.

She put everything into her preparation and training, and she knew she'd reach the finish line. But the big question lingered. Could she win?

Chapter 16

On race day, CJ woke at four in the morning. She'd spent the last twenty-four hours on her own. Kate, who'd arrived two days before, and Nick both respected her space. They both understood the pressure she put on herself, and the time to celebrate and catch-up with her friend could wait until the race ended.

On the walk from the hotel, she focused on today. Her day.

The team agreed to meet outside the swim-to-bike transition room inside Monona Terrace at 6:00 to help each other with their wetsuits, but first body-marking. She stood in line, waiting to be called to the next available volunteer with the large black sharpie.

A young brunette called CJ over, and she lifted her shirt sleeve to have her number inked on. A ripple of pleasure skimmed through her when the young girl wrote the letter P for "pro" on her calf instead of her age. Reality set in, and she smiled, thinking of what Nick said yesterday, *"You're under no pressure to win, okay? I want you to relax and race your best possible race. I am so proud of you."*

CJ placed her bottles on her bike, checked the tire pressure and gears, then threaded her way through the crowd to meet the boys. The area pumped with music and comments from the race director. Energy crackled in the air as more than twenty-one-hundred athletes readied themselves to start. The weatherman predicted a scorching day with temperatures rising into the low-nineties—a reminder to sip fluids every fifteen minutes, whether she felt thirsty or not.

"CJ. CJ," Kate shouted. Only athletes were allowed inside the transition area, so Kate stood on the other side of the fence, waving with enthusiasm. A nice looking young man stood smiling beside her. Gregory looked just like his pictures.

She went over to hug her friend. "Thanks for being here."

"Photographer reporting for duty." Kate held up her camera, then poked Gregory in the ribs. "I'd like you to meet my tongue-tied son. He volunteered to help at the aid stations."

"It's my way of saying thank you for Berlin. It was like—awesome." His cheeks colored. "It's great to finally meet you. I'm so excited about seeing your first pro race. Man, this is so cool." Eyes resembling his Mother's sparkled with youthful energy. "I'd better run before I'm late to my post. We'll be out there supporting you. Good Luck, CJ."

"It's going to be a long, hot day from what I hear." She shook his hand, then added an impulsive peck to his cheek. The color rose higher on his cheekbones. "We, the athletes, really appreciate the hours you guys put in. Thanks, and hey, remember to have fun out there."

He scampered off to fulfill his duties for the day.

"What a great kid." She touched Kate's arm. "Did he really volunteer on his own, or did you strong arm him?"

"Exclusively his idea, and since the college has a team racing, he persuaded his professor and a bunch of others to volunteer." Pride marked her tone. "Look, this is your day. Go have a spectacular race. I'll be waiting for you at the finish." Kate waved her away with a smile.

When she got inside, she found the guys applying body glide, getting ready to wrestle into their wet suits. Though the day called for the nineties, the lake held well below the seventy-eight degree mark, which allowed for wet suits. She whispered a thank you to God, because wearing one gave the swimmer better buoyancy, and right now, CJ appreciated any available advantage.

Nick gave last-minute instructions, hyping each of them to have a good race. "No pukin'," he said as he high-fived each of the guys.

He came to her, pulled her into his arms. "You're prepared and ready. Stay in your zone. Relax, and enjoy your day."

"I want to win so badly." She pulled away just far enough to see his face.

He smiled that heart-stopping smile then kissed her. "I want you to remember something—no matter what happens, no matter where you place, you'll always be my star." He kissed her again. "Good luck, babe. I'll be out there rooting for you."

"I want to make you proud."

"You already do."

"Awe." Her teammates sighed behind her. Then each of them added their "good lucks."

She took in a huge breath, then exhaled before stepping into the right leg of her wetsuit.

* * *

Before she knew it, CJ treaded water in the lake, a small group of professionals surrounding her. Calm washed over her, an unusual feat at 6:40 the morning of a big event—her event. During every other race, she relaxed when she hit the halfway mark of the 2.4-mile swim.

She thought of Yogi and once again smiled—Nick's words bolstering her.

Bella Zeebroek moved closer, touched her shoulder. "I keep eye on you, but I wish you goot race."

"You, too," she replied. "Stay safe, race strong."

"I heard you're fierce competition." Sophie Kessler angled over. "May the best man win."

CJ smiled. "I still can't believe I'm racing as a pro. I'm awed to be here with you."

Several other competitors drew in deep breaths, closed their eyes, then blew the air from their lungs in an effort she understood well: that need to release the pent-up tension that made one's heart flutter just before plunging into the water for the start of a very long day.

For the first time ever, the gerbils in her stomach remained at bay, her limbs loose. Her mind clear, her goal set—Team Fear US deserved a winner.

The cannon boomed, and the small group of professionals took off. Unlike the washing machine effect of the age-group mass start, where thousands of bodies fought for the same space, and one worried about being swum over and drowned, this felt tranquil. It boosted her confidence and her arms reached even farther as she slipped into the line of fast swimmers.

In other races, she had experienced panic as hands struck her back, pushed her under. The coughing after gulping water as she fought not to drown, until her heart settled, but with this group, it felt more like an occasional tap here and there, hands fluttering against feet, elbows thumping. It allowed her to relax a little and focus on her form. The swim was a blip in the whole of the day.

One loop, so no worries about lapping the age-groupers. CJ took advantage of the space and motored.

She concentrated on lengthening her body with each pull.

When she made it to land, her feet grabbed the earth with relief, and she ran, got peeled out of her wetsuit and headed up the helix into the building. *Holy cow, how many turns before reaching the top?* Glancing at her watch, she realized this long transition would alter her expected finish-time. She recalculated as she pulled on her socks.

She carried her cycling shoes, and raced out of the building, down the sloping ramp and into the transition. With shoes on, she grabbed her bike and dashed to the mounting line. Within seconds, she sat on her bike, coasted down the other helix, then pedaled out of town. The ride out to where the loop started was flat but technical. Soon she climbed and rolled through the farmlands. Most of the cornfields had been harvested, but a few remained untouched, their sun-dried stalks swaying in the morning breeze as if waving the riders on to their final destination.

The streets were lined with spectators, yelling and ringing cowbells—just like in New Zealand—this was a day to celebrate and cheer on the athletes visiting their home town.

Several athletes cramped and fell over on the steeper climbs, and her gut clenched. What if she pulled a Uri? Doubt flitted through her, but she pushed it aside, concentrating instead on her form. She sipped, ate an energy gel, and kept pedaling.

On her second trip up Headhunter Hill, CJ stood and powered through the climb.

She felt strong coming off the second loop, then she hit the headwinds on her way back into town. Her time held, but she struggled with the slight decrease in average speed.

She reminded herself to relax, to set her pace, and keep going.

She pictured Nick at the finish, waiting with a huge grin on his face, those gorgeous lines around his eyes crinkling as she crossed through the tape. She thought of his hands on her body when he congratulated her, the touch of his lips as he showed his delight. Passion's race—her love of racing, and a lifetime of love. They may be lofty dreams, but they kept her preoccupied, kept her from second-guessing her abilities and the secret she'd kept for months. She trained hard, and could do only what her body could do.

She'd know in about three hours' time if it was enough.

* * *

At the check-points, Nick confirmed each of their times. Three of the guys started the run, the others including CJ remained on the bike course. He prayed for her to finish strong. He wanted her to feel secure in her decision to leave her management position to race for his team. Though they'd discussed it only a few times, he knew it weighed on her mind. Her self-doubt cropped up once in a while to challenge her strength. Did she recognize the pattern? That it took about two days for her to bounce back after receiving a phone call from her mother?

He now understood the power the woman wielded, and though he wished CJ would break off communication, her large heart wouldn't allow that. She felt the pull of blood. But he so wanted to protect her, cocoon her from the negative, allow her to experience the bond of absolute love. His heart warmed; no doubt his family would accept her with open arms.

Would she handle the role of mother differently, as he would being a father? One thing was certain, she'd make beautiful babies. Thinking about that brought a smile to his face.

Uri dismounted, slapped Nick on the back as he headed for the men's changing room. "I do as you say, Coach. Heart monitor and stay steady."

"You go, boy." Nick laughed. "Right now, you're on track for top fifteen."

Lars and Val followed Uri only a few seconds down, close enough to each other to vie for position. "Kick it, guys, Uri just came through. Go get him."

"Nick." He heard CJ call, as she flew by.

She got off the bike in fourth place, a hair splitting her from the third place pro. If she remained strong, she could pick her off. Even a third place finish provided him a bargaining chip to persuade the sponsors to hang in.

"Go, CJ, you're doing great," he screamed. "You can catch her. Pour it on."

She nodded as she ran by, an incredible smile covering her face. She looked light on her feet, comfortable with her stride, which gave her the edge with 26.2 miles to close the gap on the three women ahead of her.

His heart kicked. She might just pull this off.

The Wisconsin race venue offered many opportunities for spectators to see their favorite athlete, in this case, at least eight times during the two-loop run course. After John, Pete, Simon, Big, and Dave started the run, Nick moved to his next vantage point. So far, the entire team looked strong. From his new spot, he timed the interval between the leader and CJ, calculating her chance to overtake the lead, while still checking on the rest of the team.

He moved from one spot to the next, continuing to monitor their progress.

The guys held their ground. Kyle and Hunter fought for first position among the team, Zach not far behind. Uri, his breathing steady, dashed by, saluting Nick as he passed. Lars and Val raced shoulder to shoulder, determination etched on their faces—a sprint finish waited up ahead for those two. CJ floated by, her turnover consistent and fluid, the gap shrinking with number three. Dave, who brought up the rear, carried a look of courage on his face as he chased John, Pete, Simon, and Big, but if he maintained his pace, he could finish in the top forty; overall, not bad for the team.

Kyle turned on State Street first, led the pack to the finish. He looked comfortable and strong at his current pace, and he had over two minutes on the next male. If he held it, he'd finish fifth. Nick hustled to get to the line to cheer him in.

"Come on, Kyle, nail it." Judging from Kyle's facial expression, he gave his all.

One by one, his team members crossed the finish line. The announcer called each by name and added, "Congratulations, you are an Ironman!"

Tears welled as he watched each one accept his medal. Music played, and the crowds screamed, emotion thick in the air. The late afternoon rocked with festivity.

Pride swelled his chest as the finishers hugged and high-fived.

Kyle, Hunter, Zach, Uri, Val, and Lars stood with him as CJ came toward the finishing chute. *Oh, my God.* She nipped at the lead woman's feet. They all screamed, but their cheers blended with those of the standing crowd as everyone watched the race for the win unfold.

"Come on, babe," he shouted. "Go for it!"

The lead woman, Sophie, sensed her competitor behind her, because the grimace on her face conveyed her struggle. She dug deep and popped ahead another few feet. She flew for the finish line. CJ, too, accelerated, pouring every ounce of strength into her sprint.

But in the end, it wasn't enough.

She finished second—thirteen seconds down. Bella

taking third a full minute behind.

He stepped forward and scooped her into his arms, spinning her around, before setting her feet back down on the ground. The others descended on them, adding their excitement to the celebration. Kate ran toward them, her camera bouncing against her chest, her arm pumping the air. When the fray of elation calmed, he took CJ's hand.

"Second place! I'm so proud." Emotion welled, but he caught the small flicker of disappointment that flashed in her eyes. "Wait, you better be, too," he urged. "Excellent race."

"Thirteen seconds, Nick." Tears crested and a spark of fight replaced the disappointment, her physical let-down replaced with renewed enthusiasm. "Florida. I'll do it there."

"You just earned a nice pay check. Let's celebrate that, shall we?" He kissed her. "Florida is eight weeks away." He pulled her into the crook of his arm, turned to face the clock. "Now, let's watch the others finish. John's next to cross. Three minutes behind you at the last checkpoint, though your sprint might have widened the gap."

Reporters rushed her, stuck microphones in her face. "How does it feel to get that close?"

"I'm still in shock." She breathed hard, her palm pressed against her chest. "Did I really finish thirteen seconds down from Sophie Kessler? Makes me wonder—if I'd transitioned faster, could I have caught her? If I'd picked up just one minute on the swim, could I have won?" Her smile widened. "Fuels my determination for the next race, that's for sure."

Nick's pride soared when the mics shifted in Sophie's direction. "She's a fierce competitor, this girl, she had me busting a gut to stay ahead. Second place in her fist pro race, I say we keep our eyes on her going forward."

The crowds continued to cheer as Dave crossed the line an hour later. He looked drained, but happy. "Man, that was tough," he said as he joined them near the sideline.

Kate sat among them, as each one shared experiences of the day.

"I wonder how many cramped on the second bike loop?" Simon asked. "I saw several athletes sitting at the side of the road."

"No kidding, the medical tent is filling up fast." Pete pointed in that direction.

"It was a scorcher," Big added.

"One thing's certain, we overcame the difficulties because of our training on Guam," Hunter added. "I say we keep that as our secret training ground."

Everyone nodded in agreement.

"Overall, these are the best results ever. For the first time, everyone finished...feeling strong, I might add—a definite pay-off for training on the island. I vote for it to be our new tradition. Mike offered, we'll accept."

"Here, here," the others shouted.

Excitement pumped through the group but subsided as a sturdy, broad-shouldered man approached them with determination. A moment's hesitation, a brief question of curiosity on everyone's faces, but Nick jumped to his feet.

He grabbed the guy in a bone-crushing bear hug. "What are you doing here, Shayne?"

"I need to talk to you about your father."

Chapter 17

Shayne Hart, Nick's cousin, stood eying the group, his light green eyes such a contrast to his dark hair. Good looking, but then he shared Nick's genes, right? Several inches shorter than Nick, but still as handsome in a lumberjack kind of way.

Nick seemed happy to see him, but the announcement about his father gathered his brows, pulled at the corners of his mouth. He turned in her direction, and introduced her as his star athlete…. "The woman I'm in love with."

Shayne's hand swallowed hers, as her gaze followed the line of his rolled-up shirt sleeve. Under the crisp white fabric flexed an arm the size of a substantial tree trunk, bulging against the fold, and she looked away, embarrassed. Out of the corner of her eye, she caught the snicker cresting his mouth, and she felt the blush creep up her face.

His job—president of his father's construction company—accounted for his tanned and leathered skin, his brawny build.

Nick coughed, and Shayne dropped her hand but bent down and hoisted her off the ground in an affectionate embrace. He spun her around, his massive hand gentle as he patted her back. When he put her down, he turned toward Kate.

"And who is this lovely lady?" His hand, palm up, hovered, waiting for her to reach out.

"Kate Brooks, CJ's personal race photographer." Kate placed her hand in his, making no move to extract it.

Shayne didn't seem to mind, his smile spread below that melting gaze. His lips grazed Kate's knuckles as he winked, and CJ thought her friend might faint.

"Not to mention, my best friend in the world," CJ added, catching Nick's surprised look.

"So, what's this about my father?" Nick's voice carried an edge. "Did you come to tell me he's dead? Because that's about the only news I want to hear about him."

"He's not dead." Shayne surveyed the group. "Shouldn't we discuss this in private?" He released Kate's hand, a small shrug of apology moving his shoulder, and took a step toward Nick. Placing his arm across Nick's back, he drew him from the group.

"Hey, guys," CJ addressed her teammates. "Why don't we go shower and change? We'll meet back here to cheer on the late night finishers. Let's grab a bite to eat and give these guys time to talk." She indicated Nick and Shayne with her thumb.

Mumbles of agreement rippled through the group.

"Can we get our gear later?" Dave asked in a pathetic voice.

"I'd rather eat first; I'm hungry." Hunter patted his stomach. "I'm ready for solid food."

"After all that gel," Simon groaned, "I'm ready to barf."

Chuckles and moans followed her and Kate as they meandered back to the hotel, the boys trailing behind. Evening blanketed the festive city, but the deepening twilight did nothing to dissipate the humid climate of early-September. The oppressive heat clung to her skin, making her crave a shower.

"Second place in your first pro race. You must be ecstatic." Kate threaded her arm through hers. "How long before you come back to earth?"

"I'll let you know when my feet touch solid ground."

* * *

Finding a quiet spot bordered on impossible at an Ironman race. Spectators blanketed the area; racers in search of family and friends weaved back and forth. Even the area behind the medical tent buzzed with activity, because of the number of drop-outs who needed attention.

CJ was thoughtful to take the team out of his orbit, but for how long? Would he have time to recover from whatever news Shayne brought? The subject of Mitchell Madison bristled his skin and dulled the thrill of seeing his cousin.

He walked the few blocks necessary to stand beside the lake that rippled with bodies early this morning and found an empty bench to sit on.

"What's he up to now?" He couldn't disguise the disgust in his voice. "He must want something."

"He does. He wants to set things straight." Shayne looked him in the eye. "He's dying of lung cancer and requested to see you. I know it's the last thing you want to do, but Nick, you can't let him die without clearing up the past."

"Why not?" Off the bench, he paced. "I don't owe the bastard anything."

"No, you don't. Maybe he owes you." Shayne remained seated, his hands clasped between his widespread knees. "Either way, why carry more guilt on your shoulders?"

"Guilt?" His fingers flexed, diving through his hair, though they itched to pound a nearby tree. He wanted to turn away, to hide the emotion, but faced his cousin instead.

"Oh, come on." Shayne licked his lips, sucked in a breath. "We both know you blame yourself for your mother's death."

He stilled, every nerve vibrating in his body. He closed his eyes, the rush of heat in his throat unbalancing him, surprising him after all these years. He strode to the edge of the water, wanted to throw something out there to disturb the calm.

He heard Shayne shift behind him, felt his cousin's palm flatten against his shoulder. "You need to get this out of your system, Nick. He's the only one who can help you."

"You'd think…" he expelled a breath, balled his fist against his mouth to hold in the rage that built in his chest, "…after all these years, it wouldn't hurt so much. He wanted me to feel responsible, to believe that without me, she could have lived a full and happy life."

"You were her light, Nick. Without you, she wouldn't have made it as long as she did, but hearing that from me won't clear your mind. You have to confront your father, let him share what's weighing on his soul. Hear him out and resolve for yourself if you can forgive him or not. Whether you do will be your decision, but at least you'll be able to move on and purge him from your life." Shayne dropped his hand. "Just think about it, okay?"

He nodded, his bottom lip caught between his teeth. He turned to hug his cousin, the long-held tears pushing through. He laid his forehead against Shayne's massive shoulder and let the dam break. Years of self-blame poured through him, shattering the concrete shell he'd cultivated for over twenty years.

* * *

Back at the hotel, Kate joined CJ in her room as she drew a hot bath, using the eucalyptus foaming bath Nick left for her in a basket by the tub. It also contained a scented candle, a pack of matches, and a loofa for scrubbing her skin. She lit the candle while the tub filled, then opened the card he left nestled amongst the goodies.

"What does it say?" Kate leaned against the doorframe, a dreamy expression on her face.

The beautiful picture showed a lone cyclist climbing switchbacks on a mountain, under it: *What an accomplishment!* She flipped it to show Kate. "Inside he wrote: I'm so proud. No matter your time or your rank, I know you're a winner. I love you, Nick."

"How sweet," Kate murmured. "Wonder what his cousin's like?"

She slid into the tub, her gaze fastened on her friend, a giggle escaping. "I half expected you to drool when he kissed your hand. Never pegged you as the romantic type."

"I'm not." Her chin shot in the air.

"Umm, I felt the sparks in the air. Something obviously passed between you two."

"You know how people talk about the electrical sizzle when they meet *the one*?"

CJ nodded. "Yup, happened with me and Nick, but I registered it as irritation."

"Well, this felt more like slow-moving syrup coating my insides." Kate pulled the vanity stool over to the tub, her lips pursed in thought. "Soothing—yes, a comforting warmth I've never before experienced." She sat with her back to the wall, her perfectly Frenchpedicured feet propped up on the edge of the tub. "Odd how safe he made me feel. I don't even know him."

"It's not odd." She stretched her weary legs in the warm water, her less fashionable toes playing with the bubbles at the surface. "What are you looking for in a relationship, Kate?"

"I stopped looking so long ago, I couldn't tell you." That throaty laugh echoed against the bathroom walls. "Besides, he's Nick's cousin. Let's not go there."

"Oh, let's." Scooping foam into her palm, she blew it in Kate's face. "Answer me, what do you want in a mate?"

"A partner." Kate looked surprised by her own admission but continued. "A man who accepts me as I am, quirks and all, because at this stage in my life, I don't think much will change. He'd have to respect my career, my decisions, my needs, as much as I would his. You know, fifty-fifty." She tugged at her ear, her eyes scanning the ceiling. As if embarrassed, she turned away, the cord in her neck flexing.

"Go on," she coaxed.

"I'd want his strengths to complement my weaknesses."

"You have weaknesses?"

"I'm not the most sensitive person."

"You think that big brawny guy is the sensitive type?"

"He might be. And if so, he'd be in charge of remembering birthdays and such." They both burst out laughing at that statement. Then Kate sobered. "I'd like my partner to cherish me, but that's asking too much, isn't it?" Her nostrils flared, and she grinned.

She shrugged. "Don't ask me. I'm no expert. Nick and I are still navigating."

An hour later, she and Kate straggled behind the group, so they could continue the conversation they'd started earlier in the bathroom, the boys up ahead oblivious to the subject of their feminine fantasies.

"When did you know you loved Nick?" Kate nibbled on the last of her ice cream cone.

"The day Reed died." Warmth seeped through her at the memory. "When I crawled into his lap, which was so not me. He felt like *home*. Deep down in my belly, I knew he'd keep me safe."

"He's not shy on the 'demonstrate feelings' end." Kate wiped her mouth, wadded up her napkin and searched for the nearest trashcan. "I love how he looks at you."

"Yeah, when he does, I go all soft inside."

"I think in time, he'll help you fight your insecurities."

"You mean my mom."

"Your mother loaded a mountain of heavy baggage on your tiny shoulders. I hope Nick's love releases you from her sick and selfish crap."

"Wow, don't mince words. Tell me what you really think."

Kate tugged on her arm. "What about the secrecy? When are you going to tell Nick about your leg?" Her friend stared at her in an attempt to gauge the expression on her face. Kate possessed quite an incredible and accurate deception meter.

"What he doesn't know can't hurt him."

"You mentioned getting a second opinion. Will you keep it from him after that?"

"It depends. If everything is healed, there is no need to tell him."

"What if they're not healed? What will it do to him and your relationship when he finds out you've been less than candid with him?"

"I don't know." She bowed her head, fear of his abandonment nipping at her. "I know I promised to come clean, get another doctor's opinion, but I'm only seconds off the mark. I plan to win in Florida. I'll handle the rest after the race."

"I think you're making a mistake."

"Look, I feel great. I raced strong today."

"Yes, but by keeping this to yourself, you're risking not only your career, but a relationship with the man who believes in you and has since the day he saw you race in New Zealand. Is racing Florida worth that risk?"

"I need that win."

Shaking her head, Kate walked ahead, disappointment sparking off her like static.

* * *

The team huddled near the finish line. Nick stood off to the side, a somber flare in the otherwise exuberant atmosphere. Coming up from behind, CJ wrapped her arms around his body, snuggling against his back.

"You okay?" she asked, placing small kisses on the soft material of his shirt.

"I am now." He turned in her arms, pulled her closer against his chest. She transferred tranquil peace from her body to his, heard him sigh. They remained like that for several heartbeats, one unit in a crowd. One balancing the other.

Then something shifted inside her—an overwhelming shot of uncertainty, a drug invading her bloodstream—and she wobbled. Kate's displeasure weighed on her, but what caused this wave of instability?

She hugged Nick harder, kissed him to rebalance. "You want to talk about the news?"

"Later. Kiss me again. I liked that."

"Dude!" Shayne chuckled and rolled his eyes.

"Get a room." Big slapped Nick on the back.

"Yeah, we're here to cheer on the age-groupers,

remember?" Zach elbowed Hunter, who howled like a wolf.

Kyle winked. "Just ignore them. That's what they do to us."

"Don't know we exist," John quipped. "Most of the time."

"Oh, shut up," Nick shot back as Shayne grabbed him in a wrestling hold.

CJ just shook her head. Did boys ever grow up? Her answer came as huge hands closed around her waist and hoisted her high in the air. She now sat perched on Uri's shoulder as he danced in a circle, making her dizzy.

"Uri, what are you doing?" Her voice rose, and she clutched at his ears not to fall off. "Put me down."

"We proud. You did *goot*." He circled again and again.

"I'm getting nauseous! Please put me down before I puke." That did it. Her feet touched ground within seconds, but the celebration continued.

The entire team laughed and cheered and hugged as more and more finishers crossed the line. Kate finally joined them but remained distant, using her camera as her shield.

CJ noticed Shayne inching closer to Kate and nudged Nick to watch, as well.

She turned her attention back to the finish line. Another small group of athletes entered the chute. She jumped up and down, screaming encouragement, but out of the corner of her eye, she caught a blur of movement, felt a hand touch her arm.

"CJ!"

She recognized the voice, and turned to greet her brother. Nick stepped between them, his arms crossed in front of his chest, a protective stance. She touched Nick's arm, smiled then turned back to ask, "Gordon? What are you doing here?"

"I came to see my sister race her first pro race. You were awesome."

He beamed.

His bright green eyes lit his radiant face. He came to watch her race. She grinned at him as her heart rolled over in her chest.

He pulled her into a hug, lifting her from the ground. "I never realized there'd be so many people. It took me hours to find you.

"I can't believe you're here."

"You didn't think I'd miss my baby sister's day, did you?"

"I didn't know you cared. Never thought you were interested in my hobby."

"Career," Nick corrected, sticking out his hand. "I'm her coach, Nick Madison."

"Sorry." She made introductions to the rest of the group.

"So, you're the one who got her to take a chance," Gordon addressed Nick. "Nice to meet you." He turned back to CJ. "Actually, your little announcement to the family made me think about going after my own goals. I met with my manager and charted a career plan. Decided I want to manage my own dealership. Then Dad died, and I re-examined my life again. I focused and worked hard to reach my goal. Next week, I start as the assistant manager of our sister dealership in Ft. Lauderdale, Florida."

The news shocked her. "You're moving to Ft. Lauderdale? Leaving Mom?"

"Yeah. She flipped. Carried on about everyone abandoning her—her mother, you, Dad, and now me."

CJ wondered if feeling abandoned by her own mother added frost to their mother-daughter relationship—something to investigate in the future. For now, she concentrated on her brother. She wrapped her arms around him, squeezing hard. "Gordon, I'm so proud of you."

"Thanks, Sis. You gave me the courage." He kissed her cheek, hugging her back. Then he surprised her again by pulling Nick into the hug. "Thanks to both of you."

The team cheered as another Ironman finisher crossed the line, and she hugged the two men by her side. This tribe banded together—a stronger, more cohesive core of family, friends, and lovers—and as one, they cheered the last person across the line. Closing in on seventeen hours of racing made every finish emotional, but the last one left not one dry eye among them.

The girl, probably in her late twenties, deserved the standing ovation she received.

The announcer screamed, "Congratulations, Jenny from Utah, you are an Ironman! This is her first, folks."

The roar deafened as the crowd went wild.

Tears streamed down the girl's face, but her smile lit the world. Her fatigue fled as she floated the last few feet across the line. She pumped her fists in the air for her finishing picture, and accepted her medal from the volunteer. Then she bent down, took off her left prosthetic leg, and hoisted it in the air.

"I am an Ironman!" she shouted, her face radiant.

* * *

In the quiet early morning, CJ held tight to Nick's hand as they strolled back to the hotel. Nick pushed her bike with his free hand and carried her gear bag on his back. Accustomed to trudging her own equipment, this allowed her time to bask in the glow of an amazing day. Her favorite time after every race, but tonight seemed even more magical.

This end-of-the-race-day tradition—a window of time to reflect on the day, to wind down after the exertion of racing, to process the memories—she now shared with the man she loved. For a few minutes, the over stimulation of competition disappeared in a vacuum of calm hard to describe to an outsider. Nick, though, seemed to understand.

He released her hand, wrapped his arm around her shoulder and hugged her close.

"I love this time." She walked beside him, her fingers tucked into his belt loops.

"You should be exhausted, yet you're glowing." Nick smiled.

"The pain comes later, after gear is stowed, and I collapse on the bed." Then the aches appeared, the throbbing of each muscle group confirmation of the distance covered and the effort expended. "Second place, Nick, and I almost caught her."

"I know." His eyes lit up. "I calculated as you crossed the run-start mat. Figured your opportunity to catch and pass number three, then guesstimated how long you'd need to close the gap on the next pro. But to finish just shy of that win, babe, you did great."

"I'm jazzed about Florida. Oh, and I felt the camaraderie at the pro level. We shared moments of admiration, even when we fought for the win."

He shifted, squeezing her shoulder. "You on the team raised the guys' awareness level. The entire team netted personal records. I'm so proud. But, hon, your finish brought tears to my eyes. You raced with all your heart. Your passion radiated and hummed in the air."

Tears filled her eyes and her heart pulsed. "Thanks for bringing me on this journey, Nick. You've given me so much in just five months."

"No, thank you."

When he kissed her, her insides tingled. Though her muscles sang with fatigue, she floated as she drank in the heat from his lips. And when he pulled back and looked at her, she melted. Her decision to leave retail—a bridge crossed; her life with Nick—a new world of opportunity. What else awaited?

Chapter 18

Two days later, the group shared goodbyes at the airport. CJ flew to Walnut Creek, California, with Nick to spend a few days at his house. Her brother's destination was Atlanta, to pack and plan his move to a new career. The rest of the team headed home to reunite with family and friends for the week, before reconnecting in her hometown to train for their next event.

On the plane, CJ sipped on Bloody Mary mix, craving the salt and spice. Her fingers fidgeted with the glass, and Nick reached out to still her hands, his large palm soothing.

"I can't help it, I'm bubbling with questions." She set the glass down. "Why did my mom lump her mother into her assault on Gordon? Why did she abandon my mom? What about my grandfather?"

She remembered once, long ago, asking about her grandparents. She'd learned, while still in high school, her father had lost his parents in a plane crash, but her mother refused to speak of her parents. CJ knew better than to broach the subject again. But now, she wanted answers.

Besides her family dynamics, another problem

weighed on her shoulders—this morning she overheard Nick offer the sponsors a deal. Using her second place finish as the negotiating factor, he requested they postpone their exodus until after Florida, where he hoped to secure their support for another five years at double the investment if CJ won. He sold it as leverage to sign big-name professionals next year. So now her performance in Florida determined if the team remained intact. The added pressure made her queasy.

Her mother's voice crept into her head. "You'll come crawling back with your tail between your legs," she'd said the night CJ announced her news. The risk of losing her pro status now loomed larger than the worry about her leg. She could not afford to go backward.

"What's going on in that pretty little head of yours?" Nick leaned in to plant tiny kisses along her jaw.

"Too much." She tilted her head to kiss his lips. He mustn't find out that she knew about the sponsors. "Have you decided what to do about your father?"

After they returned to the hotel on race night, they'd cuddled in bed and talked about Shayne's news. Nick apologized for keeping her awake, but she knew he needed to share. Besides, sleep never came easy after the grueling hours of a race.

Nick responded, frustration edging his voice, "I hate to see him after all these years, but maybe he regrets his actions. Better to find out and move on, than wonder years from now."

"Nick," she took his hand, lifted it and kissed his palm, "we'll do this together. I'll stand beside you and support you."

Sucking in a slow breath, he shook his head. "No, you've experienced enough negativity in your life. I won't expose you to him." He tightened his grip on her hand.

She understood the demon he faced, deduced his

need to go alone. "I'll wait at home with hugs." Resting her head on his shoulder, she asked, "When will you go?"

"Thursday."

They sat in silence for a few minutes, then Nick turned toward her. "So...how do you plan to search for answers about your grandmother? Will you speak to your mom? Do you think she'll talk after all these years?"

"I have no idea, but after learning about my father and Gordon, I wonder what other skeletons rest in my family's closets. If my grandmother did abandon my mom, it might explain my mother's inability to love those close to her." She sipped her drink. "Whatever the outcome, I'm prepared to deal with it. I simply want the truth."

"You're a brave girl, CJ. This could drive a bigger wedge between you and your mom, but you're willing to risk that for the truth. Just one of the things I love about you."

Her heart took a little tumble and she sighed. "What else do you love about me?"

* * *

Nick drove the rental car across the San Mateo Bridge and up into Walnut Creek, a small city east of San Francisco. His home, he said, sat two blocks from Main Street, which boasted an array of specialty shops and eclectic restaurants. CJ looked forward to spending time there.

When he pulled into the driveway, she gawked. His house resembled a mini-mansion, but of course, as an ex-Tour de France rider, famous in his own right, he could afford such luxuries.

The color reminded her of roasted walnuts, warm and inviting. Clean white trim bordered the dark green roof, which peaked in several spots, giving the structure character.

Inside, the main living space was lined with large picture windows. The dark chocolate and mocha tones in the fabrics complemented the cherry woods. Rugs and pillows accented with different shades of green: pear, lime, and olive. Minimal artwork—three over-sized, bold pieces—graced the few walls in the open layout. Masculine, yet cozy, just like Nick.

His back door opened to the Iron-Horse Trail. He described it as an eighteen mile, round-trip path that connected Walnut Creek to Pleasanton, cutting through Danville and San Ramon. One day they'd run it, but for now, she obeyed her coach's orders to rest and rebuild muscle strength for the Florida race.

While Nick carried their suitcases upstairs, CJ explored.

She gazed with admiration at the magnificent kitchen. The espresso colored wood appeared almost black against the contrasting white marble counters, and the stainless steel appliances gleamed. She opened the fridge and freezer then took inventory: a case of beer, one bottle of mustard, and a pound of Starbucks' coffee. She found three cans of soup and a box of pasta in the pantry. Welcome to his bachelor pad, she thought, and laughed.

"What's so funny?" He came up behind her and nuzzled her neck.

"Where is the nearest grocery store?"

"It's not far, but we'll shop later." He pulled the collar of her shirt aside and nibbled on her collarbone. "I'm hungry for something else right now."

She purred, the heat from his lips traveling through her. The aches melted from her muscles as his mouth traced other contours of her body. Feeling the hard length of him against her, she snuggled closer, an action which caused him to moan.

She turned to face him, threading her fingers in his hair, and brought his mouth to hers. Her lips, cracked from the hours of racing, feasted. He tasted of toothpaste, minty and fresh. She savored the flavor as she deepened the kiss.

"God, woman, you drive me crazy." He gathered her into his arms and headed for the stairs. In the bedroom, he settled her on the bed, looking down at her with those gorgeous eyes. "I love you—inside and out."

Her stomach tightened at his words, her heart dropping to her toes. With him, she felt beautiful. "I love you, too."

She wanted to spend the rest of her life with this man. Even with that huge question mark still dangling in her future, she wanted him by her side. The potent surge of emotion made her dizzy—a feeling so new to her— true love versus the crushes she experienced in school. Like leaving her career to become a pro, she followed her heart on this issue.

"I feel so safe with you," she said and opened her arms, inviting him in.

* * *

CJ woke up alone in bed. She found Nick closed up in his office, an odd expression on his face. He shook it off and suggested they walk to his neighborhood Starbucks, to sit outside and enjoy the September weather.

People jammed the sidewalks, the din of conversation constant, but Nick's body language bothered her. He seemed preoccupied, probably thinking about his upcoming visit with his father. But what could she do to help?

She cuddled up next to him, rubbed his back in an

effort to help him relax. "Are you worried about seeing your dad?"

"No. I have bigger issues on my mind."

He held open the door to the coffee shop, and she stepped inside, the rich scent of coffee greeting her. She breathed in, enjoying the moment. They both ordered lattes then went back outside to sit in the sun at one of the tables.

"What issues?" she asked, when they settled.

He sipped his latte as if he debated whether to share. After several moments, he said, "Hunter's leaving the team."

"What?" She sat forward too fast. Foam shot from the hole in her lid, landing with a splat on the table. She wiped it up with a napkin. "What do you mean he's leaving?"

"I didn't know if you knew. Thought he might have told you." He made a face. "He signed with QT2."

"No. He didn't tell me." Shaking her head, she asked, "Why would he sign with them?"

"Several reasons. He's worried that if the sponsors pull out, he'll be without a team. He can't afford to continue racing on his own. He also thinks he'll get more focused support from Jesse and his team of coaches, better advice to grow as an athlete."

"Well, that's bull." She set her cup on the table, crossed her arms over her chest. "You've been grooming him and Kyle for a win. He doesn't call that support?"

"Maybe he doesn't like the competition—with you and Kyle." He shrugged his shoulders. "I don't know. I'm not in the guy's head. I thought I knew my team better." His lip twisted, the arc of his brow revealing his frustration.

"Is there a chance the sponsors will bail?" She'd overheard his conversation, so she knew. Did that make Hunter a traitor or, professionally, was he looking out for his best interests? "And if they do, does that leave us all out in the cold?" A shiver of apprehension snaked up her spine. What would she do? Go back to running a store?

"I'll be honest with you." He leaned forward, rested his elbows on the edge of the table. "Your second-place finish in Wisconsin allowed me to renegotiate to keep them interested, but that doesn't mean they won't back out. They want a winner, and with Hunter leaving, we have one less chance."

"When you called me your ticket to fame, you meant it." She lined up the symbol on her cup with the hole in the lid. "More rode on me than succeeding as a first-time pro."

"Yup." He sat back, steepled his fingers under his chin. "I signed you because of your potential, your drive. I knew Reed had a chance, but you sweetened the pot. I never expected to fall in love with you."

"Then Reed got killed, putting my abilities to the ultimate test. I guess I became the team's number-one chance."

"If you do as well in Florida as you did in Wisconsin, we might be able to buy another year. If you win, we get double the value and a five-year extension. With that, we could probably persuade a big name male and a few more females to sign on, giving us more leverage going forward." She could almost see his thoughts spin.

As she digested the information, Nick's cell phone rang.

He answered, listened, asked two questions that puzzled her. Then he hung up uttering an expletive that frightened her.

"Ah, fuck."

"Now what?"

"Kyle broke his hip. Doctors surgically inserted three, four-inch screws in it. He's out for at least the next year." He dropped his phone on the table and raked his hand through his hair, a gesture she now associated with disaster.

Chapter 19

CJ slammed her phone on the desk, the urge to scream choking her. Her mother tested her patience. Their conversations always grated, but this one made her shiver. Just mentioning her grandmother frosted the earpiece.

"Everything okay?" Nick entered the room, a Zipp wheel in his hands. "I started changing your tire and heard the walls rattle."

"That mother of mine infuriates me." CJ swiveled the office chair around to face him. "Why can't we have a normal conversation?"

"You're asking me?" He sat on the couch and seated the tire on the rim. As he checked for pinch spots, he continued, his eyes focused on his task. "She seems to know what buttons to push. Why do you let her aggravate you? Seems to me, as a manager of a multi-million-dollar store, you dealt with irate customers and associates. Why can't you handle her the same way?"

She had handled angry customers and disgruntled employees with ease, set emotion aside to treat the behavior. Why couldn't she do that with her mom? Would it change the degree of their relationship if her mother realized she'd lost control?

Without a second thought, she flung herself at him. The wheel dropped to the colorful rug, as she drowned him in kisses.

"Genius—you are brilliant."

His little-boy smile melted her heart.

"You want to fill me in on the details of that travesty?" His arms looped around her, pulling her close.

"Well, she wouldn't talk about her mother, other than to suggest she's a nasty, uncaring woman who left her only family high and dry."

"Do you know anything about your grandmother?"

"Only her name—Frances Crenshaw. That's it."

Carrying her, Nick headed toward the desk. "Let's Google her." He set her on her feet and pulled his laptop over. His fingers tapped, and when he hit enter, he rubbed his hands together, imitating the voice of a mad professor. "Let's see what we can uncover."

A screen popped up with several options. She watched over his shoulder as he scrutinized the list then clicked on the second link. "Let's start here, though that's quite a list." He glanced up, stood, and pushed her into the chair. "Here, you read. I'll go open a Pinot Noir."

"We're having wine?"

"You deserve it." He smiled. "Read. I'll be right back."

She watched him leave the room then turned back to the screen.

Her grandmother, an artist, owned an art gallery in Paris on La Rue du Faubourg St. Honore. Several newspaper articles honored her work and referred to her as *Paris' Darling*. Apparently, she studied her craft in Paris and returned to the city of her passion after a tragedy.

CJ accepted the glass of wine from Nick. "Look." She turned the computer to face him. "I think we found her."

"Don't get too excited, babe. If your mother's account is semi-accurate, Frances may not want to know you." He set his glass aside and took her face in his hands. "I worry she'll break your huge heart if she refuses communication."

"I'm prepared, one way or the other, because I need answers." She touched her breastbone. "Something tells me I'm in for a surprise."

"Okay." He planted a sound kiss on her mouth. Then he turned the screen so they could both see. "How do we verify that she is indeed your grandmother?"

He brought up several more articles. One detailed the wedding of one Matthew Crenshaw to his "autumn bride" Frances, an aspiring artist he met in Paris while vacationing after college graduation. They married and lived in Atlanta, Georgia, where he accepted a financial position with a well-recognized company. Another revealed that two years into their marriage, they delivered a premature baby, a little girl named Abigail Lucette. CJ's mom.

They tracked Abigail through high school, found some of her modeling photos. Next, they found the announcement of Abigail's marriage to Burton Montgomery Fallon, the son of a prominent banker who died with his wife by his side in a plane crash only months prior.

They found Gordon's birth announcement, and another article dated two weeks after Gordon's birth, the headline read—*Devastating death of Matthew Crenshaw, a man well respected in his community.* Reading further, they learned that while Matthew crossed the street after picking up his daughter's prescription, a drunk driver ran a red light, killing him instantly.

"Forty-one years old," CJ said, shaking her head. "How tragic, yet Mom never mentioned it. Bizarre, don't you think?"

"Unbelievable." Nick pulled her onto his lap, hugging her tight.

After the obituary, they found nothing further about Frances Crenshaw in the US papers. The next article they found was in the *Paris Tribune*; dated mid-October, it welcomed Frances back to the city.

"I find it sad that my parents hid what shaped them as individuals."

"Maybe they couldn't handle their own emotions. Perhaps they felt emotion equaled weakness. Their generation believed in appearing stoic at all times."

"More like they buried the flaws in their perfect world." She sighed. "Let's keep digging. I wonder what they meant when they referred to Frances as Matthew's autumn bride."

"Don't know." Nick tapped and clicked.

They hit a few dead ends, found some trivial information, but most of what they found focused on basic Fallon family news: her birth announcement, Gordon's graduation, her track and field accomplishments, her graduation, all of her triathlon finishing times, the announcement of her turning pro, and most recently, her second-place finish in her debut race.

"Wait, go back to my mother's birth announcement."

Nick hit a few keys, found the link. "What?"

"There." She pointed at the text. "Frances turned twenty-nine prior to giving birth. So, if we do the math, my grandmother married a younger man. Hence, his autumn bride." She laughed. "You go, Grandma."

"Hot babe. You inherited that from her."

"Yeah, right." She wrinkled her nose. "Pull up the website for her gallery. She may have posted a picture, though," mentally she subtracted dates, "she's probably in her late seventies." She handed him the Post-it where she scribbled the name of the gallery—"Reves du Coeur."

"Dreams of the Heart. I like it." Nick typed in the address, hit enter.

"You speak French?" she still knew so little about him.

"*Mais oui, bien sur.* Had to learn the language for Tour press." He whispered a few short words in her ear.

"What does that mean?"

"I'll show you later." His laugh tickled her lobe, sending a delicious thrill down her neck.

A colorful homepage filled the screen, a picture of an attractive older woman in the upper right-hand corner. She had large, expressive green eyes, a devilish smile, and funky red hair. Hard to tell her age in the photo, but she had quite a youthful face. Could it be an old photograph? One taken years ago?

"What a beautiful woman, and she has talent." Nick navigated through the site, enlarging some of the paintings. "She wrote poems to accompany some of her work."

"Wow. When you stop to think she created such beautiful paintings and words," she swiped at a stray tear, "makes it difficult to imagine her as a nasty, uncaring woman."

"Maybe she mellowed with age? Or she used her art as therapy."

"It's too late to call now." She glanced at her watch. "But first thing in the morning, I'm ringing the gallery. They're...what, nine hours ahead of us in France?" She wrote down the number. "I have so much I want to ask her."

She sat hugging Nick, while absorbing the history of her family. Her family's destiny seemed to center around tragedy, emptiness, and loss. What if history repeated itself?

* * *

CJ dreamt her grandmother welcomed her with open arms, like Annalise had done with Kate and Gregory. Then she dreamt the opposite. Her grandmother cursed her, screaming she left them behind for a reason. She jolted awake, cold dread coiling in her stomach.

Why did Frances leave her only family? How could she move to another country and never look back? Didn't she care about her daughter and grandchildren?

At four-twelve in the morning, CJ stared at the digital numbers on the bedside clock. No chance of falling back to sleep now. Trying not to disturb Nick, she slid from beneath the covers, and decided to call Paris. *Just after lunchtime there. Perfect.*

She padded down the stairs and closed herself in the study. Her phone lay where she'd left it last night. Reaching for it, she dialed and almost hung up when she heard the first ring. Inhaling, she held her breath for a count of three, then let it out, a ripple of fear shooting through her.

On the sixth ring, she heard a click and a breathless, *"Oui, bonjour?"*

"Ms. Frances Crenshaw, please?"

"This is she."

"I hope I'm not disturbing you, but I'd like to ask you a few questions."

"And who might you be?" Her voice spiked with an edge of challenge—that cool detachment someone famous might take with the paparazzi.

"My name is CJ Fallon. My proper name is Cassandra Jade. I'm Abigail Fallon's daughter, and I believe I'm your granddaughter."

A sharp intake of breath at the other end of the line

225

was followed by a soft curse. "Tell me, do you have siblings?"

"Yes, an older brother, Gordon. Born September 6th, thirty years ago. Two weeks prior to Matthew Crenshaw's death. He was your husband, was he not?"

"He was the love of my life. The only true love I've ever known," the voice declared vehemently. "I have never and will never love like that again."

"Is that why you abandoned your family?"

"I did no such thing," she snapped. "They abandoned me."

* * *

Nick opened the door and strolled in just as she ended the call. The wonderful aroma steaming from the two mugs he held preceded him to the desk.

"I rolled over, and you weren't there. Figured you came down to make that transatlantic call." He handed her one of the mugs. "Did you connect with Frances Crenshaw?"

She took it and sipped the delicious brew. "Mmm. This is heavenly." She inhaled with eyes closed, throwing her head back in delight, then sipped again.

"Are you torturing me on purpose?" Nick asked, as he slid into the large leather chair.

She eyed him over her shoulder, a smile spreading over her face. "I did reach her, and we had a very interesting conversation. She has quite a passionate temper, as I learned when I accused her of abandoning her family."

"Quite tactful of you." He leaned forward, which caused several drops of coffee to slide over the rim, chasing one another down the thick olive pottery. "What else did you say?"

"Only what I've been told, of course."

"Are you satisfied with her explanation? You don't seem upset."

She nodded, a dreamy smile cresting.

The rising sun peeked through the half-opened shutters, a stream of liquid gold that slithered over the rug and dark wood floor. Birds sang from just outside the window as the morning woke up around them.

Nick stood, took her hand. "Come, bring your coffee. It's so beautiful out. Let's walk while you share her story." He guided her out the back door and onto the trail.

"You should have heard the passion in her voice when she told me how she met my grandfather. She finished her studies and attempted self-discovery. Like most artists, she planted herself at Montmartre, happily painting what surrounded her. She said she was singing an old French song when he walked by the first time. The second time he passed, she hummed, but the third time, she remained silent and stared at him. Challenged him.

"Nick, she said his eyes were like melted caramel. She compared his hair color to barley and his smile to a crescent moon turned on its side. Isn't that romantic?" Nick hugged her close and kissed her temple as he agreed.

CJ described how her grandparents fell in love, the afternoon they met over a bottle of Beaujolais at la Place du Tertre. And even though he was younger, her grandmother had no qualms about saying yes when he proposed less than a month later.

"She said she packed up everything and moved to Atlanta with him, set up an art studio in the sunroom of the house they found together. He worked and she painted. She sold some of her pieces to the local gift shops and restaurants."

"Sounds like they were happy."

She nodded. "She said she'd never love that way again. And she hasn't."

They turned to head back home. The sun now filtered through the rustling leaves of the huge trees lining the path. Runners came and went through the confetti of light, the sound of their shoes crunching the rocky dirt at their feet, small puffs of dust rising behind them. CJ's empty mug swung at her side as she drank in the tranquil environment, trying to imagine her grandmother in front of an easel.

"Why did she leave?"

"When Matthew died, she said, her world turned black. She couldn't paint, couldn't focus on anything. She tried to balance the grief with the joy of Gordon and my mother's new life, but it put a strain on their relationship. While my grandmother exhibited overwhelming emotion, my mother showed no outward signs of mourning. It doesn't surprise me. She did the same when my father died."

"That's sad."

"Tragic, really. It turns out my mother, Mrs. Abigail Fallon, pushed her own mother away. My grandmother chose to go back to Paris. A city she said was filled with passion. She opened her gallery and moved on with life."

"How could your mom lie and say her mother abandoned her?"

"Beats me. Who can explain my mother?" She twined her fingers with his. "She has no heart. Frances said she wrote my mother a letter a week for over five years, and my dear mother returned every single one, unopened. She's sending them to me."

They were back in his kitchen, Nick rinsing the cups and placing them in the dishwasher. He wiped his hands on a dishtowel, watched her with an intent look.

"At least I know where my emotions come from." She sat on a barstool and grimaced. "Passion runs in my bloodline. I'm not a freak after all."

Balling the towel, he tossed it aside and came to her. Sliding his arms around her waist, he hugged her to him. "Hon, you are the most compassionate person I know." He bent his head to kiss between her breasts. "I'm glad you learned that your enormous heart, which reaches out to people, even those who've trampled it, seems to mirror your grandmother's."

Something warm spread through her. The thought that she might share an ounce of her grandmother's appetite for life provided a place for her in this world. The secrets revealed by her father, and now this, made her feel hopeful about going into the future no matter what happened.

Florida loomed. With a new purpose, and a solid goal, CJ prepared to charge forward at full throttle with no thought of braking.

* * *

Intense colors streaked the evening sky as CJ sat with Nick enjoying a delectable Pan-Asian meal in the outdoor courtyard of Ono Maze, one of his favorite bistros. The warm, dry air kissed her cheeks and ruffled her hair.

"You're glowing," Nick said. "Have I told you lately how beautiful you are?"

Her heart shifted and butterflies fluttered in her belly. She gazed at him with love.

He smiled, but she caught the flash of another emotion deep in his eyes, and she wanted to kiss away those slight creases of tension around his mouth. Was he worried about his trip to San Diego tomorrow?

She sipped her ginger martini, toying with the stem of her glass. "Nick, are you sure I can't go with you?" Though she wanted to accompany him, she understood his need to go alone.

"Absolutely. I won't expose you to him." He looked off into the distance. "I'm not eager to see him, but I do want to know why he summoned me."

"Who knows, maybe time and the disease have mellowed him."

"I can only hope." He reached across the table and took her hand, his expression softening. "I hated him for years, but last night, I realized I pitied him instead. He gave me up to loving people, and it made me wonder, did he ever know love? I can't picture a time he smiled. Even his photos captured the permanent scowl on his face."

"That's sad, but people make their own choices, Nick." She'd learned that with her own family, though Nick turned out stronger because of his father's chosen path. Like the brush of a moth's wings, the words floated up her throat. "I love you so much."

The creases melted, and his eyes glowed. Within a blink, she stood enfolded in his arms. He kissed her as if he meant to drink in her essence. "I don't ever want to lose you."

That her grandparents' lives shattered at the height of their passion made her cling to him. "Then don't ever let go." Her arms tightened around him, drawing him in. "Then, now, and always, Nick, promise me we'll be here for each other."

Chapter 20

Nick hesitated at the front door of the Adult-Care Center, but only briefly, before he shoved the door open and marched inside. As if on a mission, he approached the reception area.

"Mitchell Madison, please." His tone sounded severe, so he shrugged and smiled at the matronly woman behind the desk. "Sorry, could you tell me what room he's in?"

She looked up, her annoyance visible. But something in her gaze softened as she looked into his eyes. Her composure shifted, and she smiled back.

"Room 401. Take that elevator. On four, go right. It's the second door on the left."

"Thank you." He hit the button.

"You're his son, right?"

"Yes, I am."

"God bless you," she whispered, as the doors closed him into the antiseptic space.

When he stepped out on four, he dodged left to avoid the young nurse who almost mowed him down. Tears flowed down her face and must have blurred her vision. A thin black man chased after her, clucking like a mother hen. "Don't let him upset you. He's an old geezer and he's on the brink of death."

"But he called me a clown-loving whore." She disappeared into the elevator, her sobs echoing through the hall.

The hair on Nick's neck stood up. They spoke of his father; he knew it even before he approached the room. The hope that time had mellowed him flew right out the window. Even with death beating at his door, the man's personality remained the same—nasty.

He took a breath, swallowed the unpleasant taste on his tongue, and entered the room.

The frail man, the bones in his face skeletal, sat in bed watching TV. His arms looked like wire coat hangers, his chest sunken beneath the cotton sheet. The set blared a trashy talk show. His untouched hospital food sat congealing on its tray.

The stench crawled up his nose, choking him. Nick wanted to vomit. Though the need to run and hide tugged at him, he stood his ground. He came too far not to face this man—the man who brought him into the world then abandoned him.

He needed to know what stirred in the old man's brain.

"You wanted to see me." He stood at the foot of the bed, trying not to focus on the broken man before him.

His father's gaze moved from the TV screen to his face, clouding then clearing as he recognized him. He grinned like a banshee, showing his yellow, smoke-stained teeth.

"I knew you'd come." Gnarled fingers reached out. "You couldn't let me die without learning the truth, isn't that right?" He coughed, his intake of air sounding lethal. "You're tainted, boy, just like your mama. She infected you with her blood. It's only a matter of time."

"You're making no sense." Nick walked to the window, because he couldn't bear to look at the old man.

He held his breath, waiting for more.

"I want you to know your fate. When your brain betrays you, what will you do? Will you take your own life?"

Disgusted, Nick turned back. "To think I came here to make peace with the bully of a man who couldn't bear to call himself my father." He combed his hand through his hair. "But that's not what you want, is it?"

"No, I want you to understand who you are. You think you're important, but that's an illusion. You're nothing but a spineless shell. Even when the world rallied for you, you threw it away. You never amounted to much and never will, because you're made of bad blood. It's in you, and you can't change that."

Rage fused his tongue, burning his throat. He wanted to tell this man to rot in hell, for surely that's where he belonged, but that would only please him. He would not sink to such depths. He wouldn't allow this devil to push him back into a world of doubt. But like unexpected damage from the aftershocks of a powerful earthquake, his foundation cracked.

"To think I prepared myself to forgive you, to put the past behind us. You're a sad old man, and you deserve nothing from me." Nick backed toward the door. "I can see now why my mother took her own life."

"She didn't, you fool. I knew of no other way to cast you both from my life."

Nick stumbled as he left the room, the old man's laughter following him. He leaned against the wall as reality took hold.

His mother hadn't committed suicide. His father had murdered her.

* * *

Bored and filled with pent-up energy, CJ thought to

subdue her anxiety, but now, she regretted her decision. Too much, too soon. She ran the thirteen miles, because the house felt so empty with Nick gone. Probably not the smartest thing.

Two scoops of powder to one bottle of water. She shook the contents of her recovery drink while standing at the sink. Her shin throbbed. The soreness radiated up to her knee, creating a sensation of tightness near the bone.

Opening the freezer, she pulled out an ice pack and hobbled into the living room. With her leg propped on two pillows, the ice pack in place, she sipped her Endurox and flipped through the list she's Googled. How did one choose a doctor?

As she scanned the list of names on her device, she wondered if Nick was still with his father. Had they compensated for lost time? Apologized for missing important milestones in each other's lives? Would the encounter bring Nick peace?

Could he forgive the parent who discarded him on the heels of the other parent's death?

She tried to imagine what his father looked like: now as an older man riddled with disease, then as a younger man with a strapping body and a dark nature. Due to the background Nick painted, she conjured a gnarled old gnome, but how accurate could that be? Nick turned out gorgeous. It seemed unfair to assume he inherited all of his looks from his mother.

Just as she went back into the kitchen to put the ice pack away, the phone rang. Where the heck was the thing? It rang again, sounding as if it came from the couch. She limped into the living room, reached under one of the throw pillows, and extracted the handset. Nick's landline.

"Hello."

"Oh," she heard hesitation in the deep masculine

voice. "Is this Nick Madison's place?"

"Yes, it is, but he's not here at the moment."

"You must be CJ." A rumble of laughter followed. "Shayne told us all about you. I'm Nick's uncle Ed."

"Oh, how wonderful. I was just thinking about all of you."

"Congratulations on your second-place finish."

"Thank you." She rubbed her shin. "I'm planning to get Nick a win in Florida."

"That's the spirit. We'll send positive energy your way."

"I appreciate that."

The friendly banter continued for a minute. Then his voice took on an edge like winter settling in after a gorgeous autumn day, the sun disappearing behind the snow-filled clouds.

"Can you tell me where he is?"

"He went to see his father."

"I got upset with my son for telling Nick about the bastard. He owes the man nothing."

"He needed to go. No matter what his father says, good or bad, Nick should hear it while the man's still alive. I'm sure Shayne did what he thought was right."

"I'm sorry," Ed apologized. "You're not to blame, but I hate that he went to listen to more of that man's lies. Hasn't he done enough damage already?"

"I understand your concern." She sighed. "As the man who raised Nick, you want to shield him from additional pain."

"Yes." His whisper sent a shiver down her spine.

"If the man apologizes, it will lift the burden from Nick's shoulders."

"You know my son—my nephew, well, don't you?"

"I'm learning more about him every day." She contemplated for a second, then continued, "but you should know that he counts his blessings every day.

Without you, Nick would not be the man he is today."
When they hung up, CJ called Nick's cell, a bit worried
about the outcome of his visit and in need of hearing his
voice. It went straight to voicemail.

* * *

The man won his battle, because whether he knew it
or not, his admission pushed Nick back into that world of
doubt. A calculated move on his father's end. Nick felt
set-up, cornered into a box with no outlet, choked by the
injustice. But maybe the disease came as punishment.

His heart pulsed, sadness and anger swimming
through his blood.

He turned off his phone as he boarded the plane for
Seattle. Sitting in his seat, he closed his eyes and fought
the demons. Helpless then, now he lacked the power to
change the past. Aunt Millie's hugs and his uncle's wide
shoulders waited a few hours away, which is why he
decided to fly home. He needed his real family to ground
him, and they needed to know the truth.

As in the past, they would help him sort through the
uncertainty. An odd twinge curled around his middle,
and he felt ten years old again. Those first six months
had been difficult, not because of his aunt and uncle—
they had loved him from day one—but to be alive when
his mother wasn't had made him feel guilty. Ashamed
that he hadn't saved her, he carried the weight of blame.
Yet, in his youth, questions consumed his mind.

As he matured, he researched her mental state to try
to understand. The two things he found did not indicate a
tendency to commit suicide. Trichotillomania—the
compulsive inability to resist pulling one's hair out, and
Coulrophobia—the fear of clowns, could have been
treated by a psychologist. Why hadn't she asked for
help?

But his father supplied the answer this morning. A fresh wave of anger gripped him like a vise clamping his throat. Nick started the rental car but sat for a moment to allow the emotion to abate. Finally, he placed the car in gear and drove toward the house where he grew up.

Three voicemails waited when he turned on his phone. CJ wanted to know how the face-off went. Big laughed as he explained that his Florida hotel room got canceled because of a mix-up with his name. They thought it was a joke, but he said he fixed the reservation, then reconfirmed the rest of the team. The last was his uncle, voicing his displeasure that Nick succumbed to the old man's wishes to meet in person. Just wait until he heard and digested the news.

He checked in with CJ as he drove. She answered on the second ring.

"I got worried," she stated after the usual greetings. "How did it go?"

"Not as I expected, that's for sure. He's a miserable man who drowns others in his ugliness. He's become more malicious with age, and like the disease that eats at him, his bitterness reeks." The other fact, he'd share later, face-to-face.

"I'm so sorry. Will it help to talk about it?"

"No." He would not regurgitate the words. "Actually, I called to tell you I decided to come home. I'm in Seattle now."

"Oh."

Was she hurt that he decided to go to his aunt and uncle? Without her?

"My uncle's pissed that I went to see the old man. It's important he understand why I did. I need a few days."

"I understand. You don't need to explain. I just wish I could hug you. That's all."

"I'll look forward to more than hugs." He laughed

for the first time today. "Remember those French words I whispered in your ear. Care to repeat their meaning?"

"Can't wait," she answered with a giggle. He caught a slight hesitation in her voice, then she asked, "Umm, can you recommend a doctor? I'd like to make an appointment."

"I've heard Beau Bissell is good. He's not my doctor. I haven't seen one in years, but his name's come up around the circuit. Why, is something wrong?"

"Not really. I ran the trail this morning, and my right leg's sore. Just a dull ache, but I'd like to rule out a stress fracture."

"Smart." Apprehension pitted in his chest, then dissolved as he thought about the race she'd completed less than a week ago. "How far did you go?"

"Thirteen."

"Hon. You know better than that. Your muscles need time to repair." He shook his head. His passionate little star had a difficult time sitting still. "What were you thinking?"

"With you gone, I got restless. But I'll go into Florida more confident if I learn it's not serious." She blew him a kiss. "Hurry home. I miss you."

"Make that appointment. I'll be home in a few days. I love you, babe." He hung up as he turned onto the familiar street.

He pulled into the driveway and blew out a breath. Before he rang the bell, he looked around his old neighborhood. Everything seemed smaller than he remembered. He'd left here seventeen years ago, coming and going after that, but memory kept the house large and luxurious. In reality, it was modest but well maintained. The yards on the street were meticulous; the large trees, their leaves starting to change color, were neatly trimmed.

The door opened, and his aunt Millie let out a

screech. "Oh, Nicholas. Nicholas. You're here." Her body, tall and willowy, was still youthful as she approached sixty. Her blue eyes twinkled as she threw her arms around him. Her soft, chestnut-brown hair, threaded with a few strands of gray, curled around her attractive face.

"I needed to come home." One simple statement spoken from the heart. He pressed his cheek to hers, the smoothness of her skin against his reassuring. He held her, absorbing her love.

"Come in. Come in." She broke away, turning to guide him through the door. "Ed, come down. We have company," she called up the stairs.

"Who is it?" His uncle's voice boomed, followed by footsteps in the carpeted hall. From the top of the stairs, the familiar voice echoed, "Oh my, I didn't expect to see you." Then the man descended two steps at a time to wrap him in a bear hug. Like Shayne, his uncle had muscular arms, a thick neck, and a barrel chest. He squeezed tight, laughing all the while. "It is good to see you, son."

"Same here." He hugged back as hard as possible.

"Let's sit." Aunt Millie pointed to the family room. "Do you want something to drink? Are you hungry?"

"No." He shook his head and patted the couch next to where he sat down. "I'm fine. Sit with me."

She did, taking his hand in hers. His uncle took the chair near the fireplace. Silence stretched while they stared at each other, smiling.

"He upset you, didn't he?" Ed said, taking the reins.

"He brought back all the doubts." Nick sighed. "I half expected him to apologize for giving me up, to want to catch up on lost time, but instead he attacked me. He called me tainted."

His aunt's hand tightened around his.

His uncle came out of the chair. "How could he say

such a thing? The bastard." He paced. "I think he tormented your mother by placing figurines in strange places around the house. She called so many times, hysterical after seeing clowns in the medicine cabinet, or in the freezer, but when I made her go back to get them, they'd vanished. I had no proof, thought maybe her imagination and her fear drove her, but my gut told me he was responsible."

"Why didn't you tell me this before?"

Uncle Ed stopped pacing, pulled the ottoman over and sat, placing his hand on Nick's knee. "I could never prove the speculation. They ruled her death a suicide, and with him out of your life, I never pursued it."

Nick placed his free hand over his uncle's, bonding the three of them. "He wanted to stir us up, and he succeeded. Without saying the exact words, he admitted he killed her."

"Oh, Nick," his aunt whispered.

"What?" His uncle jumped to his feet, his face flushed red with anger. "You called the police, right?"

"No." He shook his head. "He's dying. He'll rot in hell for what he's done."

"You can't let him get away with this."

"He'll be dead soon. That's enough for me." Defeated, Nick sat back. "Let's not dredge her death up again, please."

"We never understood her attraction to him. To us, he seemed vulgar. He criticized people and paraded around like a peacock. Sometimes I wondered if he beat her, but she never admitted it. And then..." Aunt Millie wiped a tear.

"He scared her," Nick whispered. "She visibly cringed in his presence."

"Her illness was a cry for help. I didn't listen." His uncle's massive hands flexed. "When he implied she lost her mind, she accepted it. We believed it, as well." The pain in the man's eyes brought tears to Nick's. "I should have followed through, pushed for the truth."

"I for one will be happy when he's dead." Aunt Millie crossed herself and asked for forgiveness. "The world will be a better place without him."

Nick and his uncle nodded in agreement.

"The past is done, and we can't change it." Ed swallowed, tears trailing down his cheeks. "You are my son, not his. You've grown to be who you are today because of our love."

"I know." Nick stood, pulling Millie with him. He hugged them both. "That's why I came home."

"We'll always be here for you, dear."

"His loss, our gain." Ed clapped him on the back after brushing at his tears. "So...tell us about your star athlete, the one who's staying at your house. She sounds awfully cute."

"You spoke to CJ? She didn't mention it."

"I called to chew you out. She answered. It's a good thing, too, because she got me to calm down, and see the need for your visit with that piece of..."

"Now, Edward." Millie clucked her tongue. "There's no need for obscenities."

Nick dried his own face and grinned at his aunt and uncle. Comforted once again by these loving and accepting people, he wished for CJ to experience such unconditional love.

"Well?" His aunt sat back down, a smile sweeping her face.

As he spoke, some of the pain faded. He described how CJ looked when he first saw her race in New Zealand, the chaos he put her through by asking her to alter her life, the development of their relationship while on the island, how hard he fell for her.

"As a matter of fact, how would you two like to go shopping this afternoon?"

"What are we shopping for?" his aunt asked.

"A ring." He smiled. "I've decided to propose at the Florida race. Plan to slip it on her finger just after she crosses the finish line."

Chapter 21

The day with his family delivered exactly what Nick needed. The strength of their love pulled him through his mood and confirmed his decision to ask CJ to be his wife. They found the perfect ring—a Bvlgari platinum band with a central, square-cut emerald, flanked by baguette-cut and pavè diamonds. It was beautiful, just like CJ.

His aunt acted as giddy as a schoolgirl when he asked her to model it. But she became even more excited when he offered to fly them out to the race. He wanted them there when he popped the question. In the end, seeing his father brought unexpected pleasure to his life.

Nick couldn't wait to get home. He ached to hold CJ close. With marriage on his mind, he pulled into the driveway, singing along to Sting's *Every Little Thing She Does Is Magic.*

He opened the front door, stood in the entry ready to shout for CJ, when he heard her voice carry from the study.

"No, sir. I'd rather hear what you have to say. As I said, the original X-rays showed dark spots on my tibia. A biopsy confirmed them to be holes, pseudo-tumors, my doctor called them, but they were filled with bone marrow, which indicated the bone was in the process of healing."

Nick moved, standing just outside the office door. He listened. He remained quiet, his ears perked. Why hadn't she told him about her leg?

"I raced less than a week ago and have another race scheduled in seven weeks." Her breath whistled through her teeth. The sound carried a tang of fear. "Yes. That's why I'd like a second opinion. I ran yesterday, and since then, my shin aches.... No, not a sharp pain, more of a throbbing.... Yes."

After another lengthy pause, he pressed his hand to the door, but her voice once again stopped him.

"Am I at risk if I race in November?... Yes, Monday morning is fine. Yes. Thank you."

She cut the connection.

Nick entered the room. "I'm home." He smiled at her, but his tone challenged. "Were you talking to the doctor?"

"Yes. I made an appointment for Monday morning."

"Good." He took a step toward her, stopped. "You don't seem happy to see me."

"I'm sorry." She moved then, hugging him.

"What aren't you telling me, CJ?" He backed off so he could read her expression. "Remember what I said about honesty?"

When she looked up, unshed tears shimmered, magnifying the jade specks in her eyes.

"Does any of this have to do with the night I saw you with Mike? The night I misread, according to both of you?" He cupped her chin, the pieces falling together in his brain. "What are we dealing with here? Please tell me."

She slipped out of his grip and sat on the sofa. Curling her feet beneath her, she told him about the original call from the doctor, the tests and the diagnosis. She shared every frightening detail, including her own denial at having no symptoms. Now it made perfect sense.

No wonder Mike wouldn't talk, kept pushing him to ask CJ. Damn it, he should have pressed her, forced her to reveal her turmoil. But how could he have known?

"Why didn't you tell me?" He sat on the edge of the couch, afraid she'd bolt if he got too close. "Why share it with Mike?"

"Mike happened to be available. Oh, Nick, having just walked away from my career, I feared you'd kick me off the team." Her bottom lip trembled, but she bit it to hold it still.

"Kick you off the team? Good Lord, CJ, I'd never do that."

"I know that now. But it was too soon...I didn't...I hadn't..."

He reached and took her hand. Patting it, he said, "Okay, give me a recap. We'll deal with this together."

"My doctor confirmed the spots are not cancer. The bone seems to be regenerating—healing itself—but now I'm feeling pain. A dull ache, nothing sharp, but I'm worried, Nick. What if I do need surgery?"

"Why place a rod in an already healing bone?" Under his breath, he added, "Unless it makes a pretty penny for the firm?" He stood up, walked to the desk and rested his hip on it.

"You raced Wisconsin against his wishes," he continued. "Finished strong and felt no pain. Then after a long run, you're sore, and you begin second-guessing your body."

"Yes, and with so much riding on this race..." She came to him, stepped into his arms. With her cheek pressed to his chest, she whispered, "I don't want to be stupid and risk my health, but with Hunter off the team, and Kyle out with his hip, I'm the only one who can save our sponsorship. This race isn't just for me anymore. It's for you and the rest of the guys. Maybe I should race and see the doctor afterward."

"No. You're getting that second opinion."

She trembled in his arms. "What if I've stressed the bone, as Dr. Hempstead warned?"

"It's a valid concern, one we'll deal with after seeing the doctor." He raked his fingers through her hair, tilted her face so he could look into her eyes. "Do you think carrying this burden alone might have added to your stress?"

"Maybe."

"I can tell you one thing, hon." He kissed her to ease the sting of his words. "You will not race unless this doctor gives his approval."

She shifted in protest. "But the team?"

"I love you too much to allow you to risk serious injury." He held her tight, prevented her from leaving the security of his grasp, and in his heart, he knew he spoke the truth. The team no longer took precedence. "I'm going with you on Monday. We'll ask questions and listen to what he says. Then we'll decide what to do. Okay?"

She pulled away, went to the window. Her voice quivered as she spoke. "I won't let you lose the team."

"CJ, the fate of the team does not weigh solely on your shoulders." Though she could be the factor for keeping it intact, he would no longer lay that enormous burden on her.

"After what Hunter pulled, it's my duty."

"Look, let's not make ourselves nuts." From behind, he rested his hand on her shoulder. "Uncertainty can paralyze. If we worry and conjure up terrifying scenarios, like you did after seeing the bone scan, we may make the situation worse." He let logic sway him.

"Based on the facts so far, you are not going to die. So, let's hear what Dr. Bissell has to say. Once we know, we'll make the appropriate decisions. Are you with me?"

Though she nodded, the look in her eyes betrayed her uncertainty. He knew her well enough to recognize her stubbornness.

* * *

Rain drenched the weekend, but on Monday morning the sun blinded, sipping the water from the streets like a thirsty kitten. An eerie silence hovered over them as they drove to the doctor's office. CJ snapped on the radio to cover her taut nerves, which she swore buzzed in the quiet. She flicked stations, searched for mellow tunes, then turned it off again. The noise only aggravated her.

Nick reached over and took her hand, placed her palm against his thigh, covering the top with his own. "I'm here for you." For such a simple statement, it moved her.

"Thanks." Her fingers trembled against his rock solid muscle.

"No matter what, you lean on me."

His quiet presence comforted her but also made her wonder what played in his mind. Did he worry, as she did, that this could end her career? And if it did, what would their future hold? If she went back to her old job, would they drift apart, and would he over time forget her?

Nick turned the car into the lot of the medical building and parked. When he released his seatbelt, he once again took her hand. "Are you ready?"

How could she say she wasn't?

The building bustled with people of every age, hobbling on crutches or with the help of a cane. A few sat in wheelchairs while others held firmly to a family member's arm. CJ felt odd stepping off the elevator and crossing into the waiting room under her own power, Nick by her side. Her pulse slowed, the sheer number waiting to see Doctor Beau Bissell, a well-regarded orthopedic surgeon, quelled her fears.

Patients stared at her as she signed in, accepted the new patient information sheets from the receptionist and took a seat against the far wall to complete the questionnaires. Just like her visit with Dr. Hempstead, she sat among the ill, her athletic body a picture of health.

Trying not to focus on the others, she watched Nick's face as he took in their surroundings. A small knot throbbed in his jaw as his eyes scanned the opulent office. She touched his arm to soothe him.

The waiting area was large—split in two by a wide hall of light hardwood floor, which ran from the elevator banks to the thick, darker wood beams that served as walls. The same type of beams ran the length of the ceiling and matched the color of their chairs. At the bar-like counter, several nurses collected charts or sat entering notes at the assembly-line of computers.

At least two dozen patients waited to see the doctor, but the space around them seemed too quiet. Those who spoke did so in hushed tones, as if not wanting to disturb the peace.

Nick handed her a magazine after she turned in her chart, but she stared at the article she flipped to. She reread the first sentence at least a hundred times before the nurse called her name. Tossing it aside, she grabbed Nick's hand and pulled him to join her.

At the nurse's tight-lipped expression, she tugged harder, explaining, "Nick Madison, he's my coach. I'd like him to hear, firsthand, what the doctor has to say."

The woman's facial features relaxed as she

shrugged a shoulder, a tiny smile edging its way to the corner of her mouth. She led them to exam room G, where they waited for several minutes before Dr. Bissell strolled in, her medical history in his hand.

His round glasses slid down his bulbous nose, squeezing the tip as he perused her information. He looked up and smiled at her, releasing the end of his nose from its confines by removing his glasses and placing them in the breast pocket of his lab coat.

His warm, dark eyes regarded her. "Well, young lady, let's see if we can figure out what happened." He sat on a stool beside the examination table, rolled up the leg of her jeans and replaced his glasses. He peered closely, and with a small rubber mallet, tapped and listened to the length of her shin bone.

She glanced at Nick, sitting in the corner chair, as murmurs and grunts occasionally escaped the doctor's throat.

His thick fingers probed her leg. "Does that hurt?"

She shook her head in answer, which prompted him to wheel his stool to the desk near the door. Pressing an intercom button, he requested a technician join them.

He stood when the young lady opened the door and stepped across the threshold. Reaching for Nick's hand, Dr. Bissell cocked his head, "Mr. Madison, why don't we chat a bit while Suzette gets an X-ray and MRI of Ms. Fallon's leg?"

As she followed Suzette down the hall and around the corner, she wondered what they would chat about. But her focus shifted as Suzette walked her through the process. Once in the little room, she sat on the table with a lead apron draped over her upper body, as the tech photographed three different angles of her tibia. After that, Suzette hustled her into a smaller chamber, where she changed into a pair of gym shorts and sat on the long bench of the MRI machine with both legs extended in front of her. The machine vibrated as the bench inched forward and back again.

The tech checked the films while CJ changed back into her jeans. She then followed the woman back to Room G, where she found Nick sitting alone. The air around them felt like a vacuum. She hopped onto the examination table and motioned for him to come join her.

"Waiting is the worst."

"I know. Stop chewing your lip." He stood beside her, draping his arm over her shoulder in support. He seemed nervous, too. "Maybe he'll have good news."

She expelled a breath, nodding. "What did he say to you?"

"He wanted my coaching observations. Had I noticed anything unusual—any signs of illness, change in gait, unusual weight loss—that sort of thing."

Time seemed to move in slow motion. Soft-soled shoes squeaking against the hardwood floor outside the door helped to count out the minutes. When CJ felt she'd go mad, the door opened, and Dr. Bissell entered, films in hand.

He clipped them to the lighted board and motioned them over. Pulling a pen from his breast pocket, he used it to point as he spoke. "These gray areas represent the healing voids. Three appear quite solid, a good sign, in my opinion. The remaining two are minor. They vary in their progress, but I don't believe they are anything to worry about."

He went on to explain that while the body focused on healing the three larger cavities, the production of bone marrow in the two smaller holes slowed—a natural progression of the immune system. Once the larger ones were repaired, the body would shift its focus to deal with the less significant hollows.

"You're strong. Your body is taking care of itself. I

can prescribe a calcium supplement with additional minerals to boost the repair, but this is not a serious situation."

"What are all those tiny, little lines?" Nick asked while studying the pictures.

"Again, they're nothing to worry about. Bones are porous, but like fingerprints, they all differ in design and dimension. Think of these as her unique structure."

"Is there any reason she shouldn't race?" Nick looked the doctor in the eye.

CJ drew in a long, slow breath and held it, waiting for the other shoe to drop.

"None that I can see." Dr. Bissell traced a white line on the outside of the tibia. "See this? It's new bone; her body created it as a natural splint to reinforce the tibia. Once the holes are healed, the right leg will remain stronger than the left, because this extra bone will never disappear. As your muscles develop around it, it will look beefier from behind."

"That's reassuring." Nick smiled at that news, and she relaxed. "Did you notice any additional stress spots or abnormalities in the MRI?"

"No. Other than the two small spots, the leg looks great. The body does remarkable things when faced with disease. CJ's attacked the problem." He bent over the desk, scribbled on a small square of paper, before replacing the pen in his pocket.

Tears of relief filled her eyes. Joy after months of worry pushed through her system, and she clutched Nick, hugging him tight.

He held her as if he meant never to let go. "Such great news, hon. No more stressing."

The doctor handed her the prescription. "Take these supplements and call me after your race to let me know how you placed. Good luck."

CJ floated on a cloud of elation. "I'm so happy I

made the appointment." She hugged Nick again as they reached the car.

"Me, too." He kissed her until her toes curled. "Now, you can go into Florida with less weight on your shoulders."

Chapter 22

Big, Uri, and John stood waiting as she and Nick exited the jet way. They exchanged hugs and gruff pats on the back. Uri picked her up off the floor, gave her a gentle squeeze. Big patted her on the head, and John, with the color of roses riding his cheeks, gave her a quick peck.

Nick rented a bus for the ninety-minute trek from the Orlando airport to CJ's place. He then decided to keep it as their mode of transportation through race weekend.

"Why don't you guys come with me? We'll grab the bus and load our gear while CJ meets the next plane. I'll call you with our location once we're parked, so you can send the others our way. That okay with you, babe?"

She nodded. He kissed her on the nose, and the four of them headed off.

CJ checked the monitors for arrival time and gate information. Pete, Simon, Lars, and Dave were booked on the same connector from Dallas, the plane due to land in thirty minutes. Zach's flight showed a four o'clock on-time arrival, but Val's had been delayed and would arrive twenty minutes after Zach's. If they hustled and didn't hit too much traffic, they'd pull into her driveway in time for dinner. She hoped Kate had stocked the freezer, but if not, they'd order pizzas.

She found an empty seat by the window and pulled the package of letters from her bag. Her grandmother had couriered them to her, so she would have them before they left for Florida. Why not take advantage of the time to read the first few? There were two hundred and sixty-three in total, neatly numbered in the bottom left-hand corner. Pulling out the first three, she stowed the others in her bag.

Nerves balled up in her stomach as she slipped the first one from its envelope.

As she read, the knot in her belly dissolved and shifted into a pang of sorrow for a woman she'd never met. Frances Crenshaw aptly portrayed her shock at losing the love of her life. The spirit of denial she tried to expunge by returning to Paris. Her words painted the gut-wrenching cry for her daughter's love and understanding. She reached out with such poignancy, CJ's heart ached.

How could her mother ignore this woman? How could she turn her back on her own flesh and blood? But CJ knew the answer to that question. She had felt that chill her entire life.

Her father lived a lie because of his love for her mom. Her grandmother sought emotion from a woman incapable of feeling. She herself craved her mother's approval. Why? What irresistible pull drew three passionate people toward Abigail Crenshaw Fallon?

Even now with skeletons exposed, CJ continued to think it her duty to mend the broken. Her need to tear down the fence erected by her mother intensified, and she hoped to one day enjoy the love and joy of family. Was she delusional to believe in happy endings?

The travelers around her swam in a sea of color. Through her tears, everything softened and blurred. As she wiped them away, she noticed four pairs of Converse gathering on the floor in front of her. She looked up to see her teammates' faces, grins as goofy as ever, waiting for her acknowledgement.

"If Coach made you cry, I'll beat him." Pete tousled her hair then patted her shoulder.

"Coach isn't a doof, you dweeb. Think he'd screw up a catch like CJ?" Dave slapped Pete on the back. "Bet she's crying 'cause she missed us."

"Oh, yeah, that's it." Simon laughed.

"Seriously, are you okay?" Lars pulled her from her seat, concern replacing his smile. "Why the tears, girl?"

"Just read something sad, that's all." She shrugged, giving them all hugs. "Nick has the Fear-mobile parked in A—level 2, row F, far right-hand side. Get your stuff and meet him out there. I'll wait for Zach's plane."

"We should beat Coach just for fun," she heard Pete say as they walked away, and her heart swelled. How her life had changed in six short months.

Zach accompanied her and together they met Val's flight. Then the three of them carted the boys' gear toward the bus. It reminded her of a college frat bus with all the shoving and razzing going on. Two of the guys held Simon and Pete in headlocks, the others encouraging them with whooping and hollering.

"I'm so looking forward to the next seven weeks." She punctuated that with a roll of her eyes, which made Uri reach out and pluck her off the ground.

He performed five perfect squats, using her as a human weight bar, a feat that had the others roaring.

"Now, boys." Nick laughed as he attempted to gain control of the rowdy group. "Enough horse play. Time to put our serious race-faces on. We have a challenge to meet."

"Party pooper." Big ducked his head to enter the bus, the others piling on behind him.

Non-stop laughter filled the drive time to Painter's Hill as everyone told stories about their week at home. Zach visited Kyle in the hospital and shared his news. "He made it through surgery without a problem but almost died when his wife, Carolyn, announced she was pregnant."

CJ tried to imagine Kyle as a daddy. Then her gaze slid to Nick. A surge of love swam through her as she pictured him holding a baby. Because of his issues with his own father, she envisioned him as a generous and loving dad. Did Nick even want kids? They hadn't broached the subject of marriage and children.

Her brain wrapped around the idea as the buzz continued behind her. Everyone seemed to talk at once, an uninterrupted line of conversation laced with a positive energy. And when the whole team descended on CJ's house, crashing through the front door, Kate came rushing out of the office with a vase in hand, charging as if to maim.

"Sorry, didn't I tell you we were all coming?" CJ laughed and hugged her friend.

"Thanks a lot. I aged twelve years in the last minute." Kate shook her head. "I expected you and Nick, but this explains the delivery of a very large picnic table."

CJ nodded, while Big pulled Kate against him, knuckling the side of her head. "Didn't mean to scare you, Kate. We're not a quiet bunch."

The team roared.

"No kidding," Kate responded, making everyone laugh harder.

CJ took the group on a tour before Nick herded them back on the bus to get them checked in at the hotel. She and Kate took advantage of the hour to raid the kitchen for enough food to feed this crew. Kate offered to pick up groceries in the morning.

After dinner, she and Kate sat on the deck soaking up the silence and the soft wash of the surf caressing the shore. The warm breeze fluttered about them, the moon, a crescent slice in the inky sky.

"My ears are still ringing." Kate sipped her tea. "But what a great group of handsome hunks. Lars is absolutely gorgeous."

"Looks like a blond Elvis, doesn't he?" CJ giggled.

After catching up on Frances, the second opinion on her leg ailment, and the plan for the next few weeks, CJ asked, "So, what's new?"

"I found a place in Pelican Bay—a two bedroom, two bath—right on the golf course." The excitement glowed in Kate's eyes. "It's close to work and perfect for me. You and Nick will have your privacy in less than a week."

"Kate, you didn't have to do that."

"I know. I appreciate that you let me stay here all this time, but now that you're back, it's time I found my own place."

"When do you move in?"

"This weekend. I have to have my stuff out of storage by Sunday 6 p.m."

"That won't be a problem with the team here to help."

"Hmm, interesting, all those sweaty, muscle-bound men flexing their strength, but I wouldn't want to interfere with your training. Can't afford to have your coach mad at me."

"We'll use it as one of our weightlifting days."

"Use what as a weightlifting day?" Nick asked, as he joined them on the deck.

"Kate found a townhouse near her store, and I offered the team as moving men." CJ got up to hug her man. "You don't mind, do you? Won't take us long if we all work together."

"That's what teams are for." Nick pulled away and looked at his watch. "But right now, I need my star athlete in bed. I told the guys to meet us here at six for a morning ride."

* * *

CJ had never been happier. Her house bustled with activity, like Grand Central Station, as the team trained, ate, and bonded in the weeks prior to the Florida race. Surrounded by goofy men who cheered each other on and competed at the same time, her heart shifted every time they folded her into the mix as one of them.

Nick beamed as the team continued to get stronger and faster in the Florida wind.

With the worry about her leg gone, she soared through each workout. Because racing was as much mental as physical, she homed in on each of the stronger guys, used them as a meter for her strength in each discipline.

She swam with Zach, cycled with Uri, ran with both Val and Lars.

As the weeks slid by, she noticed the changes in her body. The cut of her muscles became more prominent, her face thinned, and when she looked in the mirror, she saw the girl Sophie Kessler called fierce.

* * *

The Wednesday before the race came in a blink. So did the chaos of loading the bus and getting on the road. Some of the guys triple-checked their equipment. One shared how he forgot his transition bag and bottles once and vowed never to let that happen again. The others agreed.

Nick thought their rituals comical, and though he

kept his comments to a minimum, the slight upward curl of his lip betrayed him.

They swooped into Starbucks for their caffeine fix and hit the road singing. CJ tried to focus on the scenery as a way of relaxing, but the sound of her nine teammates crooning distracted her. She laughed as Pete made up words to a popular song, the others providing harmonious back up.

For the next few hours, the music and conversation kept her preoccupied, and before long, the bus pulled into the main area of Panama City. The roads congested with cars and SUVs streaming by with bike racks in place, holding countless brands of bicycles in an array of bright tones, created a colorful parade of high-end equipment.

Barricades blocked off the road in front of the host hotel, where workers currently erected bleachers and the chute for Saturday's finish line. Directed by police, Nick drove the bus to a side road and looped around to a parking lot a few blocks away. When he parked, they unloaded their gear.

Hundreds of physically fit bodies crowded the area, some running along sidewalks, others testing equipment, a handful carrying wetsuits to the beach for a practice swim. Many, like CJ and her team, wheeled their bike cases and carried duffel bags toward the lobby of the main hotel. To an outsider—a non-racer—it must appear bizarre to see that many buff, muscular men and lean women in one spot at one time. Her heart raced. She belonged to this fascinating club.

Check-in took forever, the volume of people processed unbelievable, and CJ utilized the time sizing up her competition. Looking at them all caused a sizzle of apprehension to shimmy up her spine. She shivered, her confidence shrinking.

"People are staring at you," Val whispered in her

ear. "Think they recognize you as the girl who almost beat Sophie?"

"No way. And looking at me doesn't pose much of a threat."

"I beg to differ," Lars quipped.

Just then, Sophie entered the lobby. She looked around, and they made eye contact. CJ waved, and the girl came over, giving her a hug. "I knew you'd be here. Think you can take those thirteen seconds from me?"

"I'm sure as heck going to try."

Sophie looked at the rest of the team and smiled. "I can imagine training with these guys would make you strong. I better have my game on."

"I'm quivering in my Converses, and I'm on her team." Dave jabbed her in the arm.

"She's our girl," Big hooted. "The best there is."

Bella joined the group, elbowed Sophie. "Oh, oh, we need Wheaties for race."

That got a laugh from everyone. Once it died down, they wished each other good luck and moved to the check-in counter.

Once checked-in with gear stowed, they regrouped in the lobby to explore. Workers erected tents and unloaded merchandise, setting up the Ironman Village in and around the hotel. Her excitement increased as she watched it come together.

By morning, the village would swarm with athletes looking to buy t-shirts, hats, mugs, and more. The shops carried everything from transition bags and bottles to wet suits and running shoes. Athletes wanting to test the newest and best equipment need only walk through each tent. One guarantee: no athlete would go home empty-handed.

Information booths stocked with brochures and free goodies surrounded the perimeter, and the endless pool stood full and ready for someone to jump in and swim.

An experienced crew set up most of the sanctioned events—they had their routine down—but it still fascinated her to observe the precision. The orchestration of such a huge event seemed flawless.

Early Saturday morning, over two thousand athletes would be off on their quest for an Ironman medal.

She, for much more than that.

* * *

That night at dinner, she watched Hunter cruise by the restaurant window, his stride cockier than normal. Would he pull off a win under his new coach's direction?

"He spit on team name," Uri cursed.

Several agreed, but John and Val said they understood his professional needs and vowed he would remain their brother, a comment that sparked a debate among the rest.

"It sucks," stated Pete. "He left. Then we lost Kyle."

"Yeah," Simon added, making a face. "How the hell do you break your hip going three miles an hour?"

"He turned around in a parking lot. Slid on wet pavement and landed just so," Zach demonstrated with the edge of his right hand smacking the hard surface of the table. "He's really bummed about missing the race."

"Hey, the rest of us are here. We're still a team with a budding star in our midst." Big raised his glass of iced tea and blew CJ a kiss.

"Hear. Hear." The rest of the voices sang out, glasses held high to salute her.

"It's time to make others fear us," Val shouted.

"No worries, Coach. We'll make you proud by proving we're not deadbeats," John proclaimed, causing the others to surge to their feet and cheer.

With this much spirit pumping between them, how

could Team Fear US not excel on Saturday? CJ said a silent prayer to remain strong and fast throughout the day.

Chapter 23

CJ awoke to the sound of footsteps and bicycle wheels rolling through the hall, the walls muffling nervous chatter. She stretched before sitting up in bed to wipe the grit from her eyes.

At 4:00 a.m. on race day, nerves killed her appetite, but as she got ready, she forced herself to eat a few bites of an energy bar. She couldn't jeopardize her nutrition today.

She stood on her balcony overlooking the beach as the crowds gathered: body-marked athletes with wet suits and goggles in hand, family members, and friends sipping coffee. She stared at the sea of bodies, dots of color concealing the sand.

Murmured excitement mixed with the soothing music from the transition area as it floated up to her floor, reminding her the day had arrived. Fear fluttered in her belly, making her queasy, but she drew in a calming breath to tamp it down.

"What a marvelous view and great picture spot. I'm going to suggest the family watch the swim from here." Nick joined her at the rail, laying his hands on her shoulders.

"I can't believe Shayne and your aunt and uncle

came."

"They're psyched to be part of your first win." Nick leaned in and kissed her. "This is it, babe. Ready?"

"I think so." Did hesitation show in her voice? "We'll soon find out. Won't we?" She went back in to gather her swim gear and bottles. Nick followed.

"Remember to use those nerves." He kneaded her shoulders. "Roll your head to relax, clockwise, now counter-clockwise. A few more times, that's good. Come, let's go check your equipment and find the rest of the team."

She closed her eyes, blew out another breath, counted to ten. "Okay, I'm ready. Let's go."

As she waited in line for body-marking and to enter the transition area, she tuned out as much noise as possible, focusing on the music that played through the large speakers placed around the village. She concentrated on enjoying the swim—used visualization as she checked her bike and set her bottles in place. Images of Guam and its beautiful water relieved some of her anxiety, almost made her look forward to diving into the ocean in just over an hour.

She gathered with the team, who found a spot on the beach where they could wiggle into their wetsuits. After they helped each other, they held hands and said a silent prayer. Afterward, they head-butted and called out their team motto, a good luck wish to all. "No pukin'."

Nick shared tips with each of the guys, then came to her. As he stood before her, their gazes locked, and she felt the powerful pull of his love.

He gripped her hands, squeezed. "When it gets tough, remember to be thankful for the beautiful gift of the healthy body and mind you have. Honor that and your passion by giving it your all. Race in your zone, babe, and show the world who CJ Fallon is. I love you."

Her eyes filled and she hugged her man, kissed him.

"I love you, too."

She checked her watch, kissed Nick once again, and moved to stand with the female pros. Swim caps on and goggles in place, they stood at the edge of the water, waiting for the long day to begin. Was it nerves that kept some of them from smiling at one another or simply a means of intimidation?

An urge propelled her to touch Sophie's arm and wish her good luck. Bella joined them, taking a second to introduce CJ to the rest of the group. A murmur of wishes followed just before the start gun blasted.

She rushed into the water, one of fifteen pro women and fifty pro men. She dove and sliced through the water, arms outstretched, before stroking in earnest. When she gained her rhythm, she focused on stretching and rolling, pulling her arm under and through the water to power past her competition.

Her hand brushed something soft, and she hesitated mid-stoke, holding her head below the surface a second longer than normal. Not someone's foot, she thought, as she searched the water surrounding her. When the jellyfish floated in front of her mask, she faltered.

A bubble of fear rose in her throat, as she spotted hundreds of them drifting in the murky water—soft white-like globes fluttering in lazy circles. The need to sprint pushed at her, but she pushed back. *Better jellyfish than sharks, right?*

The brain did funny things when faced with uncertainty. Hers reasoned, giving her the resources to move forward, her arms returning to their earlier cadence. But how much time had she wasted?

She blocked out the scene and swam—hard and fast—but without compromising her heart rate. Nick's voice, telling her to stay in her zone, fed her resolve. To win, she had to remain steady but still hold some reserve for the end.

Bodies exited the water in front of her, cutting a path around the buoy to reenter the sea for the second loop. She followed, again blotting out the image of the man-o-war. Thinking more pleasant thoughts, her arms cut the water, the slight chop of the ocean helping her roll. Lapping the slower swimmers proved treacherous, but she thought of herself as a missile and sliced through the field of bodies, arms and legs thrashing for control and space.

The population thinned, and once again the elite were out front, carving their path to the finish. Several athletes exited before her as she bolted for shore. How many were women?

She got help from the peelers with her wet suit and took off for the change tent. Bike ready, she charged for the mounting line. A few technical turns and she hit the main road. Head poised in the aero position, she geared down and pedaled. The weather cooperated with her. On this one-loop bike course, they would hit a forty-mile stretch and ride straight into the wind. That's what she'd trained for—a headwind she could plow through to annihilate her competitors. Some of the guys would not be happy, but she was pumped.

The course was flat and fast, and she ate it up, one mile at a time. The crowds thinned along the side of the road as she got to the long stretch, but that's where she hooked and drew in the leader, Sophie Kessler. Disbelief and exhilaration pounded through her as she reeled her in, passing her to take first place on the bike. What a rush! With a smile on her face and a silent cheer in her head, she flew by.

"You go, girl," Sophie called, but CJ knew as a strong runner, the girl would push to catch her on the run.

The motorcycle with the sign, *Lead Female*, rode directly in front of her. Adrenaline pumped as her legs pulled up on the pedals, and she motored back to town and into the parking lot of their host hotel. As she zipped into the transition area, the crowd roared. She smiled and nodded with purpose.

Dismounted, through the change tent, she began the run three minutes ahead of Sophie. When she saw Nick and his family standing off to the side, she put on her game face. It wouldn't do to be grinning ear to ear as she ran past them. But she couldn't hold it. Her happiness could not be contained. A huge smile broke free as she blew kisses to them.

She heard their cheers long after the first mile, carrying those words of encouragement with her as a shield. Fatigue the farthest thing from her mind, she felt strong and powerful. Her pace remained comfortable, and so far, Sophie had not closed the gap. She soared on a high never felt before—a high she knew would carry her to her goal.

Still three minutes ahead at mile eight, CJ focused on nutrition. She drank a few sips at each aid station and at ten grabbed an energy gel to go. She steadied her breathing and kept her pace consistent. The few times her energy flagged, she reminded herself she was in the lead.

This was her day.

At mile fifteen, she had two minutes twenty-one seconds on Sophie. The girl had closed in, but could she hold her off? Mentally, she calculated the gap and the remaining miles. She could still do it.

She pushed her pace, tried to build a bigger lead, and felt a sharp snap of pain in her shin. It radiated through her leg like an explosion. In mid-stride, she ignored the discomfort and reached for the ground with her right foot, but the earth disappeared beneath her. Her knee buckled, and she lost her footing, fell forward, tucking and rolling by instinct. Scorching fire shot through her limb, then went cold as another loud crack turned her world to black.

* * *

Nick sat in the medical tent with Uri, who suffered from dehydration. Once again, Uri over-extended himself on the bike course, powering through the headwind to land in the medical tent. The medic finished with the IV, his walkie-talkie crackling at his side, and Nick thought he heard CJ's race number. He leaned in closer to hear the repeat call.

"Request ambulance at mile fifteen on run course, bib number fifty-three down. Appears to be a bad break—right tibia. Need immediate assistance."

The medic grabbed his device and sprinted from the tent.

As if anchored, Nick remained motionless. He stared at Uri's pale face, disbelief clouding his judgment. Had he heard correctly? Was that CJ's number?

He flagged down another doctor and fired questions at the poor man. "That last call, what bib number? What happened? I need to know."

"Sir. Sir. Calm down." The doctor took his arm. "What concern is it of yours?"

"If it's CJ Fallon, I'm her coach. I heard the radio, but the static..." Nick sat down in an empty lounge chair, cradled his face in his hands. "Maybe I heard wrong."

"Stay here. If it is her, and she signed a communication release form, I'll fill you in as soon as I learn the extent of her injury." He moved away, shooting a sharp glance over his shoulder, before tapping into the computer on the center table.

Nick rubbed his face, a knot the size of Texas forming in his gut. Dr. Bissell gave the okay for her to race. Had he glossed over the concern for her health?

Had he lied? Dread iced his veins. His love for her pushed him to move. He, too, sprinted from the tent, pulling the race course map and his cell phone from his pocket.

He zeroed in on the fifteen-mile mark and took off in that direction, while hitting speed dial five on his phone.

Shayne answered on the second ring. "What's up?"

"CJ's hurt. Call Kate." He blurted her number. "We need the name of CJ's doctor in Atlanta. Get his number." He ran at full speed now, weaving through the crowds, her doctor's warnings echoing in his head. "Hurry, Shayne, there's no time to waste. I'm heading to the fifteen-mile mark. Call me back with the info."

He labored, sucking in deep breaths as he ran faster. He skidded to a stop when he saw four paramedics hunched over a body. All he could see was a shoe, but he recognized it as CJ's.

"I'm sorry, sir." A police officer stopped him. "You can't go over there. There's been an accident."

"I'm her coach." He tried to push through, but the cop's stocky body barred him. "I have to see her. How bad is it?"

"It's not pretty." The cop pulled him off to the side. "We'll get a report, but let them work with her. It's the best you can do for her right now. They need to stabilize her."

He paced, his mind painting all kinds of pictures. None that he liked, many that scared the shit out of him.

His phone rang.

"Yeah—did you get it?" He walked to the officer, motioned for him to write this down, recited the number. "Dr. William Hempstead III. Got it. I'll call you when I know more. No, no, you stay with Aunt Millie and Uncle Ed."

They lifted the stretcher, wheeled it toward the

rescue unit. Nick went after them.

"Excuse me, but I'm going with you. What hospital are you taking her to?"

"Local," one of the guys answered. "But the bone's shattered. She'll need to be airlifted to a trauma unit."

"Her doctor's in Atlanta. Resurgens Orthopaedics."

"Call him."

As they raced to the hospital, Nick made the call. He glanced once at CJ and paled. Her skin —a pasty hue—her leg encased in an inflatable cast. Two IV tubes were attached, one in her hand, one in her arm. She didn't look good, and his heart sank to his toes as he took her cold fingers in his.

Arrangements were made to fly her to Northside Hospital, where Dr. Hempstead would be waiting with his team of surgeons. The operating room was booked and being prepped. When he called Shayne to share the details, his cousin said he'd handle informing the team. Once done, he and the family would take the company jet and meet him in Atlanta.

Nick climbed into the helicopter with the weight of the world on his shoulders. His heart caught in his throat, his breathing ragged with fear. He sat stone-still, watching her, not knowing the outcome.

It seemed an eternity passed before he found himself seated in the visitors' lounge, waiting for word from her doctor. They spoke briefly. Nick brought the doctor up to date. Then Dr. Hempstead wheeled CJ directly into surgery to assess the damage.

A nurse offered him coffee. He turned it down. His stomach pitched as he took a seat in the far corner of the room and began to make phone calls. First Shayne to update him. Next Kate. She gave him additional phone numbers, offering to make the calls to CJ's family herself. He almost let her but then decided he needed to do it. It gave him purpose. Otherwise, he'd go nuts.

"Oh, my God, it's like Dad all over again," Gordon responded, his voice a whisper of fear. "Please tell me I'm not going to lose my sister, too."

Frances Crenshaw wept as he explained the situation, while Mrs. Fallon sounded indifferent. How else could he describe her reaction or lack of one? Her voice remained crisp, almost business-like, when she responded, "Northside Hospital? I see. Well, how bad can it be?"

He shared only the facts as he knew them and hung up feeling chilled to the bone. Her lack of emotion and concern froze the little bit of blood he had left in his fingertips. This woman rivaled his father in the "piece of work" department. She'd let her own mother walk away, closed off communication with her. Would she even care if her daughter died?

Something dark snapped inside him. Part of him wished she would stay away. CJ deserved better.

* * *

Ten long and exhausting hours later, Aunt Millie, Uncle Ed and Shayne arrived, worry and concern written on their faces.

"I haven't heard anything yet."

"What is taking so long?" Shayne's patience frayed.

"I've been asking myself that same question for hours." Nick took Millie's hand, needing her calm assurance. For the last hour, he'd been ready to crawl out of his skin.

"Could no news be good news?" his uncle asked.

"I certainly hope so, dear." Millie's lips pursed, and she blinked, fighting the sheen that brightened her already brilliant blue eyes. "Edward, please sit down. Your pacing is making me nervous."

"Yeah, Dad." Shayne coughed. "Come. Sit here."

"We waited for the team to finish, told them what we knew. They're terrified for her, waiting for phone calls to update them. I can make them once we hear." His uncle's need to be useful rounded the edge in his voice. "They said they'd collect her gear and handle everything at that end."

"Great. Thanks." Nick threw his untouched, cold cup of coffee, one of many, in the trash. "Waiting sucks. Ten hours is insane."

As they continued to wait, Nick filled in his family on the details of CJ's prior doctor visits, including the warnings Dr. Hempstead had issued months earlier. He explained the second opinion with Dr. Bissell and his approval for her to race.

"But when I told Dr. Hempstead that I'd seen the X-rays—seen the dark gray shading of the three holes that were healing—he asked me if I noticed any tiny lines that resembled pencil marks" Nick continued, "I did see fine lines and asked about them." He pinched the bridge of his nose. "Dr. Bissell explained they were her bone's fingerprint."

"What did Hempstead say to that?" Shayne shifted and placed his hand on Nick's shoulder, squeezed it in comfort.

"Hempstead grunted, turned on his heel, and announced he'd better get in there," Nick answered. "That did not make me feel better."

Another hour ticked by, the silence deafening, but in his head, Nick replayed the conversation over and over again. Fatigue weighed on him, and he prayed for CJ to survive.

In the wee hours of the morning, the doctor approached. His scrubs were soaked with sweat and splotches of blood. His face mask hung around his neck, exposing the beard stubble on his face. He looked war-torn, ready for a shower and some sleep, but in contrast, his eyes were very clear.

"She's in recovery." His deep baritone lacked pep. He did that strange vee thing around his nose that CJ once described and huffed out a breath. "Would you like to speak in private, Mr. Madison?"

"No, sir. My family is here to support us."

"As you wish." Hempstead planted himself on a small table facing them. "As I said, she's in recovery. She will be fine in time, but there is one major adjustment she will have to make. Having family and friends to support her will make all the difference. Has her immediate family been notified?"

"Yes, sir. Her brother is on his way from Florida. Her mother..." Nick shrugged, not knowing how much to say.

"I've spoken to the woman many times, but this news may motivate her."

"What news? Did you insert a rod in CJ's leg?" Nick asked with impatience.

Hempstead reached out as if to take Nick's hand, hesitated. "We were unable to save the leg. Amputation below the knee was the only measure to save her life."

Nick jolted as if punched in the chest. He shot out of his seat, anger and disbelief crawling up his neck. "You took her leg? Without consent?"

"We had no choice. The bone shattered beyond repair. Would you have risked her life to save the leg? We couldn't. Mr. Madison, one splinter traveling to the heart would kill her. We eliminated that risk. She's strong, athletic. She'll get through this. With the right attitude, the right support, she'll be up and racing again by her thirtieth birthday."

"Oh, Lord." Nick dropped back into his chair, thinking of her reaction. The hurdles she'd faced so far in her life were nothing compared to this. What if she couldn't handle it?

"A disability is only as limiting as the person allows it to be, Mr. Madison." The doctor stood, pointed to a small cubical at the far left of the hall. "She'll sleep for a while yet. Why don't you go in there and look up Ossur online. They manufacture prosthetics and orthotics. Check out the Flex-Foot line. It's designed for athletes.

"Many of my patients lead active lives and swear by the line." Hempstead looked him in the eye. "Look, once the shock subsides, the future will beckon. She'll fare better with some concrete answers, which you can provide for her."

Uncle Ed found his tongue. "Doctor, are you saying she'll be able to participate in Ironman races in the future?"

The doctor nodded. "If she believes in herself, there's no reason she can't race Ironman distance again. As long as her spirit remains intact, she should live a healthy and happy life." His words were meant to comfort. "Right now, I need a shower and a cup of hot coffee. I'll find you when she's ready for company."

He disappeared behind the double doors, leaving them in a state of confusion. CJ was alive and would heal but without part of her right leg. Nick jammed his hands in his pockets, searching the faces of his family. His left hand closed around the small round box he planned to present to her at the finish line. He asked her to change her life, and now... *Oh, God.* How could she not blame him?

What would this do to her?

Chapter 24

Nick pulled the ring out of his pocket, shaking his head as the weight of blame descended. Tears burned. He'd never felt so helpless in his life. What if she pushed him away? How would he get her through this? He knew how much CJ feared regretting her decision to leave her career for his team. Would she now curse meeting him?

"Nicholas, she'll need time to adjust. This is devastating news." Millie placed her hands on his shoulders. "What she'll need from you is a firm shoulder to cry on, a loving arm to support her, and your tenacity to get her racing again. Once she's able to recognize her own strengths and abilities, not her shortcomings, she may consider marriage. Until then, she won't be objective."

He nodded, allowing his aunt to wrap him in a hug. He needed his family's support as CJ would need his. He would protect her. He would shelter her. But he would also push her from the nest when the day came to test her wings. Deep in his heart, he also knew he'd wait below with a safety net, ready to catch her in case she couldn't fly.

* * *

CJ's eyes fluttered, closed, and reopened, focusing on Nick's face. He sat on her bed, holding her hand. When it seemed her vision cleared, her eyes huge in her colorless face, he leaned forward to kiss her lips. They were cracked and dry, not only from her time on the race course, but from the hideous hours in surgery.

"Where am I?" Her gaze shifted to circle the room, pausing on each face, landing on the nurse who stood by the door. "All I remember is my knee buckling, and my ass kissing the ground before everything went dark."

She lifted her hand, stared at the connected tubes. Tears welled, and Nick's heart paused. She looked so frail. He swallowed the lump in his throat, trying to hold back tears of his own, as the nurse hit the buzzer.

Within minutes, the doctor stepped into the room. "How are you feeling, young lady?"

"Dr. Hempstead?" The color of her eyes deepened in confusion. "Why are you here?"

"I'm taking care of my patient. Do you feel any pain?"

She shook her head but raked him with an odd look. "My leg felt like it exploded just before the world went black, but now, I feel nothing. My whole body is numb." Her tears spilled, a reaction that undid Nick. His emotions swamped him, and he could no longer hold his.

In the past, Nick evaded emotions. Now, he couldn't seem to escape them. From the day he'd met her, they kicked to life inside him. Though that frightened him, the fear he now recognized in her eyes killed him. Guilt sliced his heart. How would she cope with life? And with their relationship?

The doctor took her hand from Nick's, motioned for him to take a seat, then turned his attention to her. "You are doing remarkably well after being in surgery for hours. We tried to repair the bone, but it didn't just snap, it shattered. You remember the tiny lines on your x-ray? Like fissures in aged china, if struck against a hard surface, would explode into millions of tiny fragments. That's what happened to your tibia."

"I…"

The doctor squeezed her fingers, held one finger from his free hand to his lips to silence her. "We tried to save the leg, but amputation below the knee was necessary to save your life. There were too many bone fragments to risk one reaching your heart."

What little color she had drained from her face.

"Your residual limb should heal quickly, and within the week, you should be up and about. You'll start rehabilitation with an IPOP—Immediate Post-Operative Prosthesis—and when the swelling subsides, we'll have you fitted for some special limbs. Ossur has an incredible athletic line made of carbon-fiber. They'll have just what you need to get back on the race course."

"No." Her head burrowed into the pillow as if she wanted to block out his words. Her eyes closed, her lips moved, a strange sound emerging—she did not want to hear the truth.

When Nick moved to hold her, she glared at him.

"CJ, listen to me." The doctor took hold of her chin, forcing her to look at him. "There is no reason for you to change your lifestyle. You'll adjust. Once you've relearned the basics, mastered balance, you'll race again." He stepped back. "This is a lot to digest. You're exhausted. Rest, and we'll talk again later. You have an incredible support group here. They believe in you, and in time, you'll do the same."

After the doctor left, Nick suggested his family go find a hotel nearby to get some rest. He planned to stay by her side.

In the quiet of the room, her spirit broke and more tears fell. Hot, fluid misery flowed unchecked, and it tore at him, settling a weight in the center of his chest. How could he comfort her? What could he say?

He said nothing, simply held her in his arms and cried with her until she had no tears left.

* * *

CJ experienced waves of emotion as she lay in that hospital bed. She pictured the girl they watched finish the Wisconsin Ironman, her heart swelling, as she remembered the standing ovation the girl received.

Then her stomach pitched. Because she lost her leg.

She made a huge mistake. Walked away from security to explore the unknown, and look what it got her. No matter how she looked at her situation, she realized, she'd let everyone down.

Nick remained by her side, even when depression took hold, and she yelled at him to leave her alone. She was never good enough whole, how could he love her now?

Gordon admitted he didn't know what to say but sat with her and cried. Like a sick joke, she gained a sincere big brother but lost a limb.

The team visited every day and bullied her to fight.

Big wore his distress on his face. "You're not a quitter, CJ. Prove it by getting strong."

Simon spoke with conviction, "We won't give up on you. When you're ready, we'll take you back to Guam. We'll bring our families, so we can stay as long as it takes to get you strong enough to score that win."

Zach stared at her, a determined line firming his lips. "Yeah, you're my hero. You can't give up. I won't let you."

Uri whispered, "All the day you sit and feel sorry is another day you lose. You must move, be winner."

It pissed her off. "Fuck you. You are not the one

missing half a leg." Temper seethed, bringing fresh, hot tears to her eyes. "You have no idea how I feel."

"You're right, we don't," Dave soothed. "But at least you have some fight in you. You're not going to die, CJ, so use your anger to get back on your feet."

Like pulling a stopper, CJ's anger drained, and she looked at these men with a small bubble of laughter escaping her throat. "Back on my foot, you mean."

They glanced at each other, a bit unsure, but the laughter followed, and for the first time in days, her shoulders relaxed. The weight lifted from her, even if only temporarily. The peaks and valleys exhausted her, but it took her mother's visit to push her over the edge.

"You see, dear, you've ruined your life. Can you live with the fact that you're damaged goods?" The icy disgust was clear in her voice.

Like a spear jabbed in a wound, her mother's perception shoved her into action. She took her first steps that afternoon, hobbling about twenty-five feet, Nick smiling by her side. Pain and humiliation almost stopped her, but the burning desire in her gut for her mother to realize she had been put on this planet for a reason made her get up and try again. She would prove her worth.

Could she, like that girl, be an inspiration?

Later that night, when her mother returned to once again crumble her resolve, CJ took a stand, and she did it with an audience. "I'm sorry, Mom, that you think I'm less of a human being because I'm missing an appendage, as you put it, but I have people in my life who accept me as I am." She scanned the room, smiling at the people she now thought of as family. "If you can't do that, so be it. It's your loss, not mine."

Her team stood and cheered. Her mother's expression pinched. CJ continued to punctuate her point. "Everyone here except you sees my strength, even when I'm weak."

"Well, if that's how you feel." Her mother stood and glided to the door, her icy façade cracking. "Come, Gordon."

"No, Mom, I'm staying," Gordon responded. "I choose to support my sister."

With her back rigid, her mother prepared to sail out of the room without another word.

"Wait. Mrs. Fallon." Nick stood. "There is one more thing."

That stopped her in her tracks, her brow hiked, curiosity getting the better of her.

"CJ, this isn't how I envisioned doing this." Nick took her left hand, and all eyes rested on him as he spoke. "I planned to give this to you as you crossed the finish line." He pulled a tiny odd-shaped box from his pocket and flipped its lid, revealing a magnificent emerald and diamond ring.

She gasped. He sank to one knee. "Will you marry me?"

The room erupted in shouts and hollers as he removed the ring and slipped it on her finger. Her gaze moved from the ring to her mother's face, which twisted in a look of distaste, but before she could respond, her mother bolted, leaving the room with the door swinging shut behind her.

The noise died down. An eerie silence settled, and when CJ looked at the ring again, she burst into tears, huge sobs erupting.

"It's only fair to warn you, I won't take no for an answer." Nick kissed each of her knuckles, smiling into her eyes. "I understand you may need time, but I refuse to live without you. You are my other half. I need you to be whole."

* * *

Two weeks of rehab proved an emotional rollercoaster for CJ, the high points when she gained strength, her spirit soaring as she took normal steps and remained upright. The lows came when she stumbled or fell, her courage teetering on the brink of insanity. Twice now, she left her bed thinking she still had two feet. They weren't the most graceful face-plants, but she felt lucky to hurt only her pride.

She spent her alone time reading the rest of Frances' letters, which Nick had been thoughtful enough to bring. One early morning when she couldn't sleep, she called Paris. The concern in Frances' voice brought tears to her eyes. She asked CJ to call her Meme, and they chatted about life and how things could change in an instant.

"One of the things I learned after Matt died was that life shrinks or expands based on the risks we take and the courage we display," her grandmother said. "You will get through this."

She found courage in her grandmother's words, and in time, she began to accept her own Fate, though many questions remained unanswered.

She would survive, but what was her purpose?

She thought about her second opinion. Should she sue Dr. Bissell or take responsibility for her own foolishness? Hadn't she wished for him to say there were no concerns, tell her she could race without worry? She'd prayed to hear those words. After over-analyzing the situation, she could blame no one but herself.

She crawled into bed after another intense hour of therapy. Her leg throbbed, her stump was swollen, and the phantom sensations—like her toes itching right now—freaked her out. The doctor promised they would decrease in sensitivity after a few months.

Nick fluffed her pillow, helping her adjust and settle, when the door swung open and the team filed in.

Uri carried a huge stuffed tiger, and Big handed her a stack of magazines.

"So, how's it going?" Simon asked, as the guys filled chairs.

CJ hugged the tiger to her chest. "Still adjusting, having good days and bad." She grinned as she stroked the animal's fur. "The doc explained that he took a piece of leftover bone to bridge my fibula to my tibia. He screwed them together so my residual limb could handle more pressure while running. Right now, I'm having a hell of a time learning to walk. The thought of running seems eons away."

Several guys looked like they'd swallowed lemons. "Can we stop with the details?" Big scrunched his nose and coughed.

"You're such a wimp, Big," John hooted.

"Oh, yeah, and you like all this stuff?" he shot back.

Lars came to sit beside her. "Okay, gentlemen, enough. We're here to cheer her up." He picked up one of the magazines and flipped it open. "We wanted you to see this."

CJ stared at the full page ad. She took the magazine from Lars, her hands shaking. It resembled one of the storyboards Nick had shared with them at dinner in her home while they were training for Florida. Except instead of the sponsors thanking CJ for her race results, it wished her a speedy recovery—*CAN'T WAIT TO SEE YOU BACK ON THE RACE COURSE*—read the caption in bold print across the bottom.

The flood gates opened, her heart dropping to her toes. A sob escaped as she spoke her thoughts. "I'll never race again."

"Fate loves the fearless." Zach clucked. "You will race again. We'll make sure you're strong enough and fast enough to annihilate the other pros."

"You can't stop pursuing your dreams," Dave

added.

"Now's as good a time as any to share this." Nick wrapped his arm around her. "The sponsors agreed to renew our contracts with two conditions: CJ, you have to race again. After that, they want you to coach with me. They expect you to use your progress to motivate others. You'll widen our field."

"We can call them Team Fear US2," Zach said.

"No added pressure, right?" Her tears came faster and harder. What if she wasn't an inspiration? What if the world saw her like her mother did, as a broken freak?

Nick must have sensed her doubt because he hugged her to him. He kissed her cheek and looked at the boys. "With these lugs, you have no choice; you will gain enough strength and speed to conquer that comeback. We won't let you fail. Right, guys?"

"That's right, we're here to help you make history," Simon agreed. "Amputees have been racing for years, but as age-groupers not pros. You can do it, CJ. We know you can, because you're incredible."

"Amen, sister," Big shouted.

And with that, CJ had a new goal—to cross the finish line as the first pro amputee.

Chapter 25

"Where are you taking me?" Nick took her crutches from her and helped her settle in the passenger seat of the car.

"It's a surprise." He came around and slid into the driver's side. "Tomorrow is Thanksgiving, and since the doctor said you needed a few days off, we're taking the weekend. You've worked thirty hours a week since surgery. You deserve a break."

Her residual limb ached, rubbed raw by the IPOP, which she would do without until Monday. She hadn't ventured out in public yet, and hobbling around without her leg made her vulnerable. Would people stare at her? Would they see her as disfigured?

"I don't know that I'm ready for this." Her breath caught as if someone tightened a band around her chest. "What if I can't handle people's reactions?"

"You'll be fine," Nick reassured.

He drove north on the 400, the highway that led to her mom's. Her heart raced. After that last visit, why would he take her there?

"You've got me to lean on. What more do you need?" Nick seemed oblivious to her angst. But her heart settled as he drove past her mother's exit.

"A leg would be nice." She laughed, but it sounded hollow.

Nick reached over and squeezed her hand. "Remember, you're an Ironman—my Irongirl."

Outside, the day was cold and gray, and though most of the trees had lost their leaves, a few held fast to a colorful array. The wind yanked at them, trying to pull them from their perch, to add them to the blanket of color below.

Soon, the trees would be nothing but wood skeletons standing naked against the winter sky, exposed to the elements, unprotected. A chill ran up her spine, and she burrowed deeper into her jacket. "I'm scared, Nick."

"I know."

"I've been thinking about this whole coaching deal. What makes them think challenged athletes will accept me as an authoritative figure when I've been uninjured most of my life?"

Nick switched off the radio, even though only background music played. "Your experience as an athlete, and dealing with this crisis, not to mention your strength and sensitivity. How could they not be drawn to your vulnerabilities and your huge heart?"

He glanced at her then and turned his attention back to the road, which curved and twisted along Lake Lanier. "Do you doubt what you have to offer?"

"Well, yeah." She shifted in her seat, unable to get comfortable. The rock on her finger didn't help. Every time she looked at the beautiful ring, she faltered. "Nick, what if I can't do it? What if I can't race? What if I'm not an inspiration? I've already let the team down once."

"You won't fail. Trust me." His lips pursed, and he sighed. "Look, I know this is scary. Worse even than leaving a stable job to test your athletic abilities, but you are stronger than you give yourself credit for."

"I wish I believed you."

"What's the alternative? Go back to running a store? It's a way to make a living, but racing is your passion."

"Look where it got me."

"How will you know if you don't try?" He turned down a gravel path and pulled up in front of a large wood cabin. When he cut the engine, he turned to face her, and flashed that brilliant, heart-stopping smile. He took her hand, pointed at the ring. "Partners, sweetheart. We're a team. We can do this together."

He pulled her toward him and kissed her, the heat from his mouth traveling down the length of her body. How could she not believe him? This man had believed in her since day one, and even now after a tragedy, he trusted that she could motivate others. Could coaching become her new passion?

Someone tapped at her window, and she almost jumped out of her skin. "Are you guys ever coming out of there?" It was Lars, and most of the team stood grinning behind him.

"Yeah, come on, we've got serious partying to do." Pete pulled open her door. Several hands reached in to help get her out of the car.

Uri picked her up and carried her up the stairs. Nick followed with crutches in hand.

Inside, Kyle hobbled over on his own set of crutches, a pretty young woman by his side. "This is Carolyn, my wife," he introduced. "CJ Fallon, and you know Nick Madison."

"This is the girl you spent five months on an island with?" The edges of her mouth tightened.

"Your husband did not just carry her through door." A striking blonde sauntered over and popped Uri in the arm. "My man, he has to prove he is strongest."

That wiped the pout off Carolyn's face and had the

others laughing. Several other women joined them, and more introductions were made: Uri's wife—Beata; Dave's girlfriend—Lisa; Simon's girlfriend—Josie; and Zach's wife—Brie.

"What a wonderful surprise." CJ turned to Nick, who shrugged and shook his head.

"Don't look at me. I didn't plan this." He pointed at the guys. "They rented the cabin and made all the arrangements."

John grinned. "His job was to get you here."

"Yeah, no one said anything about seducing you in the driveway," Simon hooted.

Big and a couple of the girls blushed.

"No hospital food for you on Thanksgiving," Dave said as he carried wood over to the fireplace, got the blaze going, to make the large, open room feel cozy.

An assortment of finger food crowded a large wooden table, and the scent of apple cider filled the air. A ripple of delight swam through CJ's blood. They did this for her.

"Lovely ring." Beata, Uri's wife, took her hand, scrutinized the setting. "When is wedding?"

"Oh…" Flustered, she didn't know what to say.

"I hoped to get help this weekend. She hasn't yet said yes to me or the deal." Nick patted Kyle on the shoulder. "Some of you have more influence with her than I do."

"What's up with that? Two no brainers as far as I'm concerned." Big looked offended, standing with his arms crossed over his chest.

"Umm, I've had a few things on my mind, like learning to stand on my own."

"Why do that when you can lean on Coach?"

"That's what I said." Nick shot her a look that made her giggle. "She won't listen to me."

"We've got the weekend to strong-arm her." Kyle

swung his crutch to take hers out. "It'll be a crutch of a showdown."

Everyone rolled their eyes and shook their heads, except Carolyn, who turned away.

Brie touched Carolyn on the arm. "They're teammates, family. You know…like brother and sister."

Kyle stepped over, wrapped his arm around his wife. "She's one of the guys." He kissed his wife and her posture changed, a sweet smile spreading across her face.

She shrugged as if apologizing. "It's the hormones," she said as she rubbed her belly.

"Well, you're simply glowing," CJ replied.

Fatigue sapped her, so she hopped over to a chair, sat with a sigh.

"You're looking pretty good yourself," Zach said. "A bit tired but strong. Any word on when you can start training?"

"I've done a lot of research on the Ossur line. Are you getting a Flex-foot?" Val asked.

"The doc said I'm healing fast. I'll get fitted in a few weeks." She touched her bandaged leg, still a bit uncomfortable being the center of attention. "I've read quite a bit about athletes who've lost limbs. All their recovery periods differ, and many adjustments are made over the course of time, but some come out stronger and faster than before."

"We'll get you ready to challenge the able-bodied."

"Yeah, Guam here we come. Athletes better Fear US."

"How cool would it be if you dropped out of sight and came back to pound the competition?"

"That's kind of the plan." Nick stood as tires crunched on the gravel outside. "Oh, good, they're here. I invited the rest of the family."

* * *

Thanksgiving dinner rocked, the table laden with too much food, the wine flowing. Christmas music played in the background, and the laughter never lulled. Aunt Millie told the story of how Nick decided to propose and the ring-shopping adventure, making Nick blush, the others teasing him. Shayne asked about Kate, which in turn got him teased by Nick.

One of the guys suggested this become their new tradition. "Like training on Guam, Thanksgiving meal could be ours."

"We'll watch our family grow." Simon elbowed Kyle.

"Maybe we pick a different location each year?" Kyle laughed and threw his biscuit at Simon.

A mini food fight ensued, and CJ's heart bubbled with love.

As the laughter died down, Uncle Ed cleared his throat. "Well, missy, are you going to give Nick what he wants for Christmas?"

"What could Nick want for Christmas?" Shayne asked, and all eyes turned toward CJ.

"Hmm, let's see, a wedding on Guam before we kick off the new training season?" Nick stood, his champagne glass raised, challenge flashing in his green eyes. "What do you say, CJ?"

Chapter 26

What could she say but yes? CJ had never experienced such love and support, had never been accepted simply for herself. In the last nine months, she'd experienced loss and heartache but also she'd learned the true meaning of family.

Hearts defined it, not bloodlines.

On Christmas Day, she felt like a little girl, giddy to find the goodies under the tree. Having been in retail since college, CJ thought of Christmas simply as a day off sandwiched in a grueling schedule of sales and long days, but now here she sat on a tropical island ready to marry the man who'd discovered her on the race course in New Zealand.

"Will you sit still?" Kate slapped the makeup brush on the table. "Or you're going to miss your own wedding."

She poked out her tongue. "Nick's seen me at my worst. He's not going to care about a little eye shadow and blush."

"Humor me, okay?" Kate applied more makeup. "You know I threatened to quit my job to be here. Thank God my regional has a soft spot for you. He made it clear, however, I'd pay for this the rest of my career."

"I'm so glad you're here." CJ hugged her friend.

Kate laughed. "The sacrifices we make."

"Are you two almost ready?" Gordon poked his head in the door. She made him cry on Thanksgiving when she called to ask him to walk her down the aisle, but today he was all smiles. He came over to stand in front of her. "You look gorgeous."

"Why thank you, sir." She stood up and twirled around to show off her Vera Wang gown and almost lost her balance. She grabbed his arm to steady herself, applying her weight evenly between her good leg and her new Talux carbon fiber, fashioned with a high-heeled pump. She let out a full-throated laugh, unembarrassed by her near mishap. "I'm still not that stable. You may have to hold me up."

"I'm honored to." He crooked his arm, and she slipped her hand in to grasp his bicep. "Ready to go?"

Kate picked up her bouquet and handed CJ one perfect sunflower, the flower she chose to carry for Nick. From the small room at the side of the chapel, the three of them made their way to the front door.

CJ sucked in a breath as they waited for the march to begin. The soft pinks and violets of sunset bathed the building in a luminous glow. The huge glass windows shimmered. White caps played on the ocean beyond, while island birds serenaded.

Joy, so pure, filled her, and she prayed she wouldn't cry.

As the music started, everyone stood and turned to face her. She squeezed her brother's arm, nodding she was ready.

White Poinsettias and miniature Christmas trees strung with twinkling lights lined the pews, the altar candles glowed, but when she gazed at Nick, the spark in his eyes undid her.

Tears brimmed as she focused on the man she

loved. He stood proud, his smile beaming. She sensed his nerves, yet he looked calm and oh so handsome with Mike and Shayne standing by his side.

As she followed Kate up the aisle, she took it all in. There sat her grandmother, Frances, in the first pew, already wiping at tears. All of her teammates with their significant others filled the other side, and the rest of the chapel held the staff from Mike's Resort and many of the island people she'd met while training.

Only one person chose not to attend, but CJ would not allow that to dampen her day. These were the people who cared.

Gordon stopped. Lifting her veil, he kissed her cheek then placed her hand in Nick's. As he stepped back, everyone behind her sighed, and she turned to find out why.

Each of her teammates joined Gordon and now stood behind her and Nick in a stance that spoke volumes. The tears spilled over, and she squeezed Nick's hand.

"I'm right where I belong," she whispered before the priest stepped forward to take over.

They said their vows and exchanged rings, platinum bands with the engraving—*You are my reason.* She was home.

* * *

No regrets—that's how CJ chose to live, and with that came no animosity. She selected tropical stationery and a dark purple pen from the drawer and began to write.

Dear Mom,
I'm sorry you chose not to come, but I've enclosed pictures so you can share in my wedding day. In "the

family"—you'll see all the people who have accepted me as I am and don't want me to change. Even with the loss of my leg, they've been here for me. They held me up until I could once again stand on my own, and they remain by my side to support me and encourage me.

Did you recognize the beautiful redhead in the fashionable jade suit as your mother, Frances? Yes, Gordon and I have gotten to know our grandmother, who happens to be quite passionate. There is a hint of sorrow lingering in her gaze when she speaks of you, but there is still love.

Her heart is pure, her empathy powerful.

She painted our wedding gift: Field of Sunflowers. Fitting, as Nick's first gift to me was a sunflower. He gave it to me that night that now seems so long ago, the night that forever changed my life.

I've come home, Mom. Having never fit anywhere before, I've found love, the genuine, unconditional kind, and though it still scares me, I've embraced it. How I wish you could feel it, too.

Which brings me to my invitation—one I will make once but will leave open for eternity. If you want to belong to this wonderful family, you'll have to make the next move. Just let me know, and we will open our arms to you. Until then, well—I love you.

A single tear rolled down her cheek, landing softly on the signature, blurring the edges. The signature read: *your loving daughter forever, Cassandra Jade Madison.*

"Are you sure you want to do this?" Nick came over as CJ folded the letter and stuffed it into the envelope with half a dozen pictures.

She smiled up at him as she sealed it. "I don't even know if she'll read it, but you once told me to make choices without regret. I'm opening the door; she'll have to step over the threshold. But if she chooses to, we'll have come a long way."

Nick pulled her into his arms. "You have such a huge heart. Have I told you how lucky I am to have seen you race that day in New Zealand?"

"Don't ever stop telling me." She kissed her husband, dizzy with the knowledge that he'd picked her out of a crowd of more than two thousand. What had drawn him to her? He said it had been her strength and determination, and even though both had been tested this past year to the limit and beyond, her life had expanded in a way she had never dreamed possible.

Love and acceptance were now part of her existence and that made life all the more sweeter.

Epilogue

Two years later

CJ sat at the skirted table with her husband and coach, Nick Madison, in a room overflowing with reporters. Never before had Ironman Florida drawn such a huge crowd, but then, no one in the history of the race had attempted what CJ planned to accomplish at tomorrow's race.

She'd trained hard for this. Secluded on Guam with her teammates for almost two years, she pushed herself harder than ever, not only to complete the race, but to compete with the best athletes in the sport.

In the last few days, careful not to advertise her state, she wore jeans and stayed out of view. But soon the world would know.

Nerves bunched in her stomach as she scanned the faces, cameras, and microphones before her. Nick must have sensed her unease, because he reached over and took her hand, squeezing it beneath the cover of the table cloth, so no one else would see.

He smiled, his green eyes bright with encouragement. "You'll be fine," he whispered, leaning in close. "Ready?"

She expelled a breath as the room buzzed with anticipation.

Finally, a reporter, standing off to the left, spoke. "Two years ago at this very race, you were an unknown, a new pro making her mark on the world when you collapsed."

"You were leading the women's race when you went down," a perky reporter shot from the right. "But we heard nothing more about you. Why?"

"Yeah, what happened that day? They whisked you away, and you disappeared, literally dropped off the face of the earth," a gray-haired man shouted from the back.

"Now, you're back with something to prove. What exactly do you intend to do tomorrow?" another guy asked.

"I'm here to win." She flashed her biggest smile and combed her fingers through her short, sassy hair in an attempt to camouflage the fear skimming through her.

"How do you plan to do that?" another guy, sitting in the front row, asked. "While you haven't raced in two years, the other pros have been setting records."

She dipped her head to acknowledge that statement.

"My circumstances changed, but my passion remained strong. I'm here to prove that dreams can be achieved with drive, the right mindset, and the support of loved ones."

This time her fingers closed around Nick's. Emotion welled, the sheen of tears blurring her vision. But when she locked gazes with one of her teammates, she smiled.

Uri nodded, showing his silent approval, then stood up and voiced his support. "She strong like bull. She show you."

"With the fire she has in her belly, she may stomp some of the male pros, too," Kyle added, bringing her entire team to their feet.

As their applause died down, the same guy with the thick gray hair pushed to the front. He swept the crowd with his gaze then turned to face her, microphone extended. "You vanish after making a splash as a pro, and now you're here to win! Tell us how that's possible?"

"My team makes it possible," CJ said as she stood up.

She moved to the front of the stage and bent to pull up her pant leg. The room went silent, all eyes riveted.

"Oh, my God," yelled the perky reporter. "Your leg?"

"As I said, my circumstances changed, but I've learned that change can be powerful. I plan to prove that tomorrow."

Applause spread through the room as fellow athletes stood, bringing several reporters to their feet, as well.

"I'm back. I'm strong. I'm here to prove Team Fear US should be feared." She motioned for the team to join her, and the crowd went nuts.

* * *

CJ stood on the beach among the other pros. An unusual calm settled over her as she waited to push the start button on her chrono watch. She closed her eyes and said a silent prayer, asking the gods to keep her strong throughout the day.

"No pukin'" the guys' earlier voices echoed in her head with Nick's "You're ready"—words that boosted her confidence, made her feel strong. Unlike the others, who would run into the water, CJ had to hop, but she'd practiced that as well as changing her prosthetics to keep her transitions below two minutes.

She could do this.

The cannon blast pierced the air, a puff of smoke hanging in the early morning sky. The sun just peeked over the horizon, turning the heavens a murky blue. She plunged her face into the icy water and started swimming. A helicopter circled overhead, the sound of its whirling blades mixing with the rush of arms as they thrashed in the water. There was contact as everyone vied for position, but it was minor. Within minutes, she found her rhythm.

After exiting the water, hopping to reenter for the

second loop, CJ focused on breathing and pulling. She surged forward in the frenzy of activity as she lapped the field. Threading through the sea of legs, her arms rotated, cutting the water like propeller blades. A hand struck her back, pushing her under. Instead of air, she gulped a mouthful of water, choking and swallowing more. Hands and feet pummeled her, keeping her just below the fray.

Fear of drowning made her fight. Sputtering, she rose above the surface and clawed her way through the chaos until she slipped into the long thin line at the front. When the swim-finish arch came into view, she picked up her pace. A volunteer waited with a chair and her running leg, which she'd have to change again for her cycling one.

"And here comes CJ," the announcer called over the PA. "54:31—great swim, and eighth pro woman out of the water."

With blood pumping, adrenaline surging, she raced through the change tent and grabbed her bike. At the mounting line, she swung her leg over and clipped in. Checking her heart monitor, she geared down and settled into a brisk but comfortable pace.

She'd worked hard with the boys to break the five-hour mark. The plan to take the lead came into play. On the flat and fast course with little to no wind, this would be her day.

Her heart soared as she scorched by the crowds lining the roads. They screamed words of encouragement, clanging cowbells and blowing horns. Concentrating on the rotation of her pedals, the smooth round strokes that moved her along the hundred and twelve miles of pavement, CJ absorbed those cheers, using them like fuel in her blood. Her legs worked like the pistons of a finely tuned machine, pumping with power. One by one, she picked off the female pros, passing several of the men, as well. For each, she gave a fierce nod and a bright smile.

They too called out. "Keep it up, CJ."

"You're doing great."

"Show them how fierce you are."

"Like a flame at back, you burn. You go, girl."

She passed several of her teammates, who also celebrated with her. Big pumped his fist in the air, screaming, "There's our girl. Show 'em how it's done."

Val came out of the aero position long enough to whistle.

Lars grinned like a cheetah, shooting her a thumbs up. "You're going to win this thing. Do it, Irongirl."

She motored, thanking all of the volunteers as she sped through the aid stations. They gave their day to support her and her fellow athletes. These races couldn't take place without them and the many officers who blocked or directed traffic.

On a high, she ate a gel, sucked on her jet stream, and pedaled for the win. She slipped by Uri with four miles to go. Her chest puffed with pride as he blew her a kiss.

A volunteer took her bike, another handed over her transition bag. With a grin and another thank you, she raced to the women's change tent. Back in her running leg, she took off.

She spied Kate at the side of the road, camera ready. Was that Shayne standing with her? Breathing hard, trying to find her rhythm, CJ focused on her heart rate, elevated at the moment. She needed to gain control. It wouldn't do to pull a Uri. She thought of Reed, running with her in New Zealand, and a calm settled over her.

Again the streets were lined with well-wishers, their shouts as loud in the late afternoon as they were at seven this morning. Kids lined up to dole out high-fives, and CJ responded to the enthusiastic banter with a huge grin.

She floated, the steady click of her carbon fiber foot hypnotizing. Mile by mile, she closed in on the finish, her lead solid. Each mile marker brought her that much closer to her goal. With this win, she'd be able to recruit other challenged athletes and get Team Fear US2 started.

The twenty-mile mark.

Fatigue slipped in, her pace slowing. She grabbed some water at the next aid station and forced down a gel. One foot in front of the other, she repeated in her head. *Keep moving.*

Her stump throbbed from the friction of each step, but she continued to push forward. She had a strong lead, so she could afford to slow a bit. But at mile twenty-four, like an invisible hand, the wall reached out and sapped her strength.

She slowed to a walk, the pain radiating up her thigh. Sitting at the side of the road, she removed her leg, repositioned the liner, then reattached it, hoping to ease the discomfort. She got up and walked the next mile, each step more painful than the last.

With 1.2 miles to go, she had to keep moving, but it became more difficult to believe she could. Again, she stopped to readjust her leg, and again, she walked.

Several of the men she passed on the bike now ran by her, touching her on the arm, encouraging her with words.

"You can do it, CJ."

"Keep moving, girl. You've got it."

"You're so close."

A cramp seized her good leg, forcing her to sit. She massaged it to work out the knot, but when she tried to stand, defeat crawled on her back, the weight of failure holding her down. Damn it, she'd worked so hard.

She dropped her head to her knees and cried. Hugging her shins, she let the misery flow. Hard, hot sobs escaped unchecked. A hand gripped her shoulder, and CJ looked up to find Sophie standing over her.

"Come on, CJ, you're going to make it." She held her hand out for CJ to grasp.

Shaking her head, CJ waved her on. "I'm done. I have nothing left. This is your race now. Go get that win."

"No. I was at that press conference yesterday. You're an inspiration to the world. I won't let you give up."

"But I can't..." The tears poured down her face.

"Yes, you can. Grab on." Sophie once again stuck her hand out. "We'll cross that line together."

As Sophie helped her stand, CJ saw the next pro woman closing in. "Bella's coming. She's tough. She won't stop. I won't let you blow this race because of me. Please, go."

Sophie shook her head. "I won't leave you."

Bella drew up next to them and stopped. "What, you give up so close to finish?"

CJ couldn't believe it. She stared at her in awe. "You guys can't do this."

"Do what?" Bella took her arm. "Encourage fellow athlete to finish what she start?"

Flanked by these two women, CJ hobbled toward the finish, touched by their generosity, but pained that she ruined their race. She couldn't allow them to forfeit a win for her.

"Look, I appreciate what you're doing, but I can't cross the finish with you. You two have to race for the win. It's only fair." She ignored the pain and inched forward. "I'll finish, thanks to you, but one of you deserves that win."

Male athletes continued to pass them, the crowds thickening along the side of the road. As they rounded the last corner before the finish, Uri joined them.

"Next female pro not far behind, come we go," he urged.

"Ladies, please. Sprint for the win," CJ begged.

"Yes, go. I finish with teammate." Uri pushed at the two women. "Go. We come behind."

"When we get to the chute, we'll sprint," Sophie said, and Bella nodded. "We're almost there, so let's keep moving."

The four of them picked up the pace, CJ digging deep for the strength to continue. The announcer called names, the crowd roared, and just as they entered the chute, the two women patted her back and took off.

"We see you on podium," Bella called as she lengthened her stride, and the spectators screamed as the two women raced in earnest to cross the line first.

Sophie edged by a split second ahead.

Uri took her hand. "Come, we run last steps for picture."

With her teammate by her side, tears streaming down her face, CJ forgot the pain and ran the last few feet to claim third place. Kyle, Zach, Aunt Millie, Uncle Ed, Kate, and Shayne stood off to the side, cheering for her and Uri. Nick and her brother Gordon waited just ahead. When she saw their faces and the tears rolling down their cheeks, her heart fluttered in her chest.

Nick stepped forward and wrapped her in a hug. CJ had never felt so complete. Pure and powerful love warmed her insides. After a few minutes, Gordon and the others came over to share hugs and congratulations, and to watch the rest of the team finish.

By midnight, as the last participants crossed the line, emotionally exhausted but exhilarated as well, CJ turned into her husband's arms. She stared into his beautiful eyes, touched his handsome face, and kissed his gorgeous lips. She sighed into his chest.

"Now it's time to grow our family. Tomorrow, we start recruiting for Team Fear US2."

~ ~ ~

ABOUT THE AUTHOR

Christine Mazurk is a business woman and Ironman triathlete with a passion for writing stories about "heart." Her business experiences and participation in endurance events have allowed her to live and travel the world with her husband and two cats.

She believes everything happens for a reason.

Their two 18-year-old cats passed away three months and three days apart, and though she and her husband agreed to wait at least a year to adopt new kittens, their feline guardian angels in heaven had a different idea. Thirteen days after the second one passed, on a cold, wet Christmas Eve, a little black kitten—now named Tango—found them. Soon after, they adopted her brother—another all black kitten—and named him Samba.

They all live happily in whatever State they currently call home.

Sign up for Christine's newsletter, "The Heart of Change" on her website:
www.christinemazurk.com

Like her author page:
www.facebook.com/christinemazurk

Connect with her on Twitter:
www.twitter.com/christinemazurk

Dear Reader,

Thank you for taking the time to read PASSION'S RACE. I hope you enjoyed meeting CJ, her coach, Nick, and her twelve male teammates, while following her on her athletic journey. My husband and I lived on Guam for four years, and I enjoyed revisiting the island through CJ's and Nick's eyes.

Many of you have asked about Mike Dawson, Nick's best friend and owner of the resort where the team stays. I'm happy to share that his story, PASSION'S SPIRIT, will be available soon. If you had fun getting to know the unique personalities of CJ's teammates, you'll be reacquainted with most of them while I introduce you to a few new faces.

I want to say a special thank you to the readers who read the first edition of PASSION'S RACE. Because of its success, I was able to add content and a new cover that speaks of the athletic journey of the four books planned for this series.

PASSION'S PROMISE, book three in the series, is PJ's story as an adult. You'll meet three-year-old PJ Madison in Mike's book.

HART'S PASSION, book four, is Kate Brooks' story. I've gotten questions about what happened to CJ in the two-year period after her collapse. This book is about Kate's journey, but you'll get glimpses of what CJ was doing during that time.

Thank you again for spending your time with my characters. If there were any you especially enjoyed, please consider leaving a review at your favorite online retailer. If you have questions, or want to share specific feedback, please feel free to contact me.
mazurkchristine@gmail.com

Happy Reading....

Coming Soon
PASSION'S SPIRIT

Chapter 1

Mike Dawson waited outside of Customs, watching for the team to come through the doors. In previous years, he'd been able to see them coming through the large glass window, which was now walled off for extra security.

He glanced at his watch and looked up just in time to see a gorgeous brunette stride through the door, pulling her cell phone from her bag. The serious look on her face conveyed she meant business as she stepped to the side to make her call.

Determined look or not, she was hot. Her tailored pants made her legs seem endless, and the button front shirt only enhanced her lean physique. The angles of her face and high cheekbones lent an air of mystery, her full mouth, the promise of a steamy kiss. Mmm, a tasty flavor of the month.

The island footprint was tiny, so he was bound to run into her somewhere. How long would she be on the island, and how long before he could entice her to hang out and play?

He heard a squeal and turned as a flash of color flew in his direction. "Uncle Mike!" Three-year-old PJ Madison, carrying her purple hippo blankie, ran from her parents straight into his arms. He bent to catch her and she gripped his face with her tiny hand, planting a loud, wet kiss on his cheek.

A surge of love shot through him. Dang, was she cute.

She snuggled her head against his neck and

yawned.

"How's my sleepy boo? Long flight, huh?" He hugged her tight, then dipped her to look into her face. She giggled, clinging to him.

Her father, Nick Madison, his best friend since age twelve, coach to the able-bodied pro triathletes, clapped him on the back, then pulled him into a hug, sandwiching PJ between them.

CJ, Nick's wife, an ex-pro who now coached the challenged athletes, joined them, hugging from the side, and they stood for a minute, a tight unit—a family.

A burst of greetings shattered their quiet as the rest of the group descended. Most were familiar faces, the ones from the original triathlon team, Team Fear US, the pros Nick coached. They came to Guam each year to train.

There were a few new faces Mike didn't recognize.

CJ stepped back and made the introductions.

"Oscar, aka Kumquat." She pointed to the guy in the bright orange wheelchair. "And Brent." A young kid with a prosthetic leg much like CJ's. "This is Mike, the owner of our base-camp, the resort we stay in."

CJ Madison had been coaching the challenged athletes, Team Fear US2, for several years now, and though most preferred to participate in local races or simply worked with her to live a healthy life-style, both mentally and physically, it seemed these two wanted to compete in the endurance arena.

"This is an awesome opportunity," the kid said. "I'm excited to be here, to challenge myself with the longer distances."

Big, the 6'5" redhead, placed his hand on the young man's shoulder. "This is the place to do it."

"Wait 'til you swim in water," Uri, the blocky German, plucked PJ from Mike's arms, sat her on his massive shoulder, then pulled Mike in for a one-armed bear hug.

"Simon and the rest of the team members opted to stay home and train through our personalized online program," Nick explained as he organized the troops.

The group moved to collect bike-cases and luggage, but CJ took his hand and led him in the opposite direction. "I want to introduce you to our new team doctor."

He looked around, spotted an older, distinguished looking, white-haired man, but when CJ stopped in front of the brunette with the cell, his heart stalled.

Shit, there goes the flavor of the month. Not only would she be staying at his resort, working for Nick and CJ, but she worked in the medical field. Off limits for sure.

"Natalie Walsh, Mike Dawson." The girl looked up and her full lips tipped into a smile, showing straight white teeth. The color of her eyes, when they locked with his, reminded him of summer pears—light green with tiny flecks of sunshine.

His tongue tripped, and because no greeting came out, CJ elbowed him in the ribs.

"Say hello, you dolt."

The beauty gave him the once-over then stuck out her hand. "A pleasure to meet you. I've heard so much about you, the resort, island living. Not that I'll have much time for enjoying it."

"She never relaxes," CJ volunteered with a laugh.

"I do," green-eyes shot back with a very serious look on her face. "When I run."

"Yeah, that's it," CJ replied with a sly grin and a twitch of her eyebrows.

That got a slight frown out of Ms. Walsh before she said, "Okay, so maybe running helps clear my mind."

CJ touched the doctor's arm but looked at Mike when she spoke. "All that clearing has made her a phenomenal runner. I've tried to talk her into competing—she'd leave everyone in the dust—but she refuses."

The doctor blushed, deep rose sweeping those incredible cheekbones, and he wondered if there wasn't more to her running.

In a flash, the blush faded as her smile returned. Her chin came up a hair, and her shoulders squared. "Besides, as I remember it, I never got to start the 10K I signed up to do, because my doctoral-duties took precedence."

CJ laughed. "Guess that was my fault, or one of my athlete's, anyway, but look what came of it. You got a bunch of crazies to treat and prevent injuries with, and we contracted one heck of a good doctor."

A sexy one at that, Mike thought. He felt the mutual admiration that passed between the two women, not just professionally, but on a personal level as well, and something in his belly pulled.

"You going to tell me the story, or what?" he asked, intrigued by their banter, wanting to learn more about how they met.

"We'll have plenty of time for that," CJ answered. "Right now, we need to move. My hunk of a husband is giving me the eye."

The girls headed toward the resort vans, which the team had loaded with all of their belongings. The noise level—that of excitement and reacquainting—rose higher.

Mike followed, watching the sway of the doctor's hips, and wondered how the hell he'd be able to steer clear of her.

* * *

Natalie had successfully shoved the anger at her

brother into the recesses of her heart as CJ introduced Mike, the owner of their home for the next five months. The smile she pasted on her face and the joshing with CJ seemed to cover the ire well enough, but as they scooted into the resort vans, the heat generated from her brother's messages rose to the surface.

She took this job and the travel requirements that went with it to break away from his constant demand of her. She needed the distance and the time-change to create her own space, to examine her future and decide what she wanted in life, instead of being at Travis's beck and call all the time.

But what did she want, other than peace of mind?

A movement in the rearview mirror caught her eye, and she looked up to see Mike's soft, summer blues locked on her. They seemed to drink her in, and a strange sensation swam through her. She now understood why CJ classified him as "dangerous to the female gender."

She hadn't missed the sculpted features and dreamy blue eyes, or the sunny blond hair that looked as if he combed it with his fingers, those loose waves spiking around his forehead. And that day's growth of beard, which added a pinch of rogue to the happy-go-lucky guy he'd been described as, made him even more handsome.

He was attractive, but she'd been warned about his casual playboy ways, and there was really no reason for CJ or Nick to worry. The last thing she wanted was a relationship of any kind.

She had enough in her life to deal with.

She broke eye contact, looking out the van window, and became mesmerized by the colors in the mid-April sky. Pink cotton-candy clouds floated across the light blue background, the horizon edged with the color of lemon drops. Lush green lined the road as they cruised toward Mike's Resort. She knew Guam was tropical— she'd looked at pictures on the Internet—but in person it was even more beautiful.

Drinking in her surroundings allowed her to forget her troubles for a brief moment—before her brother's whining re-entered her head, and a knot formed at the back of her neck.

She sighed and looked down at her watch, calculating; distance to the resort, time to unpack, team dinner at seven. That left her exactly forty-five minutes for a run.

Less than an hour to sweat out the frustration that clung to her shoulders like a demon. Just one more attempt to leave the past behind and move into the future. One more attempt she knew would fail.

Made in the USA
Charleston, SC
02 November 2014